HARD

NEWS

HARD NEWS

JEFFERY WILDS DEAVER

A PERFECT CRIME BOOK

DOUBLEDAY

NEW YORK   LONDON   TORONTO   SYDNEY   AUCKLAND

Mys.

A PERFECT CRIME BOOK
PUBLISHED BY DOUBLEDAY
a division of
Bantam Doubleday Dell Publishing Group, Inc.
666 Fifth Avenue, New York, New York 10103

Book design by Bonni Leon

DOUBLEDAY is a trademark of Doubleday,
a division of Bantam Doubleday Dell Publishing Group, Inc.

Library of Congress Cataloging-in-Publication Data

Deaver, Jeffery
    Hard news / by Jeffery Wilds Deaver.
        p.   cm.
    I. Title.
PS3554.E1755H37   1991
813'.54—dc20   91-14140
                                                      CIP

ISBN 0-385-42121-4
Copyright © 1991 by Jeffery Wilds Deaver
Printed in the United States of America
December 1991

1   3   5   7   9   10   8   6   4   2

FIRST EDITION

FOR IRENE

HARD NEWS

CHAPTER ONE

Rune watched the tape once, then again, and decided the man was innocent.

She sat in a deserted corner of the Network's newsroom, which wasn't really a room at all, but a huge open space, twenty feet high, three thousand square feet, divided up by movable partitions, head-high and covered with gray cloth. The walls were matte black, scuffed and chipped. To get from one side of the studio to the other, you had to dance over a million wires and around monitors and cameras and computers and desks. A huge control booth, like the bridge of the Starship *Enterprise*, looked out over the room. Overhead were theatrical lights on black-painted poles. A dozen people stood in clusters around desks or monitors. Others walked purposefully, carrying sheets of paper and blue cardboard cups of coffee and videocassettes. Some sat at computers, typing or editing news stories.

Everyone was in shirtsleeves, everyone was busy.

Rune was hunched over the Sony 3/4-inch tape player and small color TV that served as a monitor.

A tinny voice came out of the small speaker. *"I told them back then just what I'm telling you now: I didn't do it."*

The man on the screen was gaunt, with high cheekbones and sideburns. His hair was slicked back and crowned with a Kewpie-doll curl in front. His face was very pale. When Rune saw him, she thought: Nerd. This dude is a positive greaser. . . . He wore a tight gray jumpsuit, which under other circumstances—say on West

Broadway in SoHo—might have looked pretty chic. It even bore a label with the name of the designer, who wasn't, however, Giorgio Armani or Calvin Klein, but the NEW YORK STATE DEPARTMENT OF CORRECTIONAL SERVICES.

Off camera, an interviewer asked, *"You'll be up for parole, when?"*

"Parole? Maybe a few years. But, hell . . ." The thin man looked at the camera quickly, then away, as if he'd uttered an obscenity. *"A man's innocent, he shouldn't be out on parole, he should just be out."*

Rune watched the rest of the tape, listening to him tell about how bad life in prison was, how nobody in the warden's office or the court would listen to him, how incompetent his lawyer had been. She was surprised, though, that he didn't sound bitter. He was more confused, baffled—somebody who can't understand the justice behind a sudden accident, like a plane crash or car wreck. She liked that about him; if anybody had a right to be obnoxious or sarcastic or just simple feisty, it was somebody innocent who was in prison. But he just talked calmly and wistfully, occasionally lifting a finger to touch a sideburn. He seemed scared of the camera. Or modest or embarrassed.

Where was he born? In high school, had he been— What did her mother call them?—a hood? How did he get arrested?

Does he have family?

A wife somewhere? Maybe children? How would it be to have to visit your husband once a month? Was she faithful to him? Did she bake him cookies?

Rune freeze-framed a nice tight close-up. She looked at his smile and knew, without a doubt, that Randy Boggs wasn't guilty of murder.

She started the tape again and stared at the dully-colored grain on the screen.

"You want to hear what it's like to be in here?" Now, at last, bitterness was creeping into the voice. *"Let me start at the beginning of my day. Do you want to hear about that?"*

"Tell me whatever you want."

"You wake up at six, and the first thing you think is, hell, I'm still here. . . ."

A voice from across the room: "Rune, let's go. We've got an overturned something on the BQE."

The Model was standing up from his desk, pulling on a tan London Fog trench coat that would keep him ten degrees warmer than he needed to be on this April afternoon (but that would be okay because this was a *reporter's* coat). He was an up-and-comer—one of the hotshots covering metro news for the local O&O, the Network's owned-and-operated New York TV station. Twenty-seven, Midwest handsome (the word "sandy" somehow seemed to apply in a vague way), a round pleasing face, eager, sharp. He spent a lot of time in front of mirrors. Nobody shaved like The Model.

Rune was his cameraman, and he hadn't been quite sure what to make of being assigned an auburn-ponytailed twenty-two year old, who looked a bit like Audrey Hepburn, and was just few inches over five feet, a couple ounces over a hundred pounds. The Model would have preferred a pickled, chain-smoking technician who'd worked the city desk from the days when they used sixteen-millimeter Bolexes. ("I really want us to be a team, Rune," he'd said sincerely. Rune had responded, "Dynamic Duo, sure," in a tone that was somewhat less than sincere.)

But she shot damn good footage. And so far all she'd made him was mystified, not angry.

He carefully made sure the belt wasn't twisted, then fitted it through the plastic buckle. (He always did this, and, even more than the Ken-doll haircut, it made him a serious dweeb in her eyes.)

"Rune, come on."

She chose not to hear.

The first thing you think is, hell, I'm still here. . . .

"Rune, let's roll. This is great, it's ammonia. An overturned tanker truck. Boy, that is gonna screw up rush hour real nice. Ammonia. Are we lucky, or are we lucky?"

Rune shut the tape off and joined The Model at his cluttered desk. "I think I want to see her." She looked vacantly across the newsroom at a nest of intense journalists, hunkered around a computer monitor.

"Her?"

"You know who I mean."

The Model's face broke into a wrinkleless smile. "Not Her, capital H?"

"Yeah."

The Model laughed. "Why?"

Rune had learned one thing about TV news: Keep your back covered, and your ideas to yourself, unless they pay you to come up with ideas, which in her case they didn't. So she said, "Career development."

The Model was at the door. "You miss this assignment, you won't have any career to develop. It's ammonia. You understand what I'm saying?"

"Ammonia," Rune repeated. She wound a paisley elastic silkie around her ponytail, then pulled on a black leather jacket. The rest of her outfit was a black T-shirt, yellow stretch pants and cowboy boots. "Just give me ten minutes."

He took her by the arm, aimed her toward the door. "You think you're just going to walk into Piper Sutton's office?"

"I'd knock first."

The Model laughed. "Let's go, sweetheart. Double time."

"Isn't ammonia dangerous?"

"Yeah, tape the trigger down. That way, you pass out, the Icky'll keep on taping."

They took the elevator down to the ground floor of the four-story building that occupied a whole square block on the Upper West Side. The building had been an armory at one time, then had been bought by the Network, gutted and rebuilt. Outside it was scabby and dark and looked like it ought to be housing a thousand homeless people; inside was a half-billion dollars' worth of electronics and TV celebrities. A lot of the space was leased to the local O&O station, but most was for the Network, which recorded a couple soaps here, some talk shows and a bad sitcom that, rumor was, would be canceled mid-season. The rest of the square footage was devoted to Network News.

In the equipment room beside the parking garage, Rune checked out an Ikegami video camera with an Ampex deck and a battery pack. Rune and The Model climbed into an Econoline van. She grabbed the lip of the doorway and swung up and in, the way she liked to do, feeling like a pilot about to take off on a mission. Gregory Peck in *Twelve O'Clock High*. The driver, a scrawny young man with a long thin braid of blond hair, nodded at Rune and started the van, telling her that he'd managed to get tickets to the Fine Young Cannibals concert at the Beacon.

"The what?" The Model asked.

She forgave him. Midwesterners. Pete Seeger, Woody Guthrie. Labor union songs.

Rune said, "It's like a classic group."

"Group? A rock group?"

For God's sake, he's only twenty-seven. What's he listen to, the Stones?

And the driver was telling him how good FYC was, and how the lyrics on their latest hit went, when The Model waved his broad Midwest hand and said, "Interesting, but we got ammonia on the BQE. Let's move."

Which the kid did, glancing at Rune and squealing into the street, as if he was striking a blow for contemporary rock music. East, Uptown, east again. He never missed a chance to spin the tires and squeal around turns. He knew his way around the city, this boy did, shoving the van into side streets and squeezing in front of trucks and cabs to make right turns from left lanes. He managed to miss the big traffic jams. He caught a lot of red lights; occasionally he stopped for one.

Rune sat in the back of the oily-smelling truck and loaded the deck, tested batteries, and cleaned the lenses and the eyepiece of the camera, while she listened to The Model mumbling leads for the big ammonia story. She paused, looking out the window at people on the street as they watched the van, with its sci-fi transmission dish on top and the call letters of the TV station on the side, running up at an angle. Sometimes, sitting in the truck like this, Rune would wave at the curious. But today she was distracted.

The first thing you think is, hell, I'm still here. . . .

I'm still here. . . .

I'm still here.

"So, why can't I just walk into her office and talk to her?"

The Model snapped, "Because she's the anchor."

As if nothing more need be said.

Rune trudged beside him through the scuffed corridor that led from the elevator back to the newsroom. The worn carpet was sea-blue, the parent company's corporate color. "So she's an anchor. Does that mean she's not human, or what?"

"Go make an appointment, you want. She'll be too busy to talk to you." He was in a bad mood because, yes, it was an ammonia truck and, yes, it had tipped over, but no one had told the station that the truck was empty. So, no spill. It even had the courtesy to roll over onto the shoulder, so that rush hour traffic wasn't disrupted much at all.

"You're just upset because you didn't get to say 'snarled,' " Rune said.

The Model glanced at her. She loved his pink cheeks. She hoped that when she was twenty-seven, she had skin like his.

It was tough to keep up with his pace. She wheezed, "Every traffic reporter loves to say traffic is snarled. That is a totally great word. *Snarled.*"

"I'm not a traffic reporter."

They arrived in the studio, and Rune replayed the tape she'd shot of the truck. The Model looked at it and seemed to be trying to think of something critical to say.

Rune bounced on her toes. "Look, look. I got the sunset. There on the side of the truck. That ridge of red, see—"

"I see it."

"Do you like it?"

"I like it."

"Do you mean it?"

"Rune."

As the tape was rewinding, Rune said, "But Piper's like ultimately my boss, isn't she?"

"She's Network, you're local. It's a strange relationship."

"I live in Manhattan. I'm used to strange relationships."

"Look," he said patiently. "The President of the United

States is in charge of the Army and Navy, okay? You see him talking to every PFC's got a problem?"

"This isn't a problem. It's an opportunity."

"Uh-huh. Piper Sutton doesn't care diddly-squat for you, dear. You have an idea, you should talk to Stan."

"He's head of local news. This is national."

The Model asked, "What's the story?"

Rune was quiet.

"Don't you trust me?"

"It's not a matter of trust—"

"Which means you don't. Okay, fine. . . ." His voice was sarcastic. "But I'm hardly interested in your stories, Rune. Nothing personal, but you're just a cameragirl."

"Girl?"

"Cameraperson. I'm not saying you don't have potential. But you're a technician."

Technician. But she was smiling, as she asked, "What do you know about her?"

"Her with a capital H again?" The Model looked at Rune for a moment in silence.

Rune smiled coyly. "Come on, please?"

He said, "You ought to know as much as I do. You read *New York* magazine. Sutton started out, where I am, a reporter for the local in New York. I think she went to the University of Missouri Journalism School. Anyway, she did beat reporting, then she moved up in the ranks and became head of radio news, then executive producer for radio. Then she got tapped as a reporter for the Network. She was overseas a lot, I know. She was in the Mideast, and she got an award for covering the Sadat assassination. After that, she anchored the weekend edition, then *Wake Up With the News.* Finally, they tried to move her into the parent. Something pretty big, like executive VP in charge of O&O's. But she didn't want it. Somehow she finagled her way into *Current Events.* And there she is.

She makes a million dollars a year. Lives on Park Avenue. Lady is hot shit in the world of broadcast journalism, and ain't gonna want to spend a couple hours having a confab with the likes of you."

"She hasn't met me yet," Rune said.

"And she devoutly wants to keep it that way."

"How come everybody talks about her like she's some kind of dragon lady?"

The Model exhaled a sharp laugh through his nose. "You'll see."

"No, come on. Tell me."

"Forget about it. You don't trust me."

"I don't trust you, but I like you."

"I like you too, Rune, which is why I'm not going to ruin your evening by telling you anything more about Piper Sutton."

CHAPTER TWO

"What do you want?" the woman's raspy alto voice barked.

She was in her early forties, with a handsome, broad, stern face. Her skin was dry and she wore subtle, powdery makeup. Eyes: deep gray-blue. Her hair was mostly blonde though it was masterfully highlighted with silver streaks, every strand terrified into place with spray. She wore a cream-colored suit with a burgundy silk blouse and matching red shoes. Names like Bergdorf, Bendel and Ferragamo applied, but Rune had no idea which name went with which article of clothing. The woman sat behind a large Chippendale reproduction desk, under a wall filled with blotched and squiggly modern paintings and framed photos of her shaking hands with or embracing a couple of presidents and some other slick, gray-haired men.

Audacious!

Rune did a fast eyes right. Two of the walls were floor-to-ceiling windows, looking west and south. The office was on the forty-fifth floor of the Network's parent company building, a block away from the studio. Rune stared at a distant horizon that may have been Pennsylvania. Then she turned away, reluctantly, stopping herself just in time from telling the woman that not only was the view totally fresh, but the office didn't smell like a locker room, which is what everybody knew the armory-studio smelled like but didn't admit.

Stacks of papers covered the woman's desk, and two telephones sat on a credenza behind her. To the left was a bank of four 27-inch NEC monitors, each one tuned to a different network. The sound was off, and in unison they fired an electronic hum into the air.

Rune introduced herself. "I'm a cameraman for the local station, and I—"

Piper Sutton's voice rose with gritty irritation. "Why are you here? How did you get in?" Questions delivered so fast it was clear she had a lot more where they came from.

Rune could have told her she snuck in after Sutton's secretary went into the corridor to buy tea from the ten A.M. coffee service cart. But all she said was, "There was nobody outside, and I—"

Sutton waved a hand to silence her. She grabbed the telephone receiver and stabbed the intercom button. There was a faint buzz from the outer office. No one answered. She hung up the phone.

Rune said, "Anyway, I—"

Sutton laughed briefly and said, "Anyway, nothing. Leave."

She looked down at the sheet of paper she'd been reading, brows narrowing in concentration. After a moment, she looked up again, genuinely surprised Rune was still there.

"Miss Sutton . . . *Ms.* Sutton," Rune began. "I've got this like idea. . . ."

"A *like* idea? What is a *like* idea?" Sutton's eyes were trying to burn her into a tiny smoldering cinder, and Rune felt a blush crawl across her face. "I mean, I have this idea for a story I'd like to do."

Sutton slapped her Mont Blanc pen onto the desk. "I don't understand what you're doing here. I don't know you. I don't want to know you. Go away."

Rune said, "Just give me a minute, please."

"I don't have time for this. You want me to call security?"

"You want a boost in your ratings?"

Sutton snorted a laugh, studying Rune carefully. "Make it fast, honey, then get your ass out of here."

"I want to do a story about—"

"What do you mean you want to do a story? You said you're a cameraman. Give the idea to a producer."

"I want to produce it myself."

Sutton's eyes started at Rune's young, makeupless face and worked their way down: A black T-shirt, black spandex miniskirt, blue tights and fringy red cowboy boots. Dangling from her lobes were earrings in the shape of yellowtail sushi. On her left wrist were three wristwatches with battered leather straps, painted gold and silver. On her right, were two bracelets—one, silver in the shape of two hands gripped together, the other a string friendship bracelet. From her shoulder dangled a plastic leopard-skin bag; from one cracked corner it bled a blue Kleenex.

"You don't look like a producer." She smiled.

"I've already done a film. A documentary. It was on PBS last year."

"Really? So do a lot of film students. The lucky ones. Perhaps you were lucky."

"Why don't you like me?"

"You're assuming I don't."

"Do you?" Rune asked.

Sutton considered. Whatever the conclusion was, she kept it to herself. "You've got to understand. This . . ." She waved her hand vaguely toward Rune. ". . . is deja vu."

Rune shook her head. "I don't—"

"It happens all the time. Somebody blusters their way in and says—who knows what? That they'll work for me for free for a year. 'Please try me out. . . .' Or they have an idea for a new news program or game show or special or God knows. I don't have time for crap like this. . . . Oh, note the proper use of the word *like*. As a preposition. Not an adjective or adverb."

Both phones rang at once, and Sutton spun around to take the calls. She juggled them for a while, jamming her short-nailed finger down on the hold button as she switched from one to the other. When she hung up, she found Rune sitting in a chair across from her, swinging her legs back and forth.

Sutton's face contracted in anger.

"Okay, that's it—" She reached for the phone. "You're out of here. . . ."

Rune said, "I want to do a story on a murderer who was convicted only he didn't do it. I want my story to get him released."

Sutton's hand paused over the phone. "Here in New York?"

"Yep."

"That's metro. Talk to the local news director. You should've known that in the first place."

"I sort of want this to be on *Current Events.*"

Sutton blinked, then laughed. "Honey, that's the Net's flagship news magazine. I've got veteran producers lined up for two years with programs they'd kill to air on *C.E.* You ain't getting slotted on *Current Events* in this lifetime."

Rune leaned forward. "But this is an audacious story! The man has served three years in Attica. Three years for a crime he didn't commit."

Sutton looked at her for a moment. "Where'd you get the tip?"

"I was going through some old tapes—"

"Who told you to?"

"No one. I just—"

"Your time, our time?"

"Huh?"

"Huh?" Sutton repeated sarcastically. Then, as if explaining to a child: "Were you on your time, or on our time when you were doing this homework?"

Which was a question Rune didn't have a problem with, since, the way she looked at it, almost everything she did was on her time.

"Sort of on my lunch hour."

Sutton said, "Sort of. Uh-huh. Well, so this man is innocent. A lot of innocent people get convicted. That's not news. Unless he's famous. Is he famous? A politician, an actor?"

Rune blinked. She felt very young under the woman's probing eyes. Tongue-tied. "It's sort of, it's not so much the news as it is the fact he's innocent." She was concentrating so hard on not saying *like* that a lot of *sort-of*'s were slipping through. She felt a prickle of sweat.

"Then go to law school or set up a defense fund and get him out. We're a news department. We're not in the business of social services."

"No, it'll be a really good story. It'll be sort of like . . ." Rune paused. *Sort of . . . Like . . .* She must think I'm a total dweeb. Sutton raised her eyebrows, and Rune said, "Like *Sixty Minutes*. Everybody else'll be doing stories about *us*. Good publicity. Good rating points, you know."

Rating points. They loved to talk about rating points in television.

Sutton waved her hand. "It's a small story. It's a local story. Go away."

"It could be national."

Sutton began writing on the sheet of paper in front of her. Her handwriting was elegant. "That's all."

"Well, if you could maybe just keep this. In your files,

maybe?" Rune opened her bag and handed Sutton a sheet of paper with a synopsis of the story. Sutton slipped it underneath her china coffee cup on the far side of her desk, and returned to the document she'd been reading.

Outside, the secretary looked up at Rune in horror. "Who are you?" Her voice, as abrasive as Sutton's, was high in panic. "How did you get in here?"

"My feet," Rune said gloomily, and continued toward the dark-paneled elevator bank.

The elevator doors had just opened, when Sutton stepped into the outer office. The secretary said, "I'm so sorry, Ms. Sutton, I don't know how she got in—"

Sutton waved her quiet with a swipe of her arm. "You," she called to Rune in a voice like steel on stone. "Back in here. Now."

Rune about-faced and trotted back toward the office. Sutton, close to six feet, towered over Rune. She hadn't realized the anchorwoman was so tall. She hated tall women.

Sutton slammed the door shut behind them.

"Sit."

Rune did.

When she too was seated, Sutton said, "You didn't tell me it was Boggs."

Rune said, "He's not famous. You said you weren't interested in somebody who wasn't—"

"You should've given me all the facts."

Rune looked contrite. "Sorry. I didn't think."

"All right, Boggs could be news. Tell me what you've found out."

"I saw a tape of him, one done in prison a year ago. He says he's innocent."

Sutton blinked. "And?"

"And, that's it."

"What do you mean, that's it? That's why you think he's innocent? Because he said so?"

"I believe him."

"You *believe* him?" Sutton laughed again. She opened her desk and took out a pack of cigarettes. She lit it with a silver lighter, every movement clean. There seemed to be no smoke or ash coming from her cigarette. "You believe it when he says he's innocent?"

Rune looked around the room, trying to think up an answer to defend herself. Being studied by Piper Sutton knocked most of the thoughts out of her head. All she said was "Yep."

Sutton said, "I guess I'm looking at quite a judge of human character. You're, what, the Edgar Cayce of justice, huh? You get the vibes that this man's innocent, and that's that. Listen, dear, at the risk of sounding like a journalism professor, let me tell you something. There's only one thing that matters in news: the truth. That's all. You've got a goddamn *feeling* this man is innocent, well, goody for you. But you go asking questions based on un-supported rumors, just because you get some kind of psychic fax that Boggs is innocent, well, that bullshit'll sink a news department real fast."

Rune looked hurt. "I was going to do the story right. I know how to research. I know how to interview. I wasn't going to go with anything that wasn't . . ." *Corroborated* or *collaborated*? She wasn't good with soundalike words. ". . . backed up."

Sutton calmed. "All right, what you're saying is you have a hunch, and you want to check it out."

"I guess I am."

"You guess you are." Sutton nodded, then pointed her cigarette at Rune. "Let me ask you a question."

"Shoot."

Sutton gave a splinter of a glare.

"I'm not suggesting that you not pursue this story."

Rune frowned, sorting out the *not*'s. They didn't quite seem to add up, but she got the gist.

Sutton continued, "I would never suggest that a reporter shouldn't go after a story he feels strongly about."

Those negatives again. . . .

"But I just wonder your efforts aren't a little misplaced. Boggs had his day in court, and even if there were some minor irregularities, well, so what?"

"But he's innocent. I know it."

Sutton's matte face scanned the room slowly, then homed in on her. She said quickly and in a low voice, "Are you sure you're not doing a story about you?"

Rune blinked. "Me?"

"Are you doing a story about Randy Boggs or about a young journalist?"

"I know he's innocent. I—"

Sutton smiled again, a smile with a child's fake innocence, and said, "What are you concerned with? Telling the truth about Boggs or making a name for yourself?"

Rune didn't speak for a minute. "I think he's innocent."

"I'm not going to debate the matter with you. I'm simply asking the question. Only you can answer it. And I think you've got to do a lot of soul-searching to answer it honestly. . . . What happens if—I won't say it turns out he's innocent, because I know he's not—but let's say, if you find some new evidence that can convince a judge to grant him a new trial? And Boggs gets released pending that trial? And what if he robs a convenience store, and—"

"He wouldn't—"

"And kills the owner in the process?"

Rune looked away, unable to order her thoughts. Too many double negatives. Too many tough questions. What the anchorwoman said made a lot of sense. Rune hadn't

thought about it that way. She said, "I think he's innocent. I'm going to do a story about it."

But her voice was uncertain. Then she said firmly, "It's
a story that's got to be done."

Sutton gazed at her for a long moment, then asked,
"You ever budgeted a segment on a news program? You
ever assigned personnel? You ever worked with unions?"

"I'm union. I'm a camera—"

Sutton's voice rose. "Don't be stupid. I know *you're*
union. I'm asking if you've ever dealt with the trades, you
as management?"

"No."

Sutton said abruptly, "Okay, whatever you do, it isn't
going to be as sole producer. You're too inexperienced."

Which, even though it was insulting, didn't upset Rune
too much because it seemed to mean that she was maybe
going to do *something*. She began to smile. "Don't worry,
I'm like real—"

Sutton's mouth twisted. ". . . enthusiastic, a fast
learner, willing to put in long hours? Is that what you
were going to say?"

"I'm good is what I was going to say."

"Miracles can happen," Sutton said, pointing a long,
wrinkled finger at Rune. "You can be associate producer.
You can report and you can . . ." Sutton grinned brutally, *"like* write the story. Assuming you write more ar-
ticulately than you speak. But I want somebody looking
over your shoulder. If there is a story, I don't want it
fucked up."

Rune stood up and put her hands on the desk top. Sutton leaned back and blinked. Rune said, "I'm not a kid! I
came here to tell you about a story I think is going to be
good for the Network, and all you do is insult me. I didn't
have to come here. I could've gone anywhere. I could've
just sat on the story and done it myself. But—"

Sutton laughed and held her hand up. "Come on, babes, spare me, please." She picked up her pen. "You want to do the story, go see Lee Maisel. You'll work for him."

Rune stayed where she was for a moment, her heart pounding. She watched Sutton's slow, careful handwriting as she read a contract dense as the classified section in the Sunday *Times*.

"Anything else?" Sutton glanced up.

Rune said, "No. I just want to say I'll do a super job."

"Wonderful," Sutton said without enthusiasm. Then: "What was your name again?"

"Rune."

"Is that a stage name?"

"Sort of."

"Well, Rune, if you're really going to do this story, and you don't give up halfway through because it's too much work or too tough or you don't have enough chutzpah—"

"I'm not going to give up. I'm going to get him released."

Sutton ignored her. "If you're really going to do it, don't talk to anybody about it except Lee and me. I want status reports regularly. Verbally. None of this memo bullshit. Got it? No leaks to anyone. That's the most important thing you can do right now."

"The competition isn't going to find out, I'll be—"

Sutton was sighing and shaking her head the same way Rune's algebra teacher had when she'd flunked for the second time. "It's not the competition I'm worried about. I'm worried that you're wrong. That he really is guilty. If we lose a story to another net, well, that happens. It's part of the game. But we do a story and it's wrong . . . that shouldn't ever happen. No way. No how. And it's not going to happen on any program I'm anchoring. Comprendo, honey?"

"I'm not wrong."

The woman looked at her for a long moment. Rune tried to keep contact with Sutton's dark eyes, but finally had to look away.

Sutton broke the tension with a question. She sounded amused and baiting. "I'm curious. Do you know who Randy Boggs was convicted of killing?"

"I read his name, but I don't exactly remember. But what I'll do—"

Sutton held up a hand to cut her off. "His name was Lance Hopper. Does that mean anything to you?"

"Not really."

"It ought to. He was head of Network News. He was our boss. Now you see why you're playing with fire?"

CHAPTER THREE

Rune said, "I didn't think it was any big deal."

Lee Maisel was a large, balding bearded man in his fifties. He wore brown slacks and a tweed jacket over a tieless button-down dress shirt and a burgundy and beige argyle sweater. He smoked a meerschaum pipe, yellowed from smoke and age. The pipe was one of a dozen on his desk. He didn't look like a man who made, as executive producer of the country's most popular TV news magazine, over one million dollars a year.

"I mean, how was I supposed to know who Lance Hopper was?"

"How indeed?"

Maisel and Rune sat in his large office in the Network's portion of the old armory building. Unlike Piper Sutton's office in the parent's high rise, Maisel's was only thirty feet in the air and overlooked a bowling alley. Rune thought that was super. Being down with his troops. Yeah! Maisel even looked like a general. She could picture him in khaki shorts and a pith helmet, sending tanks after Nazis in North Africa.

Rune was sitting in front of a large Mister Coffee. She looked at it with a wrinkled nose as if the pot contained the harbor-bottom sludge that the coffee resembled. He said, "Turkish." He poured a cup for himself, and raised an eyebrow. She shook her head.

"Piper really rides on hyper, doesn't she?" Rune asked. Then it occurred to her that maybe she shouldn't be talking about Sutton this way, at least not to him.

Maisel didn't say anything about her editorial comments, though. He asked, "You don't grasp the significance?"

"All I know is Piper said Hopper was our boss."

Maisel turned and dug through a stack of glossy magazines on his credenza. He found one and handed it to her. It wasn't a magazine, though, but an annual report of the Network's parent company. Maisel leaned forward and opened it to a page near the center, then rested a thick, yellow fingertip on one picture. "That's Lance Hopper."

Rune read, *Lawrence W. Hopper, executive vice-president.* She was looking at a tall, jowly businessman in a dark suit and white shirt. He wore a red bow tie. He was in his fifties.

"You understand what you've done?"

"No, not exactly."

He chuckled. Rune decided she liked Maisel. He looked like a professor. Rune had never been to college, so she'd never had any professors, but she thought that if she ever did go, she'd take courses from anybody like Lee Maisel.

"Boggs was convicted of killing Lance Hopper. Now, I knew Lance. Knew him pretty well actually. Most of the people around here did. He was a good man. Tough, but he made Network News what it is today. When Boggs was convicted, you should've heard the applause in the newsroom. . . . Now, here you come and say he's not guilty. Well, there are people who work here who aren't going to be happy to hear that."

Rune said, "I don't *think* he's innocent. I know."

"You know?" Maisel said softly. "Look, I interviewed Boggs myself. He's a drifter. He's never had a decent job in his life. I happen to agree with the jury. Most people agree with the jury. Now, if you're right, and he's innocent, you're going to be pretty unpopular around here, and you aren't going to win any awards from the judge and prosecutor either. And if you're wrong, you'll still be pretty unpopular, but not around here, because you won't be working here any more. See the significance?"

"But what difference does it make? If he's innocent, he's innocent."

"You want my opinion, forget the story. You want to work for *Current Events,* we can probably swing a transfer here."

"I want to do this story. That's all. He's innocent. I want to get him out." Rune shook her head and closed her eyes briefly. "Just imagine that you're in jail for something you didn't do. For three years! God, that's terrible."

"You haven't met Boggs. Why don't you find a *nice* criminal who's been wrongly imprisoned, and get him out of jail? Why do you have to crusade for a, pardon my language, asshole?"

Rune said, "Innocent assholes shouldn't be in jail any more than innocent saints."

Which he liked. Rune could tell he didn't want to smile, but he did. She said, "Look, Mr. Maisel, I'm going to do this story. I may have to do it by myself, I may have to sell it to somebody else, but I'm going to. The thing is I'd really love it to be on *Current Events.*"

He looked at her for a minute. "Piper called me and said there was a, well, an eager young thing from the local station, who—"

Rune asked, "Is that how she described me? Eager?"

Maisel dug into his pipe with a silver tool that looked like a large flattened nail. "Not exactly. That's my translation of how she described you. . . . And when she said that, I thought, oh, boy, another one. Eager, obnoxious, ambitious. But she won't have grit."

"I have grit."

Maisel said, "We'll see. You might just make a reporter after all."

"I can do the story, I really can."

"Uh-huh. You have any experience?"

"I did a documentary. It was on PBS."

"PBS? Well, *Current Events* is a hell of a lot different from PBS. It costs over a half million a week to produce. We don't get grants, we survive because of Nielsen and Arbitron. You know what our rating was last year? We had ten point seven rating points. You know what a point represents?"

"Not exactly."

"Each point means that nine hundred and twenty-one thousand homes are watching us."

"Awesome," Rune said, losing the math, but thinking that a lot of people were going to be watching her program.

"Last season we finished thirty-eighth out of eighty-five prime-time programs. So we're fighting against some of the biggest-drawing shows in the history of television. This season we're up against *Next Door Neighbors* and *Border Patrol.*"

Rune nodded and said, "Wow," even though she'd only seen one episode of *Neighbors*—the season's big hit sitcom—and thought it was the stupidest thing on TV, full of wisecracking and mugging for the camera and teenage girls with teased-up hair, who'd roll their eyes and look exasperated at their parents. *Border Patrol* had great visuals and a super soundtrack, though all that ever happened was the cute young agent and the older, wiser agent argued explosively about department procedures, then saved each other's asses on alternate weeks. *Current Events,* on the other hand, she watched all the time, her only regret about the program being that she could never get her hair to look as neat and shiny as Piper Sutton's.

Maisel continued. "We've got four segments each week, surrounded by a million bucks' worth of commer-

cials. You don't have time to be leisurely. You don't have
time to develop subjects and have mood shots. You'll
shoot ten thousand feet of tape and use two hundred.
We're classy. We've got computer graphics coming out
our ears. We paid sixty thousand dollars for synthesized
theme music by this hotshot New Age musician. This is
the big time. No sex-change operations, no dolphins saving fishermen's lives, no three-year-old crack dealers. We
report news. It's a magazine, the way the old *Life* or *Look*
was a magazine. Remember that."

Rune nodded.

"Magazine," Maisel continued, "as in pictures and
words. I'll want tape of the crime scene, old footage, new
interviews."

Rune sat forward. "Oh, yeah, and how about claustrophobic prison scenes, you know, small green rooms and
bars? Maybe the rooms where they hose down prisoners?
Before and after pictures of Boggs—to see how thin and
pale he's gotten."

"Good. I like that." Maisel looked at a slip of telephone
message paper. "Piper said you're with the local station.
Doing what?"

"I'm a cameraman."

"I'll take you off that. I'll have you assigned to me."

"You mean I'll be on staff? Of *Current Events*?"

"Temporarily."

"Super fantastic."

"Maybe. And maybe not," Maisel said. "Let's see how
you feel about it after you've interviewed a hundred people and been up all night—"

"I stay up late all the time."

"Editing tape?"

Rune said, "Dancing usually."

Maisel said, "Dancing." He seemed amused. He said,
"Okay, here's the situation. . . . You're working for me

now. Normally we assign a staff producer, but Piper wants you to work directly with me. Nobody else. I don't have anybody to spare for camera work, so you're on your own there. But you know how the hardware works—"

"I'm saving up to buy my own Betacam."

"Wonderful," he said with a bored sigh, then slid a wooden pipe toward him and took a leather pouch of tobacco from his desk.

A secretary's spun-haired head appeared. She said that Maisel's eleven o'clock appointment had arrived. His phone started ringing. His attention was elsewhere now. "Okay. That's it. Get started."

Rune blinked. "That's it? Just get started?"

"Sure."

Rune said, "I kinda thought you were going to, like, tell me what to do or something."

As he turned to the phone, Maisel said abruptly, "I'll tell you what to do. You say there's a story out there. Well, go get it."

"This ain' you."

"Sure, it is. Only what I did with my hair was that I used henna and this kind of purple stuff, then I'd use mousse to get it spiky. . . ."

The security guard at the New York State Department of Correctional Services Manhattan office looked at Rune's laminated press pass, dangling a chrome chain tail. It showed a picture of her with a woodpeckery, glossy hairdo and wearing round, tinted John Lennon glasses.

"This ain' you."

"No, really." She dug the glasses out of her purse, and put them on, then grabbed her hair and pulled it straight up. "See."

The guard looked back and forth for a moment from the ID to the person, then nodded and handed the pass back to her. "You want my opinion, keep that stuff outa yo hair. That ain' natural."

Rune pulled the chain over her head. She walked into the main office, looking at the bulletin boards, the government-issue desks, the battered water fountains. It seemed like the place where people in charge of prisons should work: claustrophobic, colorless, quiet.

She thought about poor Randy Boggs, serving three years in his tiny cell.

I'm still here. . . .

You think, hell, I'm still here. . . .

A tall man in a rumpled cream-colored suit walked past her, and glanced down at the pass. He smiled, "You're press?"

Rune didn't understand him at first. "Oh, press. Yeah. I'm a reporter. *Current Events.* You know, the news—"

He laughed. "Everybody knows *Current Events.*" He stuck his hand out. "I'm Bill Swenson. Head of Press Relations here."

She shook his hand and introduced herself. Then she said, "I guess I'm looking for you. I have to talk to somebody about interviewing a prisoner."

"Is this for a story?"

Rune said, "Uh-huh."

"That's easily done. But you don't have to go through us. You can contact the warden's office directly for permission, and then the prisoner to arrange a time to meet."

"That's all?"

"Yep," Swenson said. "Which facility?"

"Attica."

"Doing hard time, huh?"

"Yeah, I guess it would be."

"Who's the prisoner?"

She was hesitating. "Well . . ."

Swenson said, "We've really gotta know. I won't leak it. I didn't get where I am by screwing journalists."

She said, "Okay, it's Randy Boggs. He was convicted of killing Lance Hopper?"

"Oh, yeah, I think I remember that. Hopper worked for your network, right?"

"That's right. Only the thing is, Boggs is innocent."

"Innocent, really?"

Rune nodded. "And I'm going to get him released. Or a new trial or something. I don't know how it works yet."

"That's going to make one hell of a story. . . . Promise you won't quote me?" Swenson glanced up and down the halls.

"Sure." Rune felt a chill of excitement. Here was her first confidential source.

"It happens. Every year there're maybe twenty, thirty people who are wrongly convicted. Sometimes they get out, sometimes they don't. It's a scary thing to think it could happen."

"I think it'll make a good story."

Swenson started down the hall. Rune followed him. He said, "I've got a meeting now. Otherwise I'd give you the number to Attica. But you can just call Directory Assistance. Area code is seven-one-six. Ask for the warden's office."

He escorted her through the security gate and to the door. She said, "I'm glad I ran into you."

"Good luck," he said.

After she'd left, Swenson walked into a phone booth next to the security guard station. He picked up the phone and dialed a number. As he waited for an answer, he was jotting notes into a battered stenographer's notebook. When a woman's voice answered, he said, "Hi, it's Bill Stevens, give me the city desk. . . ." He waited on hold for just a minute. "Hey, Tony, save me half a column in the evening final. I've got a nice little story for you."

CHAPTER FOUR

When Rune climbed up the gangway onto her houseboat, which was rocking gently in the Hudson River near the West Village, she heard Ophelia crying. Her hand hesitated at the deadbolt, then she unlocked the door and walked inside.

"Claire . . . hi," Rune said. Then, because she couldn't think of anything else to say: "You're still here."

The young woman was on her knees, comforting her three-year-old. Claire nodded at Rune and gave her a sullen smile, then turned back to the little girl.

"It's okay, honey."

"What happened?"

"She just fell. She's okay."

Claire was a few years older than Rune. They looked a lot alike, except that Claire was into a beatnik phase. She'd dyed her hair black and pulled it straight back in a severe ponytail. She wore pedal pushers a lot and black-and-white striped pullovers. Her face was deathly white, and she wore the loudest crimson lipstick Max Factor dared make. Her only redeeming virtue, in Rune's present opinion, was that she added real nice to the houseboat's decor, which was more or less 1950s suburban.

After Claire had lost her job at Celestial Crystals on Broadway and been evicted from the fifth floor East Village walk-up, she'd begged Rune to take her in for a couple days.

"I don't know," Rune had said, "I don't think it's a good idea to stay here too long. With the baby and all. Babies shouldn't live on boats. I think I read that somewhere. It affects their, I don't remember, balance, or something."

"You don't want us to be homeless, do you?" Claire asked.

Which Rune had to consider some, before she decided she didn't think she wanted them to be homeless.

"Come on. Just a day or two. It'll be fun. Like a pajama party."

That had been six weeks ago—a month and a half that'd been like no pajama party Rune had ever been to.

That morning, before Rune went to work, Claire had promised they'd be gone by dinnertime.

Now, Claire stood up and shook her head in disgust. "What it is, that guy, he backed out. Some people, some effing people."

Rune didn't exactly remember who the *that guy* was or what he was backing out of. But Rune was now just as pissed at him as Claire was. Talk now or later? Her courage broke, and she dropped her leopard-skin bag on the purple shag kidney-shaped scrap of carpet that she'd found on the street and used for a rug. She bent down and kissed the three-year-old's forehead.

Ophelia stopped crying. "Rune," she said. "Story. Will you read me a story?" She was dressed in blue jeans and a dirty yellow pullover.

"Later, honey, it's time for dinner," Rune said, crouching down and smoothing the girl's curly dark hair. "This hair is like totally audacious." She stood up and walked into the galley of the houseboat. As she poured Grape-Nuts into a large bowl, and added chocolate chips and cashews, she shouted to Claire, "What it is, is all that garbage we use. We dye it and we mousse it and we perm it. . . . I'll bet you never touch your hair, it'd be as nice as that forever."

Claire said sourly, "Well, sure, but that would like be so boring."

Rune came back into the living room, eating the cereal and drinking a Molson Golden. "You eaten?"

"We ate Chinese."

"Ophelia too? Is that good for her?"

Claire said, "Are you kidding? There are a billion people in China, and whata you think they grew up on? Cold sesame noodles and Empire Sezchwan chicken and fortune cookies."

"I don't know—"

"So how come you're eating that crap?" Claire glanced at the cereal.

"I'm not a three-year-old. Don't you watch commercials? She's supposed to be eating that gross stuff that comes in jars. You know, like pureed carrots and spinach."

"Why? She's got teeth," Claire said.

"I like spinch," Ophelia said.

Rune said, "I was you, I'd get a book. Mister Spock. The guy on *Star Trek*. I heard he wrote a book about raising kids."

Claire said, "Yeah, the Vulcan nerve pinch. That's what I'd like to learn. Put 'em right to sleep."

"What's a Vulcan?" Ophelia asked. Then she disappeared into the bedroom, without waiting for an answer. She returned a few minutes later, pulling a stuffed dragon by the tail.

Rune made the dragon dance, then hug Ophelia. She asked the little girl, "What's her name? Do you remember?"

"Persephy."

"Very good. Persephone. And who was Persephone?"

Ophelia held up the dragon.

"No, I mean in real life?"

Claire said, "Real life?"

"She was a goddess," Ophelia answered. "She was Zeus's little girl." Rune hugged her.

Claire said, "I don't think it's a good idea you're teaching her that stuff like it's true."

"What isn't true about it?"

"About the gods and goddesses and fairies and all that shit."

"Shit," said Ophelia.

Rune said to Claire, "You're saying it's not true?" Her voice was high with surprise.

"You believe in Roman goddesses?"

"Persephone was Greek. . . . I'm not saying I believe, and I'm not saying I don't."

"I want her to grow up to be a highly grounded person."

"Oh, get crucial," Rune said. "Your goal in life is to be a downtown diva, and *you* want to teach her about reality?"

"I want her to be an adult."

Rune whispered, "She's three years old. She'll grow up fast enough."

"Not necessarily. Some people I know have resisted adulthood very successfully."

"Look, Claire—" Rune set down the bowl of cereal, then began picking out the chocolate chips.

Claire tilted her head. "Favor, please?"

"I'm broke."

"Naw, what it is is I gotta go dancing tonight. I mean, like I totally have to. Baby-sit, will you?"

"Claire—"

"I really have to go. I met this guy. . . . Please. . . . Just this once. You two get along so good."

Rune looked at Ophelia. "We get along, dude?" She

held up her hand and Ophelia crawled forward and slapped it, five high.

"Dude," the little girl said, then crawled back to Persephone. Rune looked at her face and didn't see much of Claire in it. She wondered who the father was. Claire, she suspected, wondered the same.

After a moment, Rune said, "You know, I'm not, like, too good with things like this." Rune paused, hoping Claire would pick up on the hint. But she was concentrating on putting a fake diamond earring into one of the holes on the side of her nose. Rune continued, "What I'm saying is you really've got to find a place to live."

"I didn't plan on staying this long. It's not that easy to find a place to live in Manhattan."

"But I get the feeling you're looking for a place to live where you don't have to pay any rent, and that, like, puts a major crimp in the possibilities."

"You live here and don't pay rent."

"I *bought* this place. With money."

"I had some money once," Claire said. "It was wild."

"I don't want to kick you out," Rune began.

Claire got solemn for a moment. "The truth is I'm thinking about going back to Boston. Just to get my act together for a while. What do you think?"

Hallelujah.

Rune said, "I think that's a very mature thing to do. It'll be best for everybody."

"I'll stay with my mother. She's got a nice house. I can have the upstairs to myself. It'd be like R and R, you know. The only thing that bothers me is I don't know what I could do there, exactly."

Rune wasn't sure what Claire could do here in Manhattan either, except hang out, which she could probably do in Boston just as easily and at least the streets would be cleaner. But she said, "Boston's supposed to be a wonderful place. History, lots of history."

"Yeah, history. . . . The only thing is what do you *do* with it? It's not like Tower Records or a club."

"No, history is great! I love history." Rune pointed out the window to the east. "Just look out there, picture it three hundred years ago. You know who lived there? Indians! The Canarsie Indians. And there were bears and deer and everything. This used to be tobacco fields. They called the place Sapokanikan. It means *the tobacco plantation*. Then the settlers came up here from New York City, which was all down by the Battery then. They came up here because they had all these terrible plagues or epidemics—and they saw all these fields and farmland and the place got called Green Village—"

"And now it's Greenwich Village and it's got bagels and coffeehouses and ATM machines. . . . And Tower Records, thank God."

Rune shook her head, "Oh, you're just so sitcom, it's disgusting. Just think about the pirate ships that'd sail up the Hudson River."

Claire shook her head. "Tell me what you think about Boston. You mind if I spend some time there?"

"Mind?" Feeling like she'd just gotten a package in a turquoise Tiffany's box. "I'd say it's totally excellent."

"I think I'll do it," Claire said lethargically, then yawned and pulled a vial out of her purse. "You want some coke?"

"Coke," said Ophelia.

Rune took Claire by the arm and pulled her away from the little girl. "Are you crazy? Look what you're teaching her." She pulled the vial and spoon away from her and dropped them in Claire's purse.

Claire pulled her arm away angrily. "Coke is real. Dragons and goddesses aren't."

"You keep your reality." Rune stood up and took Ophelia by the hand and led her up on the outer deck. "Come on, honey, I'll read you a story. But you've got to keep a lookout for sea monsters."

"I saw one today," the little girl said.

Rune said to Claire, "There, see."

An hour later, Ophelia asked, "One more, please."

Rune sipped her third beer and debated, flipping through the book of fairy stories. She glanced down into the galley and saw Claire doing a small line of coke off her compact mirror.

It was eight P.M. "Okay," Rune said, "one more, then off to bed."

She looked at the story the book had fallen open to and laughed. *The Snow Princess.* Which seemed like a good choice, since Claire had her own blizzard going at the moment.

" 'Once upon a time—' "

"In a land far away," Ophelia yawned and lay down with her head in Rune's lap.

"That's right. '. . . in a land far away, there lived an old couple who never had any children.' "

"I'm a children."

" 'The man and woman loved each other dearly, but dreamed about how happy they would be if only they had a daughter to share their life with. Then one winter, as the husband was walking home through the forest, he saw a snowman that some children had built, and he had an idea. He went home and together, with his wife, they built a little princess out of snow.' "

"What's snow?"

"Last winter, that white stuff."

"I don't remember."

"It comes out of the sky and it's white."

"Feathers."

"No, it's like wet."

"Milk."

"No, it's cold."

" 'Nilla ice cream!"

Rune said, "Like, don't worry about it. All you've gotta know is it's this white stuff falls out of the sky and you make princesses out of it, okay?"

"Okay."

"And then the couple went to bed and all night long they wished and wished real hard, and what do you think happened?"

"They got a little girl?"

Rune read, " 'In the morning, when they woke up, there was the most beautiful little princess, who looked just like the girl the couple had made out of snow the night before. They hugged her and kissed her and they spent all their time playing with her and taking the little girl for walks in the forest. The couple was so happy. . . .

" 'Then one day a handsome prince came riding along through the snow, and saw the snow princess playing in a snow-filled field beside the couple's house. They looked at each other and fell in love.' "

"What's?—"

"Never mind that, the thing is he wanted the snow princess to come live with him in his castle at the foot of the mountain. . . . 'The snow princess's parents were very sad and begged her not to go, but she married the prince and went off to live with him in the castle.

" 'They were very happy throughout the winter, then one day in early spring, the sun came out, strong and hot, as the snow princess was walking with her husband. . . .' "

Rune paused and read ahead in the story, to the part where the sun gets hotter and hotter and the princess melts, the water running through her husband's fingers into the ground.

"Go on," Ophelia said.

Rune said, "Well . . . the sun was so hot that the snow princess remembered how much she missed her parents, and she kissed her husband good-bye and climbed back up to the mountain village, where she moved back in with her parents, and got a job and met a neat guy, who was also made out of snow, and they lived happily ever after."

"I like that story," Ophelia said in her tone of an official pronouncement.

Claire came out on deck. "Time for bed."

Ophelia didn't complain much. She was tired. Rune kissed her goodnight, then helped Claire put her pajamas on her and get her into bed.

"You know, like for your information," Claire said, "it's much easier to meet men in Boston."

"You like want me to go to Boston with you? Just to meet men?"

"Sure, why not?"

"Because most men are like seriously damaged to start with. Why should I go somewhere where it's easier to meet men? I'd think you'd want to go where it's harder."

"What's wrong with men?"

"Haven't you noticed something?" Rune asked. "How many men do you know whose IQ matches their age?"

"You gonna marry Sam?"

"He's okay to go out with," Rune said defensively. "We have a good time."

Claire sighed. "He's twenty years older than you, he's going bald, he's married."

Rune said, "So what twenty-five-year olds've you met are such good catches? I'm twenty-two. I've got eight years until middle age. What's the hurry?"

"You move to Boston, you'll be married in six months. I guarantee it." Claire pirouetted. "How do I look?"

Like a new wave hooker.

Rune said, "Stunning."

Claire grabbed her bag and slung it over her shoulder. "I owe you one."

"I know you do," Rune said, and watched her clatter unsteadily down the gangplank on her spike-heeled boots.

CHAPTER FIVE

The note was to the point. *Sutton's office. The minute you come in. —Lee.*

She found it sitting, the next morning, on her cubicle desk in the studio.

Rune had received a lot of notes like this, and they were usually the preface to flunking a course, getting fired, or getting yelled at.

She left her breakfast of pizza and Morning Thunder tea on her desk and trotted out of the studio. In ten minutes she was standing in front of Piper Sutton's secretary. Yesterday's look of terror had been replaced by a subtle gloat.

Rune said, "I'm supposed to see—"

The woman nodded, smiling. "They're waiting for you."

"Is it okay to—?"

"They're waiting for you," she repeated happily.

Inside, Sutton and Maisel turned their heads and stared. Rune stopped, then swallowed.

"Close the door," Sutton ordered.

Rune obeyed, then walked into the room. She smiled at Maisel, who avoided her eyes.

Oh, boy, she thought. Oh, boy.

Sutton's eyes were flint. She said, "Sit down," just as Rune was dropping into the chair across from the ornate desk. She felt a shiver down her back and the hairs on her neck stirred. Sutton tossed a copy of one of the city's tabloids on her desk. Rune picked it up, and read a story circled in thick, red ink that bled into the fibers of the newsprint.

Network Wants to Free
Killer of Its Exec
By Bill Stevens

The story was short, just a few paragraphs, and it told how a reporter from *Current Events* was investigating Randy Boggs's conviction for Lance Hopper's murder. Boggs's defense lawyer, Fred Megler, had no comment other than that his client had always maintained his innocence. No one at the Network, the article said, could be reached for comment.

"Oh. Shit."

Sutton sat down and tapped her glossy fingernails on the desk top. They were as red and hard as the finish on a Porsche. "All right, how did it happen?"

"It's not my fault. He lied to me."

"Bill Stevens?"

"That wasn't his name. I was at the Department of Corrections and this guy came up to me, and said he worked for the press department and could he help me and he was real nice and he even told me things off the record, so I assumed it was okay to—"

"Assumed it was okay?" Sutton's voice rose, she lifted her eyes to the ceiling. "I don't believe it."

Maisel sighed, "This's the oldest trick in the book. Jesus. Stevens is a beat reporter. He covers the government agencies. When he sees a reporter who's new and doesn't recognize him, he finds out what the story is, then scoops everybody. You wore your press pass?"

She nodded. "I thought I was supposed to."

"And you walked right into his arms." Sutton lit a ciga-

rette and slapped the lighter down on the desk top.
"Brother."

"He seemed like such a nice guy."

"He's a charming guy, sure," Maisel said, exasperated.
"You've got to learn charming's a lot different from honest."

All ruined. My one big chance, and I blew it.

Sutton looked at her and seemed to think about saying
something nice or encouraging, but changed her mind.
She said to Maisel, "Damage assessment?"

"None of the other nets are that interested." He
touched the tabloid. "Even he didn't follow up on Boggs.
The focus of the story was that we're trying to get him
out. The fact is nobody . . ." He looked at Rune.
". . . seems to think Boggs is innocent. . . . It'll hit some
services, but so far all we've had is a couple junior reporters call Publicity for statements. Nobody like Wal-
lace or Rather, nobody from *Media in Review*. It's a pain
in the ass, but I don't think it's critical."

Sutton kept her eyes on Rune as she said, "I've already
gotten a call from Semple."

Maisel closed his eyes. "Ouch. I thought he was in
Paris."

"He is. The *Herald Tribune* picked up the story."

Dan Semple. The head of Network News, Lance Hopper's successor. Rune cringed. He was, give or take a few
miracles, God.

Maisel asked, "What was his reaction?"

"Not fit for human consumption," Sutton said. "He'll be
back in a few days and he wants to talk about it." She
sighed. "Corporate politics. Just what we need now. With
the budgets coming up in a month. . . ." Sutton looked at
Rune. "But the big danger is that another magazine or
feature program'll pick up the lead and bring out the story
at the same time we do."

Maisel said to Rune, "It's a policy, we don't spend time and money on a story if there's a chance we'll be pre-empted."

"I'm really, really sorry," Rune said. She rocked forward in the chair. "It won't happen again. I promise. I'll be so skeptical you won't believe it. I'll be obnoxious, I'll be so skeptical."

"Rune—" Sutton began.

"Look, what I'll do is ask people when I interview them if anybody else has been asking them questions. If so, I'll tell you, I promise. That way you can decide if you want to go ahead."

Maisel said, "The only weapon journalists have is their minds. You've got to start using yours."

"I will. . . . Oh, I'll think a lot more than I do now. Just like the Scarecrow."

Sutton said, "Scarecrow?"

"You know, the Wizard of Oz. He wanted a brain. Sometimes I act like my head's filled with . . ."

Sutton managed to make her face both blank and hostile at the same time. The look bled the volume out of Rune's words. Finally, the anchorwoman laughed. "All right, but anybody beats us to the punch—I'm talking anybody, a rap station, MTV, Columbia's student station —we drop the project. Lee?"

"Okay with me," Maisel said, though he was grimacing.

Lighting a cigarette, Sutton nodded and said, "This was your last strike, babes."

"I thought you got three," Rune said, standing up, retreating to the door.

Sutton tossed the lighter onto her desk; it skidded into a glass crystal ashtray. "With me, you only get one."

* * *

"Huph, if he didn't do this one, he did *something."*

The man's voice went high at the end of the sentence and threatened to break apart. He was in his late forties, so skinny that his worn cowhide belt made pleats in slacks that were supposed to be straight-cut. His white shirt billowed out in back like a sail. Rune thought he had real nice eyelashes. They were soft and dark. His face was gray and mottled, and would make occasional forays into exaggerated expressions (wonder, hatred, surprise) then snap back into its waiting state of innocent incredulity, punctuated with a breathy, nasal snort. *"Huph,* and if he did *something,* the jury says, 'Fuck it, let's convict him.' "

Rune nodded at the taut words.

The man sat at his desk, which was mounded high— yellow sheets, court briefs, Redweld folders, letters, photographs of crime scenes, an empty yogurt carton crusty on the rim, a dozen cans of Diet Pepsi, a shoe box (she wondered if it contained a fee). The office was on Broadway, on Maiden Lane. The location was small-time Wall Street—grimy, dark, crowded. Inside, the building was a network of dirty, dark, green corridors.

The office of Frederick T. Megler, J.D., P.C., was at the end of a particularly dark and particularly green corridor.

"That's what I have to deal with." The bony fingers of his right hand made a circuit of the air. *"Huph,* I get a Fred Williams from Harlem or Victor Ruiz from Bed-Sty, and they're nineteen years old and they got a yellow sheet you measure in feet, not number of bookings. And you look at them and know that these are not young men you want your children to be playing with. And, sure, they probably had a MAC-10 hidden in their Guess! jacket, along with a thousand bucks from a dealer a block away they fiended, but when the cops got them they were clean. And the way the system works . . ." He looked at Rune, and his voice rose in volume the same way his eyebrows lifted. *"The way the system works* is that they can only convict you for the crime for which you've been accused. They can't convict you because you're an asshole, or because of the three guys you wasted last year, or because of the old lady you're going to fiend tomorrow for her social security check. *Just for the particular crime!"*

"Got it," Rune said.

"Huph, so what happens?"

"I give up."

Megler's other set of bony fingers joined in. They pointed at her. "You get things like this: True story. An ADA, bless her young, virginal soul, brings some kid up on four counts. Murder two, manslaughter one and two, criminally negligent homicide. Those last counts are what they call lesser included offenses. They're easier to prove. If you can't make the first count, maybe you can get a second one, or a third one, and so on. *Huph,* okay? My client had a grudge against the vic. When the cops arrested him, probable cause based on an informer, he was found in a bar in Times Square, where two witnesses swore he'd been drinking for four hours. The vic— who got his head ventilated with three nine-millimeter slugs—was killed two hours before."

"Right," Rune said.

The voice dipped from its screech and sounded earnest. "So my client—a guy without a gun and with an alibi—got arrested. I grill the informant in court and by the time I'm through, his story's as riddled as the vic's forehead, okay? *Huph,* but what happens? *They convict my guy!* Not of murder two, which is what they should've done, if they believed the informant, but of criminally negligent homicide. That's . . ." The voice cracked. "Bullshit. You don't negligently shoot three bullets into somebody's head. The chickenshit jury didn't have the balls to get him on murder two, but they couldn't let him walk because he's a black kid from the Bronx who had a record and had said on a number of occasions he wanted to cut the vic's spleen out of his body."

Rune sat forward in her chair. "See, that's just what I'm doing my story on—an innocent man got convicted."

"Whoa, honey, I didn't say he was innocent."

She blinked and went through the facts for a moment. "I thought you did. What about the gun, what about the alibi?"

"Huph, he iced the vic, ditched the gun, then paid two buddies a six-pack of crack to give him the alibi and to perjure themselves. . . ."

"But—"

"But the point is not, is he guilty? The point is you gotta play by the rules. And the jury wasn't. You can only convict on the evidence that was presented. The jury didn't do that."

"But it worked out, in the end, didn't it?"

"No, the kid got convicted for the wrong reason."

Megler smiled and rattled Diet Pepsi cans until he found the one that wasn't empty. "Welcome to the world of criminal justice." He sipped through a bent straw until there was a slurp.

"What's so wrong with that? He was guilty, and the jury convicted him. That sounds okay to me."

"Huph, okay, let me just say one thing while you're on your high horse. Let's pretend that Fred Williams, National Merit Scholar with a ticket to Harvard Medical School, who all he's ever done bad is get a parking ticket, is walking down a Hundred and Thirty-fifth Street when two of New York's finest screech up behind him, get him in a choke hold, then drag him to the precinct and book him for rape, and he gets picked out of a lineup and goes

to trial, where the DA describes to a predominantly Caucasian middle-class jury how this kid beat, raped, and sodomized a mother of two. Then a predominantly Caucasian middle-class witness describes the perp as a black kid with razor-notched hair and basketball sneakers, and the predominantly Caucasian middle-class doctor gets up and describes the injuries. . . . What the hell do you think is going to happen to Fred? He's going to jail, and he ain't gonna be just visiting."

Rune was quiet.

"Sure, most of my clients are scum. And most of them are guilty scum. But as long as there's that one chance that a Fred Williams is going to get busted by mistake, the world's got to put up with people like me."

"Is that your closing argument?"

Megler laughed. "A variation on one of them. *Huph*, I've got a great repertoire. Blows the jury away."

"I don't really believe what you're saying, but it looks like you do."

"Oh, I do indeed. And as soon as I stop believing it, then I'm history. I'll go into handicapping or professional blackjack. The odds are better, and you still get paid in cash. Now, I've got some truly innocent clients coming in in about a half hour. You said you wanted to ask me about the Boggs case?"

"Can I tape you?"

His thin face twisted. He looked like Ichabod Crane. "Why don't you just take notes?"

"Okay, sure. If you really want. . . ." She smiled and tipped her head in a subtle replay of the request.

He smiled back. Coy was one technique that doesn't work with lawyers like Fred Megler. She borrowed a yellow pad and pencil from him, thinking that it wasn't particularly good form for a journalist to be using the interviewee's own paper and pencil.

She asked, "You represented him?"

"Yep. He was a Section eighteen case. Indigent. So the state paid my fee to represent him."

"I really think he's innocent."

"Uh-huh."

"No, I really, really think so."

"*Huph,* you say so."

"Could you tell me what happened? About Hopper's death, I mean."

Megler sat back in a thoughtful pose, theatrically. He studied the grimy ceiling. The window was open a crack and exhaust-scented April air wafted through the space and riffled stacks of paper.

"The ADA said that Boggs was driving through town from, I don't know, upstate, I think. He was walking down the street and got into a fight with Hopper over something. Hopper'd just gotten home from work and had just pulled into the courtyard of his building on the Upper West Side. The prosecutor speculated it was a traffic dispute."

Rune's eyes made a circuit of the ceiling. "Traffic."

"Hey, you asked what the ADA said. I'm telling you. I'm trying to be helpful. Am I being helpful?"

"Helpful," Rune said. "What was Randy's story?"

"Part of the problem was that he had a story."

"Huh?"

"*Huph,* you're arrested, you don't have to take the stand. *Do . . . not . . . do . . . it.* The jury can't—the judge tells them this—the jury can't draw any conclusions from the defendant not taking the stand. But Randy —against my advice, I wanta point out—did. I tell all my clients, 'Clam up from day one,' but, naw, he had to get up there. The prosecutor can introduce evidence of prior convictions for the purpose of attacking the credibility of what you're saying. But what does the jury hear? Fuck credibility, all they hear is a string of arrests for petty crimes. Next thing you know, Boggs, who's really a pretty decent guy's just had some bad luck, is sounding like Hitler. He's got a petty larceny bust in Ohio, some juvie bullshit down in Florida, GTA in—"

"What's that?"

"Grand theft auto. So suddenly, the ADA's making him sound like he's head of the Gambino family. He—"

"Where was the gun?"

"*Huph*, let me finish, willya? He was with this guy picked him up hitchhiking, a guy who was into some kind of credit card scam. This guy goes to buy some hot cards or something, and Boggs is waiting in the car. He hears a shot, he goes to look for the driver. He sees Hopper lying there, dead. He turns and runs smack into a police car."

"He had the gun?"

"The gun was off a ways, in some bushes. They said he pitched it there. No prints, but they traced it to a theft in Florida about a year before the killing. Boggs had spent time in Miami."

"Who was this other guy?"

"Boggs was hitchhiking along the Taconic and the man picked him up. They drove into the city together."

"Oh, wow," Rune said, eyes wide. "A witness. Totally excellent. Did you find him?"

Megler looked at her as if enthusiasm and the flu were pretty much the same thing.

"Yeah, right. Even he's real, which he isn't, a guy who's involved in a credit card boost's gonna come forward and testify? *Huph*, what're you smoking, honey?"

"Did Randy describe him?"

"Real specific. Name was Jimmy. It was late, it was dark, et cetera."

"You don't believe him?"

"Believe, not believe, what difference does it make?"

"Any other witnesses?"

"Good question. You want to go to law school?"

You don't want my answer, Megler.

The lawyer said, "That was the big problem. Forget his taking the stand. What fucked him, excuse me, what did him in was this witness. The cops found someone in the building who described Boggs and then later she IDed him in a lineup. She saw him pull out a gun and ice Hopper."

"Ouch."

"Yeah, ouch."

"What was the name?"

"How would I know?" Megler opened a file cabinet and retrieved a thick stack of paper. He tossed it on the desk. Pepsi cans shook and dust rose. "It's in there someplace. You can have it, you want."

"What is it?"

"The trial transcript. I ordered it as a matter of course, but Boggs didn't want to appeal, so I just filed it."

"He didn't want to appeal?"

"He kept claiming he was innocent, but he said he wanted to get the clock running. Get it over with and get on with his life."

Rune said, "I saw in the story that the conviction was for manslaughter."

"The jury convicted on manslaughter one. He showed reckless disregard for human life. Got sentenced to fifteen years. He's served almost three. He'll be eligible for parole in two years. And he'll probably get it. I hear he's a good boy."

"What do you think?"

"Huph, about what?"

"Is he one of your guilty clients?"

"Of course. The old I-was-just-hitchhiking story. You hear it all the time. There's always a mysterious driver or girl or hit man or somebody who disappears. Bullshit is what it is. Yeah, Boggs is guilty. I can read them all."

"But if I found new evidence—"

"I've heard this before."

"No, really. I'm like totally certain he's innocent."

"Look, in New York it's almost impossible to get a conviction overturned because of new evidence." He squinted, recalling. "It's got to be the kind of evidence that would've changed the outcome of the case in the first place, and you have to be able to show you made diligent efforts to find the evidence at the time of the trial."

"But if I did find something, would you handle the case?"

"Me?" He laughed. "You're talking a lot of hours. I bill at two twenty per."

"But he's innocent."

"So you say. Come up with fifteen, twenty thousand for a retainer, I'll talk to you."

"I was hoping you'd do it for free."

Megler laughed again, hearty. Since he had no belly, it seemed to be his bones that were jiggling under the slick polyester skin of his shirt. "Free? I don't believe I'm familiar with that word."

CHAPTER SIX

What's that?

Rune lay in her bed, her arm around the stuffed dragon, wishing it were Sam or any ex-boyfriend (or ideally a new boyfriend) and tried to figure it out.

What's wrong with this picture?

She felt the boat gently rocking in the Hudson. Heard the baritone grind of a boat engine that seemed near but was probably two hundred yards away—she'd learned how noise carries on the water.

So what was it? What was missing? What wasn't here that ought to be?

The tie-dye sheet had tangled around her feet, a percale Gordian knot. Her white Joy of Movement T-shirt had ridden up above her breasts, and her hair was in her face. Rune was a restless sleeper. She untangled her feet and pulled the shirt down. She brushed a crescent of pizza crust out of the bed and sat upright.

Well, it was silence. That was part of it.

But more.

It was the silence that comes from the absence of a human being.

Rune realized that Claire was gone.

It was eleven, and by now Claire always had her Walkman plugged in—like it was a dialysis machine for her brain. Even upstairs, in the houseboat's bedroom, Rune usually could hear the raspy chunk of decibels murdering Claire's eardrums.

But today, nothing.

Rune went into the white-enameled head, thinking: Maybe she got up early to go shopping.

Maybe she'd actually gone out and gotten a job.

Both of which Rune thought were about as likely as what actually happened.

Claire had moved out.

Rune, downstairs, standing in the middle of the living room, grinning like a kid on Christmas eve, read the note.

Totally fresh.

About how Claire appreciated (spelled wrong) everything Rune had done for her in the past couple weeks (six and a half), even though she was a moody bitch a lot but that was good because if she could live with Rune, she could live with anybody (Rune, trying to figure who the *she*'s were and not liking the conclusion).

Claire explained that she was going home to her mother's in Boston, like she'd said, how she was going to think about school again. She spent a long paragraph, the last, talking about how happy she was that Rune and Ophelia were such good friends and how they'd gotten along so well, because—

The smile vanished.

—she knew Rune would take good care of the girl. . . .

The letter missed the table completely and fluttered to a rough landing on the carpet. Rune ran into the small storeroom in the bow of the boat, the room that Claire and Ophelia shared.

The room that was now Ophelia's exclusively.

Goddamn it!

The little girl was lying asleep on top of Claire's futon, her pillow, a mutant stuffed animal that may, at one time, have been a rabbit.

Son of a bitch. Claire, how could you?

Rune did a fast survey. The room was pretty much cleared out. Claire had taken her clothes and jewelry, and whatever other objects (some of them Rune's) had filled the dust-free squares and circles and trapezoids on the top of the dresser.

Everything, gone—except for Ophelia's toys and clothes and a poster of the Jackson Five that Claire had kept, waiting for it to become chic enough to put up again.

Son of a . . .

Rune ran outside to find the letter again.

. . . bitch.

The closing paragraph of the letter said only that she hoped to be back some time to pick up Ophelia and to give her the home she needed and deserved.

Rune was sweating. She actually felt her scalp prickle. Her fingers left stains on the paper.

Hoped to be back? *Some time?*

No address. No phone number.

She didn't even know Claire's last name.

Rune went back to the room and searched carefully. All she found was a bra under the bed with the initials penned on the side—C.S. But Rune thought it looked a little small for Claire and remembered that one of her boyfriends had been a transvestite.

Rune sat down in the middle of the room and picked up a toy, one of her favorites. A wooden penguin on a stick. His broad plastic feet were on wheels. Rune ran him back and forth, the flapper webs slapping on the wooden deck.

I don't want to be a mother.

She wasn't even married. Hell, she didn't even have a serious prospect for a boyfriend.

Claire . . .

Slap, slap, slap.

The jogging penguin woke up Ophelia.

Rune sat on the futon. "Honey, did you talk to your mommy?"

"Uh-huh."

"Before she left?"

The little girl rubbed her eyes.

Oh, they're so damn cute when they do that. Come on, kid, get ugly. . . .

"Uh-huh."

"Did she say where she was going?"

"Uh-uh. Can I have some juice?"

"Honey, did your mother say where she was going?"

"Bawden."

"Boston?"

"Uh-huh. Juice?"

"Sure. We'll get some Ocean Spray in a minute. Where in Boston?"

"Grandma's house."

"Where is your grandmother's house?"

"Bawden. I want some juice."

"Honey, what's your mother's name?"

"Mommy."

"No, I mean her last name?"

"Mommy."

Rune said, "Did she say anything before she left?"

Ophelia rubbed her eyes again and said, "Zoo."

"The zoo?"

"She said you'd take me to the zoo."

"That's what your mommy said?"

"Uh-huh."

"Did she say how long she'd be gone?"

Ophelia frowned for a moment, then extended her arms as wide as they'd go, and said, "Long, long time."

Rune picked up the stuffed rabbit. "Oh boy."

Ophelia said, "Juice."

Sam Healy was in his late thirties, over six feet and lean. His thinning hair was combed straight back, and his moustache drooped over the corners of his mouth. He resembled a cowboy, at least when he was wearing what he now wore—a plaid shirt, jeans and black boots. His profession: a detective on the NYPD Bomb Squad.

They sat in Rune's houseboat, where he spent an occasional night, and she leaned forward, listening to him as intensely as if he were telling a rookie how to dismantle a C-4 charge. She asked, "How often should I feed her?"

Healy said, "You're too nervous about this, Rune. She's a human being. She eats three times a day."

"How about medicine?" Rune's palms were glistening with sweat. "Should she be taking medicine?"

"Well, is she sick?"

"I don't think so."

"Then, why would she need medicine?"

Rune said, "She's like a baby. I thought you always gave medicine to babies."

"Probably vitamins is all. You can ask her."

"Oh, Sam, it was fun playing with her and reading to her, but this—this is like really, really serious."

"They're very resilient. They bounce."

"Oh, God."

"You ought to get a pedia—"

"Oh, God, what if she falls?"

Healy sighed. "Pick her up."

"I'm not ready for this, Sam. I can't be a mother. I'm trying to do my story. I'm. . . . Oh, God, does she wear diapers?"

"Ask her."

"I can't ask her. I'd be embarrassed."

"She's, what? about three? She's probably toilet trained. If not, you should start pretty soon."

"No way. Forget about it."

"Rune, kids are wonderful. When you and Adam and I go out, we have a great time."

"But he's *your* son. That's different. I don't want one of

my own. I'm too young to be a slave. My life is over with already."

"It's only temporary, isn't it?"

"That's sort of the part I'm not too sure about. . . ." Rune looked toward Ophelia's room. Her voice was panicky when she said, "You think she drinks too much juice?"

"Rune . . ."

"She drinks a lot of juice. Maybe I'm turning her internal organs permanently red. . . . See, that's the kind of stuff you've got to think about."

"You have to think a lot less than you are."

"Sam, I can't have a kid with me when I interview people. What am I—?"

"I'm going to give you the name of the day-care center we used to take Adam to. It's the best in the city. And some of the women there work nights as baby-sitters."

"Yeah?"

"People live with children every day. Look at the bright side: You didn't have to go through labor."

Rune sat close to him and lay her head on his chest. "Why do I get myself into things like this?"

"She's a sweet little girl."

Rune put her head in his lap. "They're all sweet when they're asleep. The thing is they wake up after a while. It's like a bad habit they have."

He began rubbing her shoulders.

"That's nice."

"Yeah," he said, "it is."

He rubbed for five minutes, his strong fingers working down her spine. She moaned. Then he untucked her T-shirt and began working his way up, under the cloth.

"That's nicer," she said, and rolled over on her back.

He kissed her forehead. She kissed his mouth, feeling

the tickle of the moustache. It was a sensation she'd gotten used to, one she liked a lot.

He kissed her back, his hand, still inside her T-shirt, worked its way up. He disarmed bombs, he had a very smooth touch.

"Rune!" Ophelia called from the bedroom.

They both jumped.

"Read me a story, Rune!"

Her hands covered her face, and she wailed, "Oh, Sam, what am I going to do?"

CHAPTER SEVEN

The train left pretty much on time and sailed out of the tunnel under Park Avenue, rising up on the elevated tracks like an old airplane that just couldn't gain altitude. Her head swiveled as she watched the red-brick projects, clusters of young men on the street. No one wore colorful clothing. It was all gray and brown. A woman pushed a grocery cart filled with rags. Two men stood over the open hood of a beige sedan, hands on their wide hips and seemed to be confirming a terminal diagnosis.

You wake up in the morning, and you think. . . .

The Amtrak train sped, and the scenes flipped past more quickly. Rune, leaning forward, climbing onto her knees, felt the lurch as the wheels danced sideways like a bullfighter's hips and they crossed the Harlem River Bridge. She waved to passengers on a Dayliner tour boat, as they looked up at the bottom of the bridge. No one noticed her. Then, the Bronx—plumbing supply houses and lumberyards, and in the distance, abandoned apartments and warehouses. Daylight showed through the upper-story windows. Good bargains in real estate there, she thought.

Rune tried to doze. But she kept seeing the tape of Boggs's face, broken into scan lines and each scan line a thousand pixels of red, blue, and green dots.

. . . hell, I'm still here.

The way their eyes looked at her—not envious at all—was weird.

She'd figured she'd get catcalls, or whoops or "Yo,

honey," or at least long gazes thick with curiosity or fas-
cination, as if they'd forgotten what it was like to flick a
Medeco open with that satisfying ratchet sound and just
stroll out into broad open country. To see the gray-green
hills in front of them, and the pale asphalt roads and the
orange Burger Kings and gaudy Toys "R" Us and utility
poles and Toyotas and dumpsters right there—right in
front of them, close enough to touch.

But nope. They looked at her the way assembly line
men'd glance at a plant visitor, someone walking timidly
between tall machines, careful not to get grease on her
good shoes. They looked, they ignored, they went back to
mopping floors or talking to wives or brothers or not doing much of anything.

She was an outsider, sure, but that was just a part of
the routine.

The warden's office had checked her press credentials
and guards searched her bag and the camera case. She
was then escorted into the visitor's area by a tall guard—
a handsome black man with a moustache that looked like
it was drawn above his lip in mascara. Visitors were separated from the prisoners by thick glass partitions and
talked to each other on old, heavy black telephones.

Rune stood for a moment, watching them all. Picturing
what it would be like to visit a husband in prison. So sad!
Only talking to him, holding the thick receiver, reaching
out and touching the glass, never feeling the weight or
warmth of his skin. . . .

"In here, miss."

The guard led her into a small room. She guessed it
would be reserved for private meetings between lawyers
and their prisoners. The guard disappeared. Rune sat at a
gray table. She waited. She studied the battered bars,
and thought the metal seemed stronger than anything
she'd ever seen. As if wind and rocks and sandstorms

had tried to wear through it, and had scarred but not dented the steel.

She was looking at the metal when Randy Boggs entered the room.

He was thinner than she'd expected. He looked best straight on; when he turned his head to glance at a guard (questioning if she was his visitor), his head became birdish. Like a woodpecker's, though his hair was longer than in the tape she'd studied, and the Dairy Queen twist was gone. It still glistened from the oil or creme he used to keep it in place. His ears were long and narrow and he had tufts of blond, wiry hair growing out of them. She saw dark eyes, darkened more by an overhang of bone, and thick eyebrows that reached toward each other. His skin wasn't good; in his face were patches of wrinkles like cities in satellite photos. But Rune thought it was a temporary unhealthiness—the kind that food and sun and sleep can erase.

Boggs looked at the guard and said, "Could you leave us?"

The man answered, "No."

Rune said to the guard, "I don't mind."

"No."

"Sure," Boggs said, as cheerful as if he'd been picked for first baseman in a softball game. He sat down and said, "What for you want to see me, miss?"

As she told him, she found she was agitated. The excitement, maybe. The surroundings. But there was more than that. She realized. It wasn't her; it was Boggs himself. The intensity of his calmness. Which didn't really make sense, but she thought about it and decided that was what she sensed: He was so peaceful that she felt her pulse rising, her breath coming quickly, on his account. She forced herself to calm down. Rune had interviewed people before. She'd put the camera in front of them, washed them in the hot light from Redhead lamps, and then asked them questions. She'd gotten tongue-tied some, and maybe asked the wrong questions, because she wasn't so good with politics and Washington and all the stuff that was on the first page of the *New York Times*. But one thing about her was that there was nothing she was afraid to ask. Interviewing, she was good at. For some reason, she'd found, people like to talk. And for an even more obscure reason, people particularly liked to talk to her.

Boggs, though, took some convincing.

"Fact of the matter is, when you told me you wanted to come talk to me, well, I's about as happy as a farmer in a July hail storm." He spoke in a soft voice; a slight Southern accent licked at his words.

"You don't like reporters?"

"I don't mean this personal, directed at you, miss, but you're the people convicted me."

"How?"

"Well, miss, you know the expression media circus? I'd never heard that before, but when I read about my trial afterwards, I found out about that. I wasn't the only person who felt that way. Somebody got interviewed in *Time* said that's what my trial was. I wrote a letter to Mr. Megler and to the judge saying that I thought it was a media circus. Neither of them wrote back."

"What was a circus about it?"

He smiled and looked off, as if he was arranging his thoughts. She decided he looked like a repairman. Rune pictured him—the prison uniform was part of it—in overalls politely explaining what was wrong with an Olds 88's transmission.

"The way I see it, there was so many of you reporters all over the place, writing things about me, that the jury got it into their head that I was guilty."

"But don't they . . ." There was a word she was looking for. "You know, don't they keep the jury in hotel
rooms and things?"

"Sequester," Boggs said. "You think that works? I was
on *Live at Five* the day I was arrested, and probably
every other day up till the trial. You think there was one
person in the tri-state area that didn't know about me? I
doubt it very much."

Rune had told him she worked for *Current Events,* but
there was no visible reaction; either he didn't watch the
program or he didn't know that it was on the Network,
the employer of the man he'd supposedly killed. Or
maybe he just wasn't impressed with reporters in general. He glanced at the Betacam sitting on the table beside Rune. "Had a film crew in the other day. Were shooting some kind of cop movie. Everybody was real excited
about it. They used some of the boys as extras. I didn't
get picked. They wanted people looked like convicts, I
guess. I looked more like a clerk, I guess. Or . . . what
would you say I looked like?"

"A man who got wrongly convicted."

A long second ticked, then another. And Boggs smiled
an interstate cloverleaf into his face. "You got some good
lines. I like that. Yeah, that's a role I've been acting for a
long time. Nobody's bought it yet."

"I want to get you released."

"Well, miss, seems like we've got a lot in common."

"I talked to Fred Megler—"

Boggs nodded, and his face held an expression of disappointment, but not contempt. "If I had money to hire
me a real lawyer, like those insider traders and, you
know, those coke kingfishers you see on TV, I think
things might've been different. Fred isn't a bad man. I just
don't believe his heart was in it. I reckon I'd say he
should've listened to some of my advice. I've had a little

experience with the law. Not a lot of which I'm proud of, but the fact remains I've seen the inside of a courtroom. He should've listened to me."

Rune said, "He told me your story. But I knew you were innocent when I saw you."

"When would that've been?"

"On film. An interview."

The smile was wistful. He kept evading her eyes. It bothered her. She thought it was shyness, not guile, but she didn't want shifty eyes on tape.

Boggs was saying, "I appreciate your opinion, miss, but if that's all you have to go on, I'm still feeling like a six-ounce bluegill on a twenty-pound line."

"Look at me and tell me. Did you do it or not?"

His eyes were no longer evasive; they locked onto hers and answered as clearly as his words, "I did not kill Lance Hopper."

"That's enough for me."

And Boggs wasn't smiling when he said, "Trouble is, it don't seem to be enough for the people of the state of New York."

CHAPTER EIGHT

Two hours later Randy Boggs got to: "That's when I decided to hitch to New York. And that was the biggest mistake of my life."

"You were tired of Maine?"

"The lobster business didn't work out like I'd hoped. My partner—see, I'm not much for figures—he kept the books, and all this cash coming in didn't no way equal the cash going out. I suspicioned he kept the numbers pretty obscured and when he sold the business, he told me he was letting it go to a couple creditors, but I think he picked up good money. Anyways, I had me maybe two, three hundred bucks was all, and two new pair of jeans, some shirts. I figured I'd be leaving that part of the country before another winter come. Snow belongs in movies and in paper cones with syrup on it. So I begun thumbing south. Rides were scarce's hens' teeth, but finally I got me some rides and ended up in Purchase, New York. If that isn't a name, I don't know. Purchase. . . . It was raining and I had my thumb out so long it was looking like a bleached prune. Nobody stopped, except this one fellow. He pulled over in a—we call them—a Chinese tenement car. Big old Chevy twelve or so years old, you know, could ride a family of ten. He said, "Hop in," and I did. Biggest mistake of my life, miss. I'll tell you that."

"He say what his name was?"

"Don't matter much. Said 'Jimmy,' but I told him, 'Dave,' in answer to the same question. I just had a feeling this wasn't a person I wanted to open up with a real lot."

"What happened after you got in?"

"We drove south toward the city, making small talk. 'Bout women mostly, you know the way men do. Seeming to be put down by women, and saying how you don't understand them, all the while really bragging that you've had so many. You know what it's like. Complaining about having to use, you know, protection nowadays all the time. That sort of thing."

"Was he going south?"

"He said he was only going to New York City for a day or two, but I was thankful I was getting a ride at all, I figured worse came to worst, I could get a Greyhound ticket to get me on my way to Atlanta. In fact I was thinking just that, when he looks over at me and says, 'Hey, son, how'd you like to earn yourself a hundred bucks.' And I said, 'I'd like that pretty well, particularly if it's legal, but even if not, I'd still like it pretty well.'

"He said it wasn't real illegal. Just picking up something and dropping it off. I told him right away, 'I've got a problem if that'd be drugs you were talking about.' He said it was credit cards and since I've done a little with them in the past I said that wasn't so bad, but could he maybe consider two hundred. He said he'd more than consider it, and said if I drove he'd make it two hundred fifty. And I agreed was what I did. We drive to this place somewhere. I didn't know New York, but at the trial I found out it was on the Upper West Side. We stopped and he got out, and I scooted over behind the wheel. Jimmy, or whatever his name was, walked into this courtyard."

Rune asked, "What did he look like?"

"Well, I wasn't too sure. I oughta be wearing glasses, but I'd lost them overboard in Maine, and couldn't afford to get new ones. He was a big fellow, though. He sat big, the way a bear would sit. A moustache, I remember. It was all in profile, the look I got."

"White?"

"Yes'm. Don't believe I'd've gotten into the car otherwise."

"Describe his clothing."

"He wore blue jeans with cuffs turned up, engineer boots—"

"What are those?"

"Short buckled boots. Black. And a Navy watch coat."

"Weren't you a little nervous about this credit card thing?"

Boggs paused for a minute. "I'll tell you, miss. There've been times in my life—not a lot, but a few—when two hundred fifty dollars hasn't been a lot of money. But then it was, just like it would be now, and when somebody is going to give you a lot of money, you'd be surprised what stops becoming funny or suspicious. . . . Anyway, I sat for about ten minutes. The car was idling. I had me a cigarette. A couple. I was real hungry, and was looking around for a Burger King. That's what I really wanted, one of those Whoppers. There I am, feeling hungry, and I hear this shot. I've fired me enough pistols in my life to know a gunshot. They don't boom like in the movies. There's this crack—"

"I know gunshots," Rune said.

"Yeah, you shoot?"

"Been shot at." Ego, sure, but it gave her a kick to say it.

Boggs glanced at her, decided she wasn't kidding, but didn't go after it. "I walk carefully into the courtyard. There's a man lying on the ground. I thought it was Jimmy. I run up to him. Oh, I'm not saying I was trying to be a hero. If I'd seen somebody else, somebody who maybe had a piece on them, sure, I would've been burning rubber. But the courtyard was empty. So I go up to this guy, and see it's not Jimmy, and I lean down and say,

'Mister, you okay?' And of course he isn't. I see he's dead. I stand up fast, and I just panic and run."

Boggs smiled with a shallow twist of his lips. "And what happens? The story of my life. I run into a police car cruising by outside. They collar me and that's it."

"What about Jimmy?"

"I glanced around and seen the car, but Jimmy was gone."

"Did you see any gun?"

"No, ma'am. I heard they found it in the bushes. There wasn't any of my prints on it, but I was wearing gloves. The DA made a big deal out it I was wearing gloves in April. But I got me small hands. . . ." He held one up. "I don't have a lot of meat on me. It was real cold."

"You think Jimmy shot Mr. Hopper?"

"I pondered that a lot, but I don't see why he would have. He didn't have any gun that I saw, and if it was just a credit card scam, Hopper wouldn't've been in on that. Credit cards're small potatoes. I think Jimmy had the cards on him and seen the cops, and maybe figured I really did kill that Mr. Hopper. Never saw him again."

"But you told the cops about Jimmy?"

"Well, not the credit card part. It didn't seem that was too smart. So I kept mum on that. But sure I told them about Jimmy. Not one of them—to a man—believed me."

Not even your own lawyer, Rune thought. "But he might've seen the killer?"

"Could've been. But who is he? Where is he?"

"There isn't a lot to go on, what you've told me."

"I understand that. I'm not asking you to help me. Way I see it, it's pretty much hopeless. I was just biding my time waiting for parole. I've given up anything else happening."

Rune asked, "How bad do you want to get out?"

Boggs glanced at the camera. Rune stood up and

looked through the viewfinder to frame him better. What she saw troubled her because she wasn't looking at animal eyes, or criminal's eyes, which would have been scary but expected; she saw gentleness and pain and that portion of him that was still a boy. He said, "I'll answer that by telling you what it's like in here. It's like your heart is tied 'round and 'round with clothesline. It's like every day is waking up the morning after a funeral. It's like you welcome fear because when you're afraid you can't think about being free. It's a sadness so bad you want to howl when you see a plane flying by going someplace you can image but can't ever get to, no matter how close it might be, for a year or three or ten. . . ."

Randy Boggs stopped and cleared his throat. "Do what you can, miss. Please."

The chameleon sat on the wall, at an angle, frozen in space, hardly breathing.

Jack Nestor lay in bed and watched it.

He liked chameleons.

Not the way they changed color, which wasn't so spectacular when it came right down to it. It was more the way they were fragile and soft. He sometimes could get up real close to them—the ones around the Miami Beach Starlite Motor Lodge were used to people. He'd pick one up and let it walk along his massive tanned forearm. He liked feeling the baby-skin of the lizard and the pleasant tickle of its feet.

Sometimes he'd plop one down on his dark blurred tattoo, hoping it would turn to that deep bled-blue color, but it never did. They didn't change to flesh color either. What they did after a few minutes was they jumped the hell off his arm and scurried away like long roaches.

Nestor was forty-eight years old, but looked younger. He still had a thick wavy mass of hair, which he kept in

place with Vitalis and spray. It was dark blond, though
he had some timid streaks of gray. Nestor had a squarish
head and hint of a double chin, but the only thing about
his body that bothered him was his belly. Nestor was fat.
His legs were strong and thin, and he had good shoulders,
but his large chest sat above a round belly that jutted out
and curled over his waistband, hiding his Marine Corps
belt buckle. Nestor didn't understand why he had this
problem. He couldn't remember the last time he sat down
to a proper meal, roast and potatoes and bread and vege-
tables and pie for dessert (he thought it was probably
Christmas Day six years ago, when the prison cooks had
laid out a really good spread). What he ate now was just
Kentucky Fried and Whoppers and Big Macs. He missed
Arthur Treacher's Fish 'N Chips and wondered if they
were still in business anywhere. Anyway, he thought it
wasn't fair that all he was eating was these fucking tiny
meals and gaining weight.

Nestor noticed that they'd fallen asleep with two red-
and-white striped boxes in bed with them. The Colonel
grinned at him. Nestor kicked the boxes out of bed. They
tumbled open, and bones and coleslaw shreds scattered
on the floor.

The chameleon took off.

"Ooops," Nestor said.

He pulled on his T-shirt and smoothed his hair back.
He yawned and groped on the bedside table for a cigarette. The pack was empty, so he found a used one, still
an inch long, lit it, and stacked the cheap pillows against
the headboard. He sat back, yawned again, and coughed.

Flashes of sun shot off speeding car windows and burst
against the wall. The room's window, as advertised, did
overlook the beach, that much was true. However, the
view had to get across six lanes of highway, two access
roads and the hotel parking lot before it eased through

the streaked window of room 258. Nestor listened to the sticky rush of the traffic for a few minutes, then reached over and squeezed the butt of the young woman lying next to him.

The third time, when he got a little rougher, she stirred.

"No," she mumbled with a thick Cuban accent.

"Rise and shine," Nestor said.

She was in her mid thirties, with a body that looked ten years younger and a face that went ten years the other way. Her eye shadow and mascara were smeared. The lipstick, too, was a mess, and it looked as if her lips had slid to the side. She opened her eyes briefly, rolled over on her back and pulled a thin sheet up to her navel.

"No, not again."

"What?"

"Not again. It hurt last night."

"You didn't say nothing about it hurting."

"So? You wouldn't have stopped."

That was true, but he would at least have asked her if it felt any better before they went to sleep.

"You all right now?"

"I just don't wanna."

Nestor didn't want to either; what he wanted was two Egg McMuffins and a large coffee. He crushed out the cigarette and bent down and kissed her on the side of her breast.

Mumbling, eyes closed, she said, "No, Jacky, I don't wanta. I have to go to the bathroom."

"Well, I gotta have either you or breakfast. So, what's it gonna be?"

Her eyes opened slowly. "What you want for breakfast?"

He told her, and five minutes later she was in her orange spandex miniskirt struggling along the glisteningly hot sidewalk to the McDonald's up the street.

Nestor took a shower, spending most of the time rubbing his stomach with this green-handled pad with bumps on it. Somebody'd told him you did that, it broke up the fat cells and flushed them away. He thought he noticed a difference already, even though on the scale he hadn't lost any weight yet. He kneaded the large glossy star-shaped scar six inches to the left of his navel, a memento of the time a hollow-point 7.62mm slug had made a journey through his abdomen. Nestor had never gotten used to the leathery feel of the flesh. He had a habit of squeezing and running his fingers over it.

He rinsed off, stepped out of the shower, and spent a lot of time shaving, then getting his hair into shape. He dressed in a dark-green short-sleeve knit shirt, and the gray pants he always wore. Dungarees. He wondered why anybody would call pants anything that started in *dung. Shitarees. Craparees.* He pulled on thin black nylon socks, sheer like women's stockings, then strapped on black sandals.

He stepped out of the bathroom, which was filled with steam and hair spray mist, and smelled the food, which was resting on the TV. The woman was sitting at the chipped desk putting on her makeup. For a minute, looking at her buoyant breasts in the tight yellow sweater, Nestor's hunger for food wavered, but then he smelled the McMuffins, and he sat on the bed to eat.

He ate the first McMuffin quickly, then, with the edge off his appetite, lay back on the bed to read the paper and sip his coffee while he worked on the second one. He noticed she'd bought some insurance; a third McMuffin was also in the bag—to keep his appetites and his hands occupied. He laughed, but she pretended she didn't know he'd caught on.

He got halfway through the front section of the *Miami*

Herald, reading the national news, when he sat upright in bed.

"Oh, shit."

She was curling her eyelashes. "Huh?"

But Nestor was standing up, walking to his dresser, wiping his mouth with the back of his hand. He pulled out a jumble of underwear and socks and knit shirts.

"Hey, you iron these for me?" He handed her the shirts.

"Jacky, what is it?"

"Just get the iron out, okay?"

She did and spread a thin towel on the desk for an ironing board. She ironed each shirt, then folded it precisely, the way a salesman in a clothing store does.

"Whatsa matter. You get, like, bad news?"

"No, nothing. I've got to go away for a little while."

"Yeah, where you going? Can I come too?"

"New York."

"Oh, Jacky, I've never been—"

"Forget about it. This's business."

She handed him the shirts, then snorted. "What business? You got no business."

"I got a business. I just never told you about it."

"Yeah, so what do you do?"

In the bathroom, Nestor packed a Gillette double-edged safety razor, toothbrush, shave cream, toothpaste, and a box of Trojan Extra Strength condoms (a large box, the "unfamily size," he'd joked with the clerk when he bought them). He sprayed on extra deodorant, packed that too, then walked into the living room.

"I'll be back in a week or two." He hesitated, then took out his wallet and handed her two hundred and ten dollars. "I'm not back then, pay Seppie for the room for next couple weeks, okay?"

"Sure, I'll do that."

He looked at the dresser again, then said to her, "Hey, check in the bathroom, see if I left my razor?"

She walked out of the room, the high heels swaying unsteadily on the orange and brown polyester carpet.

When he could see she wasn't looking, Nestor reached back into the bottom drawer of the dresser and took out a dark-blue Steyr GB 9mm automatic pistol and two full clips of bullets. He slipped these into his bag. Then he said, "Hey, never mind, I found it. I packed it already."

She came up to him. "You gonna miss me?"

He picked up the paper and tore out the story and was about to put it in his wallet, then he unfolded and read it again. She came up and read over his shoulder. "What's that about? Some guy who's in jail?"

He looked at her with irritation and put the scrap in his wallet.

She said, "Who's Randy Boggs?"

Nestor smiled in an unamused way and kissed her on the mouth. Then he said, "I'll call you." Then he picked up the bag and walked outside into the blast of humid heat, glancing at a tiny chameleon perched in a band of shade on the peeling banister.

CHAPTER NINE

Spring in prison is like spring in the city. Weak, almost unnoticeable. You only sense it because of the air. You smell it, you taste it, you feel an extra portion of warmth. It flirts with you once or twice, then that's it. Back to work, or back to the yard. Crocuses can't break through concrete.

Randy Boggs was waiting for Severn Washington in the prison gym when the smell of spring hit him. And, damn, it made him feel bad. He'd never been to college. School for him meant high school, and this battered prison gym reminded him a lot of the one at Washington Irving High —where, twenty years before, he'd be working out on the horse or struggling to do an iron cross on the rings, and, bang, there was that smell in the air that meant they'd soon be out, and he'd have a summer ahead of him, and a couple weeks freedom before the job at the Kresge warehouse or the Army.

Damn, what a smell spring has. . . .

He thought about a dozen things that were packed away deep. Girls' small tits, and hot grass, and the chainsaw rumble of a 350 Chevy engine. And beer. Man, Randy Boggs loved beer. Now as much as then, though he knew there was no taste like the taste of beer when you were a teenager. Like you hit twenty and your tastebuds change somehow.

Randy Boggs squinted across the gym and could see the loping figure of Severn Washington, two hundred thirty pounds' worth, a broad face in between a scalp of tight cornrows and a neck thick as Boggs's thigh.

Washington had laughed and told Boggs not long after they met he'd never had a white friend in all of his forty-three years. He'd missed Nam because of his eyesight, and always stayed pretty close to home, which in his family's case had been a Hundred and Thirty-seventh Street, where there were not many whites at all, let alone any that he'd befriend.

That's why Washington had been uncomfortable when, one day in the yard, Boggs began talking to him, just bull-shitting in that soft, shy voice he had. At first, Washington thought Boggs wanted to be his maytag, but no way, of course; a white'd never be a black's old lady no matter what kind of head he gave, even for the protection of a six-foot-sixer. Then Washington decided Boggs was just another white-ass hatter, maybe methed or dusted out. But when Boggs kept it up, talking away, funny, making more sense than most people Inside, Washington decided the guy just wanted to talk.

A Southern Boy. White. Shit.

And there they were, sitting over white bread and macaroni, listening to church bells in the distance like it was Sunday dinner down on the farm.

Then he found out that Boggs'd been through Raleigh and Durham a bunch of times, and Washington's family had come from North Carolina, so Washington wanted to hear all about the state. From there, it was Sylvia's, Harlem, Dizzy Gillespie, Dexter Gordon, Eddie Murphy, Denzel Washington (no relation), Class D felonies. . . .

But there was another foundation for the friendship between the two: Allah.

Late one night, after he'd finished reading his Koran, after he'd dozed without dreaming, Washington suddenly woke and understood why Boggs had come and talked to him: Because it was Washington's job to befriend Boggs, and maybe even convert him. He thought about this for the rest of the long night. Allah was calling on Severn Washington to be a prophet to this white man, and Washington couldn't thank Allah enough for giving him one that was funny and pretty decent, even if he didn't talk about pussy as much as a man ought.

He told all this to Boggs, who felt himself blushing and said, "Damn, if that's not the craziest thing I ever heard."

"No, man, that's the way it is. Your ass's safe. Me and Allah gonna watch out for you." Which Boggs thought was even crazier, but perfectly fine with him.

From the start, it wasn't an easy job. Boggs was animal feed. Scrawny, shy, quiet, a loner. He didn't deal, he didn't fuck, he didn't side. Instantly unpopular. The sort that end up accidentally dead—like not paying attention and driving a 3/4-inch drill press bit through their wrist, then bleeding to death before somebody notices them.

Or the sort that do it themselves. They may take your belt away from you, but you want to get dead in prison, you can get yourself dead, no problem.

But Severn Washington did his job. And when it became clear that Boggs was under the wing of one of the most devout Muslims in all of Attica (who also happened to be one of the largest and who was serving consecutive thirty-year sentences for the shotgun killings of two liquor-store clerks), when that news was clear in the yard, Boggs was pretty much untroubled.

Except for what he was hearing in the prison gym.

Washington, disposing of the fast greeting, "Marhaba, sardeek," then frowning as he whispered, "Yo, man, you got trouble."

"What's up?"

"Man, word up that somebody maybe gonna move on you. Move on you bad."

Randy Boggs frowned. "Me? Why?"

Washington shrugged. "Could be numerous reasons.

Maybe you dissed the wrong motherfucker. I axed a moneygrip a mine from the block, and he say he heard it for fucking certain."

"Okay." Boggs's face twisted a little. "Shit."

"I'm putting out some inquiries," Washington said, emphasizing the second syllable of the word. "We'll find ourselves out what the fuck's going on."

Boggs considered this. He didn't go out of his way for trouble. He didn't give steely killer eyes to blacks, he didn't eye anybody's dick in the shower, he didn't get cartons of Marlboros from the guards. There was no reason he could think of that somebody'd want to move on him.

"I don't know what I did. I don't think—"

"Hey, be cool, man." Washington grinned. "Hey, you walk in what? Twenty-four months. Shouldn't be too hard to keep yo ass intact that long."

"This place, man, I hate it so much. . . ."

Severn Washington laughed the way he always did when somebody expressed the obvious. "Hells yeah. Less play some ball."

And Randy Boggs said, "Sure."

Thinking, as he saw his reflection in a chicken-wire-laced window, that what he was looking at with the red-socketed eyes wasn't his living body at all, but something else—something horrible, lying cold and contracted as his blood fled from the flesh as fast as a prisoner'd run in an escape.

Thinking that despite what this huge man said, the little girl with the ponytail was the only one who was going to save him now.

Rune gave it her best.
She really did.
Ophelia was maybe three-quarters toilet trained, and

really made an effort to do what she knew she was supposed to. The remaining quarter was tough, but Rune
managed to live with it.

Then she surveyed the girl's clothes. Claire, who had
super-crucial taste in her own fashion, had bought the
poor kid only sweatshirts and corduroy jeans (corduroy!
in New York!) and blouses with bears on them. Rune took
her straight down to SoHo, to a kid's store where Rune
knew one of the sales clerks. She dropped some bucks on
real clothes: A black Naugahyde miniskirt and a couple
black T-shirts. Yellow and lime-green tights. A wad of
tooling for her hair. Jewelry was risky; you never knew
what kids would swallow. But Rune found an outrageous
studded belt and black cowboy boots (which were
slightly too big, but she figured there was only one way
the feet were going to grow, and why not buy something
that would last more than a month?). The finishing touch
was a plastic leopard-skin jacket. ("This is totally fresh,
Rune," the clerk said. "You've got a matching bag and
little girl.")

Rune paid the two hundred twenty-seven dollars,
which hurt, but she had to admit it was a good invest-
ment. She said, "All right, dude, you're looking crazy
good."

"Crazy," Ophelia said.

They'd left the store and bought some ice cream and
went window shopping.

Rune wondered if you could take three-year-olds dancing. There was a super late-night club just opening up
down on Hudson, in the old building where Area had
been years before, a totally historical place. She hadn't
seen too many children there. None, in fact. Maybe you
could get away with it early, say, just after work, about
six or seven. It seemed a shame to have a kid who looked

like a miniature Janet Jackson and not expose her to some real life in New York.

"You want to go dancing?"

"I want to go to the zoo."

"Well, the zoo's closed now, honey. We can go in a day or so."

"I wanta see the animals."

"In a day or two."

At that point, Ophelia started to scream and ran into Comme de Garcon, where she threw the ice cream into a rack of $800 suits.

The day-care center didn't work out either.

Rune did the math and figured if she dropped Ophelia off at eight, and picked her up at seven—the hours Piper Sutton suggested her crew work, at a minimum—then if she got a night sitter twice a week, she would have one hundred and eight dollars a month left out of her paycheck.

So the little girl spent a lot of time at the studio.

And when Sutton called Rune one night at what was supposed to be quitting time and demanded an update on the Boggs story ("Now, Rune. Now now now!"), Rune had to park the little girl with The Model, who, Midwestern and family-minded though he probably was, got tired of the assignment after the first hour. By nine he was spitting nails, and wouldn't even respond to Rune's offer to buy him dinner at Bojangles for his effort.

But what finally did it was the honey.

Rune had spent all Thursday taking footage of the courthouses and exteriors of the building where Lance Hopper had been killed. She'd picked up Ophelia just before the day-care center closed and had to spring for a cab to get fifty pounds of equipment and thirty pounds of child back to the houseboat.

Rune plopped her in front of the old Motorola console TV, queued up *The Wizard of Oz* and took a shower.

Ophelia, who didn't like the Kansas portion of the film, wandered off to find something to play with.

What she located was Rune's quart jar of clover honey, sitting on the galley table. She climbed up on a chair and pulled it down carefully, then sat on the floor and opened it.

Ophelia loved honey. Not so much because of the taste (although she did have a couple handfuls), as the great way it poured so slowly down the stairs.

Which was good, but what was even better was the way she could use it to paste together the videotape cassettes Rune had shot that day. She made a wall out of them, like the Wicked Witch's castle.

Then the water in the shower shut off, and it occurred to Ophelia that playing with the honey might be one of those things she shouldn't be doing. That was when she hid the rest of the evidence, pouring it inside the Ikegami video camera.

"Totally fantastic," Ophelia said, closed the door, then slipped the empty jar under the coffee table. At that point Dorothy ended up in Oz, the color part came on, and the little girl settled down to watch the film.

Rune surprised herself by actually screaming when she saw the camera. She was trying to shout that the camera had cost $50,000, but the words weren't even getting out of her mouth. Mostly, she screamed. Ophelia looked down at the camera, which was bleeding honey bad, and started to cry.

Rune dropped to her knees and picked up the camera like a hurt pet. "Oh, God, oh, no. . . ."

"Oh-oh," Ophelia said.

* * *

Only two phone calls.

She was surprised that when it came to children, you could cut through city bureaucracy pretty fast. The administrator she was speaking to told her that a protective diagnostic caseworker could be on her way in a half hour. Rune said not to bother. She'd come to their offices. The woman sounded surprised, then gave Rune the address.

She packed, which was easy, then walked to the subway. Three trains later they got off at the Bleecker Street stop and climbed to the sidewalk.

A factory.

The building looked like one of those massive, grimed factories, done in ten shades of gray, from a 1930s movie about a tough, slick-haired industrialist who learns that life with floozy blondes and martinis is pretty unsatisfying.

But when Rune considered it again, she decided the building on LaGuardia Place was closer to a prison. She thought of Randy Boggs, and almost turned around.

Almost. What she did was just pause, then shift Ophelia's fingers, still slightly sticky, into her left hand and lead her toward the squat, dark building. The whole area was sullen; this was the sickly membrane between Greenwich Village and the Bowery.

"Zoo?" Ophelia asked.

Rune didn't answer. She glanced at the mantlepiece above the door, expecting to see a carved sign starting: ABANDON HOPE. . . .

Inside, a guard directed her to the Child Welfare Administration office. Rune walked slowly toward the door, past green corridors, over green linoleum. Through fluorescent light that started life white but turned green when it hit the skin. Bile light, pore light. A man pointed to a thin black woman in a red linen suit, sitting behind a desk covered with recycled files and coffee cups.

"May I help you?"

"You're Ms. Johnson?"

The woman smiled, and they shook hands. "Sit down. You're? . . ."

"Rune."

Paper appeared, and civil servant Johnson uncapped a Bic pen. "What's your address?"

"West Village."

Johnson paused. "Could you be more specific than that."

"Not really. It's hard to explain."

"Phone number?"

Rune said, "No."

"Beg pardon?"

"I don't have a phone."

"Oh." So far she hadn't written anything. "Well, why don't you tell me why you're here."

"Okay. This is Ophelia."

"We're going to the zoo," the little girl said.

"What it is, is this. I have a roommate, I mean, had a roommate and I don't know her last name, and she left me with Ophelia. She just left, can you believe it? Blew me away. I mean, I woke up, and she was gone."

Johnson was frowning painfully, more maternal than civil servant for the moment.

"Anyway, she went to Boston, and what she did, she . . ." Rune's voice fell, ". . . ditched you know who. And I'm like, what am I going to do? See, I wouldn't mind if I wasn't working, which is usually what I'm doing—not working, I mean—only now I—"

Johnson had stopped writing. "Apparent abandonment. Happens more often than you'd think."

Ophelia said, "Rune, I'm hungry."

She dug into her shoulder bag and pulled out a can of sardines. Johnson watched her. A can opener appeared, and Rune began cranking.

Rune said, "I liked it better when they had the key."

Ophelia watched the process hungrily. "Totally awesome."

Rune looked at Johnson. "You know, the key. For the sardines. Like in the cartoons you always see."

"Cartoons?" Johnson asked. Then: "You think those are good for her?"

"Waterpacked. I wouldn't give her oil." She held up the can.

Rune tucked a napkin into Ophelia's collar, then handed her a plastic fork. "Anyway, her mother's gone, and I don't know how to find her."

"You don't have any idea? No last name?"

"Nope. Just know she's in Boston."

"Bawden."

Johnson said, "Usually what happens in cases like these is the police get involved. They'll contact the Boston police, and do a standard missing person search."

"I don't have any leads. Claire took everything with her. Except this too-disgusting old poster, and some underwear. You could fingerprint it, maybe. But they probably wouldn't be her fingerprints on it."

"Who's Ophelia's father?"

Rune frowned and shook her head.

Johnson asked, "Unknown?"

"Highly."

"Describe her mother to me."

"Claire is about my height, her hair's dark now, but we're talking it started life pretty light." Rune thought for a minute. "She's got a narrow face, but she isn't pretty. I mean, you put my feet to the fire, yeah, she's cute, but that's like as far as I'll go. I'm only saying this because I want to be as accurate as possible. And, okay, she's got a good figure, and no folds around her belly button—"

"I'm really more interested in a description."

"Okay, sure. Five three, black hair. About a hundred and ten. Wears black mostly."

"Grandparents or other relations?"

"I can't find her mother, how'm I going to know the aunts and uncles?"

Johnson said, "She's really adorable. Does she have any health problems? Is there any medicine she takes?"

"No, she's pretty healthy. All she takes is vitamins in the shape of animals. She likes the bears best, but I think that's only because they're cherry-flavored. You like bears, don't you, honey?"

Ophelia had finished the sardines. She nodded.

"Okay, well, let me tell you a little about the procedure from here on out. This's the Child Welfare Administration, which is part of the city's Human Resources Administration. We're also regulated by the State Department of Social Services. We've got a network of emergency foster boarding homes where she'll be placed for a week or so until we can get her into a permanent foster home. Hopefully, by then we'll have found the mother."

Rune's stomach thudded. "Foster home?"

"That's right."

"Uhm, you know what you hear on the news. . . ."

"About the foster homes?" Johnson asked. "It's the press that made up most of those stories." Her voice was crisp, and Rune had a flash of a different Ms. Johnson. Beneath the ruby lipstick and pseudo Ann Taylor did not beat a delicate heart. She probably had a tattoo of a gang's trademark on the slope of her left breast. "We spend weeks investigating foster parents. If you think about it, who scrutinizes natural parents?"

Good point, Rune thought. "Can I visit her?"

The answer was no—Rune could see that—but Johnson said, "Probably."

"What happens now?"

"We have a diagnostic caseworker on call. She'll take Ophelia to the emergency home tonight."

"I don't have to do anything else?"

"That will be the end of your involvement."

Rune hated civil-servant language. As if they took the words and quick-froze them. It sounded like English, but didn't work.

She turned to Ophelia and said, "Will you miss me?"

The girl said, "No."

No?

Johnson said to her, "Honey, would you like to go stay with a nice mommy and daddy? They have some children just like you and they'd love for you to visit."

"Yeah. I'm sleepy."

Rune said to her, "You'll be happy there."

Why isn't she sobbing?

Johnson said, "I'll take her now. You have her things?"

Rune handed over the bag containing the ratty stuffed animals and her clothes. Johnson looked at Rune's face and said, "I know how you feel, but believe me, you did the right thing. There wasn't any choice."

Rune squatted down and hugged her. "I'll come visit you."

It was then that Ophelia sized up what was happening. "Rune?"

Johnson took her by the hand and led her down the corridor.

Ophelia started to cry.

Rune started to cry.

Johnson stayed dry-eyed. "Come on, honey."

Ophelia looked back once and said, "Zoo."

"We'll go to the zoo, I promise."

Rune left the ugly slab of a building. Feeling an intense freedom, a thorny burden was gone.

And feeling the weight of a guilt that matched her own 102 pounds ounce for ounce. But that was okay. She had a story to do.

CHAPTER TEN

A playground you never got tired of.

Once you took the element of fear out of it (and there wasn't anything, Jack Nestor thought, that he feared), New York was the biggest fucking playground in the world.

He felt it the instant he stepped out of the Port Authority bus terminal. The feeling of electricity, and for a moment he thought: What was he doing wasting his time in piss-ant Florida? He smelled: fishy river, charcoal smoke from pretzel vendors, shit, exhaust. Then he got a whiff of some gross incense three black guys dressed up like Arabs were selling from a folding table. He'd never seen this before. He walked up to them. There were pictures of men from ancient times it looked like, dressed the same. The twelve true tribes of Israel. Only they were all black. Black rabbis!

What a town this was.

Nestor caught another whiff of the sickly sour smoke and headed off.

He walked along Forty-second Street, stopped in a couple peep shows. They didn't show the old film loops any more. The shows were computerized. And you only got about ten seconds for a quarter. He remembered in the old days they gave you a minute at least. Man, times change. He left and wandered some more, looking at the old movie theaters, the legit theaters, the grudging drivers, the suicidal pedestrians. Horns blared like mad, as if everybody driving a car had a wife in labor in the back seat. Already, the energy was exhausting him. He knew he'd be up to speed in a day or two. He remembered after he'd spent a week in New York once, then gone to visit his sister and her family in Dearborn, he was bouncing off the walls. That's what this city did to you, it charged you and it bled you. Go with it, he told himself.

He stopped and bought a hotdog and ate it in three bites. At the next street corner he bought another one. This time he asked for onions too. On the third corner he bought two more hotdogs, without onions, and stood eating them and drinking a Sprite, which wasn't a Sprite at all, which he'd asked for, but some brand of lemon-lime soda he'd never heard of. It tasted like medicine. As the vendor split a sausage to fill with sauerkraut, Nestor asked him where there was a hotel in the area.

The man shrugged. "Donoe."

"Huh?"

"Donoe."

"That's a hotel?"

"I donoe."

Nestor walked off. Two blocks later, he was somewhere in the forties, he saw a sign, "King's Court." Which was the same name as a motel he'd been to in Miami Beach once, and wasn't a bad place for a hotel he'd only spent two hours in. He remembered it being clean and cheap. It must have been a chain. Nestor walked up to the door, which opened suddenly. He hadn't noticed a tall young man, dressed in black, standing inside. The man said, "Hello, sir, take your bag?"

The Miami branch didn't, Nestor recalled, have a doorman.

He was going to say *Just checking it out,* but that sounded too much like *checking in.* "Just want to ask the desk guy a question."

She wasn't a guy, but was a young blonde woman with

a French accent and teeth that were perfect. He stared.
Injection molded teeth. She smiled at him. "Yessir?"

Looking around him. Bizarre. It looked like a warehouse with a low ceiling. Stone and metal furniture everywhere. And a lot of the furniture was wrapped up in
white cloth, even though there were people sitting on it.

"Uh, I was wondering, you have a room?"

"Certainly, sir. How long will you be staying?"

"Uh, how much would that be?"

A computer was consulted. "Three hundred forty."

For a week? Are these people fucking insane?

The question now was how to get out of here without
the blonde with the ruler-straight teeth thinking he was a
complete asshole.

"I mean by the night."

A moment's pause. Something shifted. "Actually, that
is the daily rate, sir."

"Sure. I was joking." Nestor grinned, saw no way to
salvage the situation, and left.

Only one block away, he found the Royalton Arms,
which he knew was okay because there were a couple of
dirty-looking tourists standing out in front, looking at a
Michelin guide to New York City. The desk clerk here
didn't have straight teeth at all, and he was behind a
Plexiglas bulletproof divider. Nestor checked into a
$39.95 room and took the elevator up to the seventh floor.
The room was okay. He felt good as soon as he walked
inside. It didn't overlook anything, but that never bothered Nestor. He was building a house in Florida, which
was why he was staying at the motel, and had told the
architect to keep the windows small. Nothing was sadder
to him than pale afternoon light bleeding into a room. He
gave a fast glance at the airshaft, lowered the window
and the blinds, and then lay down on the bed and lis-

tened to the battle his stomach was having with the hotdogs.

After a half hour, he clicked on the TV and watched some *Miami Vice* rerun for a while, then flipped through the channels once, then shut off the set. It was irritating not to have a remote control. He tried to think for a minute how the hotel could put one in the room, how they could maybe chain it to the wall or the table. It seemed like a lot of work, but he couldn't imagine anything in a New York hotel room not bolted down. He stripped down to his boxer shorts and sleeveless T-shirt, brushed his teeth powerfully, and got into bed.

He closed his eyes.

Snap. The pictures began.

Nestor often had trouble sleeping. He'd thought, a long time ago, it was something physical. Well, *hoped* more than *thought.* But he knew now that wasn't the case at all.

The reason for his insomnia was the pictures.

The minute his head hit the pillow (unless there were someone next to him, distracting, or at least promising distraction), the minute he was prepared to sleep, the pictures began. He supposed he should call them memories, because they really were nothing more than scenes from his past. But memories were different. Memories were like the impressions he had of his family, or his childhood. His first car. His first fuck. Maybe they were accurate. Probably not.

But the pictures. . . . Man.

A Philippine revolutionary he picked off at three hundred yards using an M16 with metal sights, the man just dropping like a sack. . . .

A black South African who thought he was safely across the border in Botswana. . . .

A coathanger binding the hands of a Salvadorian, Nestor thinking why bother? He'll have a bullet in his head in five minutes anyway. . . .

Hundreds of others.

They were in black and white, they were in color, some nearly had Dolby stereo sound.

The pictures . . .

They didn't haunt him, of course. He didn't have any emotional response. He wasn't tormented by guilt, he wasn't moved to lust. They just wouldn't go away. The pictures came into his head, and they wouldn't let him sleep.

Tonight, Nestor—energized by the city and sickened by its fast food—lay in a too-soft bed and fielded the pictures. Push one away. Then the one that took its place. Then the next. For an hour, then two. He wanted Celine next to him. He thought about her. The pictures pushed *her* away. He thought about what he was in town to do. That kept the pictures away for a while. But they came back.

Finally—it was close to three A.M.—he began to think about the blonde girl, the one with the straight teeth. With the thought of her, and a little bit of effort on his part (elbow grease was the way he thought of it), Jack Nestor finally relaxed enough so he fell asleep.

Yeah, Randy Boggs worked for me for close to two years. He come in and was looking for a job. Good boy. Dependable. He wasn't no killer. He pushed a broom with the best of them. I'm sure it was the sixties. We had the Negro problem then. Course, we still have the Negro problem. 'Bout that, I'd like to say a few words, seeing how you have a camera—

Click.

Randy Boggs? Yeah, I knew the Boggs family. Boys I

don't remember. Father was a mean motherfucker. Man, the—

Click.

Randy? Yeah. We had this lobster business. But—you got the camera rolling? Okay, let me tell you this story. The wife and I were one time over to Portland, and we were driving in the Chevy, we always buy American cars, even if they're a pile of you know what. So we were driving along and there were these three lights in the sky, and we knew they weren't planes because they were so bright. Then one of them—

Click.

For one week, Rune had traveled. She'd shot thirty-seven hours of half-inch videotape.

Atlanta. Bangor. Pittsburgh. Raleigh.

Her life became an endless circle of long hours by herself, of flying on airplanes and staying in hotels that somebody else paid for, of tense meetings at the Network, of interviews that sometimes careened out of control and sometimes worked, of a lonely houseboat, of a chaotic editing room. (One morning she woke up to find that she'd fallen asleep with the Betacam next to her—which wasn't so scary as the fact that she'd slept with her arm around it all night.) She gave up late-night clubs, she gave up West Village writers' bars. Even gave up seeing Sam much. Piper Sutton was too busy for her, though the anchorwoman would swoop by Rune's cubicle occasionally for a status report, like an eagle grabbing a squirming trout in its talons.

Maisel was the one she spent the most time with, and he in turn spent a lot of time playing the role of stern headmaster with a near-hopeless student.

"Didn't you put a sponge on the mike?" he'd ask, incredulous.

"I forgot."

"It sounds like a goddamn hurricane, Rune."

"You can hear what he's saying. It's just kind of wooshy is all."

Maisel would growl, "You do it right or you don't do it."

"You want me to go back and shoot it again, Lee? . . . All the way to Attica just for that one quote? It'll take me another two days."

He'd just look at her.

"Aw, Lee," she'd say, "I don't care. It doesn't make that much difference. . . ."

Five minutes later, she'd call the Network's travel desk to order the tickets.

Weeks of talking to wackos, to people too pleasant to be successes despite their desires, people too scattered to be crooks despite their inclinations, people who were spouse beaters, saints, smart, stupid. She talked to Randy Boggs's brother. Two cousins, an aunt. His mother wasn't all with it—a kind woman but one whose mind was always a step or two away from the conversation. But she *was* a mother, and Rune figured a quote from a mother about a son in prison would carry some serious weight. She talked to two of his teachers. She interviewed people he worked with.

But if there was one common denominator to the chaotic hours she spent it was something she already knew: Everybody—those who were related or those who remembered him—one way or another said that Randy Boggs couldn't be a murderer.

CHAPTER ELEVEN

"Come on, Sam. Please?" She'd tried charm, and now she was trying pleading.

But Sam Healy was a detective who disposed of bombs for a living; it was tough to talk people like that into anything they didn't want to do.

They were sitting on the back deck of the boathouse, drinking beers and eating microwave popcorn.

"I just want to look at it. One little file."

"I can't get access to the files in the Twentieth. I'm Bomb Squad. Why would they even talk to me?"

Rune had spent a lot of time trying to decide if she was in love with him. She thought she was in a way. But today wasn't like the old days—whenever they were—when you were either in love or you weren't. Love was a lot more complicated now. There were degrees, there were phases of love. It kicked in and out like a compressor in an air conditioner. She and Sam could talk, they hit the same wavelength a lot of times. She liked the way he looked like a man in a Marlboro ad. She liked the way his eyes were completely calm and deeper than any eyes she'd ever seen. But what she missed was that gut-twist, that weight-losing obsession with the object of your desire that was Rune's favorite kind of love, even though it was totally rare.

Also, Healy was married.

Which, oddly, didn't bother Rune that much. At least he was separated, and had no problem being bluntly honest about the times he saw Cheryl. Rune looked at his marriage like an airbag in a car—a safety feature. Maybe when she got older, if they were still together, she'd force him to make a decision. But for now, that was his business. He let her know where they stood. All she wanted was honesty, and to be able to go out with somebody who kept you guessing. And no boyfriend kept you guessing like one on the New York City Bomb Squad.

Rune said, "They got the wrong man."

"I know your theory about Boggs."

"I don't need to prowl around the evidence room. I just want to read one file."

"I thought you wanted to be a reporter."

"I am a reporter."

"Reporters don't cheat. It wouldn't be ethical to use me to get information."

"Of course it would. You know about unnamed sources. Come on, you can be my Deep Throat."

"It's a murder investigation. I'd get suspended for leaking information."

"It's a murder *conviction.* It's a closed case."

"The transcript is public record. Why don't you—?"

"I've got the transcript. I need the police report. It's got the names of all the witnesses and the bullet angles and pictures of the exit wounds. All the good stuff."

"I've got no pull at the Twentieth. There's no reason for them to release a homicide file to me. You stand just as much of a chance as me of getting it."

"Sam." She kissed his neck.

"There's nothing I can do. Sorry."

"Sam." She backed away. "The man is innocent. He's serving time for something he didn't do. That's terrible."

"You can talk to the public information officer. They'll give you the department's story."

"Bullshit is all he'll tell me."

"She," Sam said. He stood up and walked into the galley. "You have anything substantial?"

"Well, first, everybody I've interviewed said that no way in the world could Randy Boggs kill anyone. Then—"

"I mean to eat."

"Oh." She turned a squinting gaze into the galley. "No."

"Don't mope."

"I'm not. I just don't have anything substantial. Maybe some Fruit 'N Fiber cereal."

"Rune . . ."

"A banana. It's pretty old."

"I can't get the report. I'm sorry."

"A can of tuna. That's a pretty icky combination, though, you mix it with the cereal. Even with the high fiber."

Healy wasn't buying it. "Sorry, hon. I can't do it." He walked back with pretzels and cottage cheese. "So where's your little girl?"

She was hesitating. "I took her to Social Services."

"Oh." He was looking at her, his face blank. Not saying anything, eating the cottage cheese, offering her a fork she wasn't interested in.

She said, "They seemed like they were a good bunch of people there. They were, you know, real professional."

"Uh-huh."

"What they'll do is keep her in a foster home for a while, then they'll track down her mother. . . ." She was avoiding his eyes, looking everywhere else. Studying his buttons, the stitching of his shirt seams, the trapezoid of floor between his shoes. "Well, it was a good idea, wasn't it?"

"I don't know, was it?"

"I had to."

"When I was a portable, walking a beat, we found kids sometimes. There's any suspicion of neglect or abuse, you have to bring them in, or get a caseworker out to see them."

Rune said, "Those people are okay, aren't they?"

"I guess so."

She stood up and paced slowly. "What was I supposed to do? I can't take care of a baby."

"I'm not saying—" Healy began.

"I know you're not. You're not saying anything! You're just looking at me."

"You did what you thought was right."

Clench, loosen. Her short, unpolished nails dug into her palm, then relaxed. "You make it sound like I gave her away to the gypsies."

"I'm just a little surprised is all."

"What am I going to do? Keep her with me all the time? I'm trying to make a film. I can't afford a baby-sitter—"

"Rune—"

Volume and indignation rose. "You make it sound like I abandoned her. I'm not her mother. I don't even want her."

Healy smiled. "Don't be so paranoid about it. I'm sure they'll take fine care of her. Have some cottage cheese. What's in here?"

Rune looked. "Apple? Pear? Wait, I think it's a zucchini."

"Should it be that color?"

She said, "It's only until they find her mother."

Healy said, "Just a couple days probably."

"I did the right thing, didn't I, Sam?"

"Sure you did."

Healy capped the cottage cheese.

Rune stood at the round porthole, looking out over the water, at the way the lights in Hoboken made lines in the waves like runway approach lights. With her eyes she traced them to the land and back again. She watched them for a few minutes, until they were shattered by a passing speedboat. When the colors began to regroup, she turned to Healy and said, "Sam, I really need that file."

He said, "Let's go get something to eat."

"Can't we talk about it?"

He pulled on his blue jean-jacket. He was smiling in an infuriating way that he had. A smile, but it was more some kind of jamming device. Was he listening to her? Was there a message getting through?

"Well?" she asked.

"Pizza might be good. What were you thinking about?"

She smiled coldly. "It's not pleasant, Sam. You don't want to know."

Piper Sutton sensed the power she had over him and it made her uncomfortable because it was purely the power of sex.

And therefore a power she couldn't exercise.

As she looked at the man across the desk from her, she crossed her legs, and her cream-colored stockings whispered in a reminder of that power. She was sitting in an office exactly two floors above hers—the penthouse of the parent company's monolith.

"We'll have coffee," the man said.

"No thank you."

"Then I will."

Dan Semple was a trim forty-four, compact, with short salt-and-pepper hair curling over his forehead in bangs. He was not—like Piper Sutton or Lee Maisel or Lance Hopper—a newsman. He had sold advertising time for local stations, then for the Network, and eventually he had moved into entertainment and then news programming. The lack of reporting experience was irrelevant. Semple's talent was for money—making it and saving it.

No one in the television business was naive enough to believe that high-quality journalism alone was enough to make a network a success. And, with a few exceptions, no one was surprised when Semple was given Hopper's job as director of Network News. The similarities were obvious: Hopper had been a great newsman in the incarnation of a son of a bitch; Dan Semple was a great businessman in the body of a cold megalomaniac.

Although one thing he wasn't the least bit cold about was Piper Sutton.

She had had affairs with various Network executives in the past—only those men, however, who were on a corporate level equal to hers or lower. Sutton didn't give a shit about rumors and gossip, but one of her few rules of ethics was that she wouldn't use her body to advance her career; there were plenty of other ways to fuck those you worked for.

The affair with Semple had lasted one year, when they were both, in different departments, on the ascendancy. But that had been four years ago. Then came Hopper's death, one consequence of which was what Sutton had predicted would happen: Semple was named Hopper's replacement. The day after the board announced the appointment, she walked into his office to say how happy she was for him; she'd known how much he'd lusted after the job (though mostly she was pleased because she knew Semple would stabilize a department that had been battered for several years by Hopper, who was described in a rival network's obit as a "psychotic drill sergeant"). Sutton had taken Semple's hand, kissed his cheek, congratulated him, and told him the affair was over.

Since that time, Semple'd waged an almost adolescent campaign to win her back. Although they saw each other often and dined together and attended benefits and formal functions, she'd decided that their intimate days were over, and that would not change as long as he headed the department she worked for. He didn't believe her when she said it was a hard decision for her as well, though it was. She was attracted to him physically and he was as strong and decisive as she was. Sutton had settled for weaker men in the past, and there she'd made a mistake; she had the ex's to prove it.

This tension was an undercurrent in every conversation she and Semple had, which were many, because she considered Semple, rather than Maisel, her boss. It troubled her that, although Semple respected her immensely for her ability, he *desired* her only on the lowest level. The power over him was the power of a courtier, not a reigning queen, and that infuriated her—the same as her continual refusal to resume the affair stung him.

"How was Paris?" she asked.

"Comme çi, comme ça."

"Ha."

"How is it always? The same. Paris never changes."

The coffee arrived. The executive vice-presidents had their own dining room, which delivered their requests for food or beverages on Villeroy & Bosch china, carried on parent-company-logoed lacquered trays. Semple poured a cup and sipped it.

"Tell me about this story."

Sutton did, quickly, without emotion.

"Her name is Rune?"

"Some kind of stage name bullshit. She was with the O&O."

"What does Lee think?" Semple asked.

"Slightly more in favor than I am. But not much."

"Why are we doing it, then?" he asked coolly.

Semple's dark eyes scanned Sutton's blouse, and she

was glad she'd worn the wool suit jacket over the white silk. But only a part of his eyes was seeing her flesh. What the other part was considering, and what was happening in the brain behind those eyes was a complete mystery to her. It was one of his most magnetic qualities —that she hadn't been able to fathom him. It was also one of his more frightening.

She answered, "The girl said, in effect, that if she didn't produce it for *Current Events,* she'd do it independently and sell it elsewhere."

"Blackmail," he snapped.

"Closer to youthful fervor."

"Closer to blackmail," Semple corrected softly.

"I'm not too worried. She has more balls than intelligence."

Semple didn't answer. He sipped more coffee. Sutton remembered that he liked to sit naked in bed in the morning, with a tray resting on his lap, the cup and saucer directly over his penis. She remembered too wondering if he did that because he liked the warmth.

He asked, "What does she have so far? Anything?"

"Nope. Nothing substantial. Lots of background footage. That's all. And she's been at it for a while."

"So you think there's a chance it'll just go away?"

Sutton avoided his eyes. "She's young. I'm keeping a close eye on her. I'm hoping she gets tired of the story."

After a pause, Semple said, "Well, it will be interesting to see how it turns out."

Sutton didn't respond.

Semple looked out the window for a moment. "I dined at a wonderful restaurant. It was off St. Germain."

"Really?"

"Superb. I wish you'd been there with me."

"Yes."

"Michelin was wrong. I have to write and urge them to give it another star." And he uncapped a fountain pen and wrote a note on his calendar reminding him to do just that.

C H A P T E R   T W E L V E

Sleep working. That's what I'm doing.

Rune had been sitting at her desk, in the same curvature-of-the-spine pose, for six hours. The close air of the studio was filled with the buzz of a dozen yellow jackets, and she found—it made her giggly—she'd forgotten how to read.

She stood up and stretched; a series of pops from her joints momentarily replaced the buzzing. She shut off the monitor and left the studio, then the building. She took the chrome necklace of her ID from around her neck, and slipped it in her leopard-skin bag.

She wanted to go home, to climb into bed, to hug Persephone and to fall into a bliss of sleep.

The cool, electric-scented city night air woke her up, and she saw from the clock on the MONY tower that it was early, only eight P.M. Early. Rune remembered when quitting time had been five. She continued down Broadway, past the pastel carnival of Lincoln Center—pausing, listening for music, but not hearing any. Then she continued south, deciding to walk home, a couple miles, to get the blood back in her legs. Thinking of what she needed to do for the story. Get her hands on the police report of the Hopper case was the number one item.

Then she'd have to talk to all the witnesses. Get Megler on tape. Maybe interview the judge. Find some jurors. She wondered if there was an old priest who knew Boggs. A Spencer Tracy sort of guy. *Ah, well, now, sure I'd be knowing the boy Randy, and I'll tell you, he helped out in soup kitchens and took care of his mother and left*

half his allowance in the collection plate every Sunday,
when he was an altarboy. . . .

A lot to do.

She walked through Hell's Kitchen. Her head swiveled
as she went down Ninth Avenue. Disappointed. The de-
velopers were doing a number on the area. Boxy high
rises and slick restaurants and co-ops. What she liked
best about the neighborhood was that it had been the
home of the Gophers, one of the toughest of the nine-
teenth-century gangs in New York. Rune had been reading about old gangs lately. Before she got waylaid by the
Boggs story, she'd been planning a documentary on them.
The featured thugs were going to be the Gophers and
their sister gang, the Battle Row Ladies' Social and Ath-
letic Club (aka the Lady Gophers). Not a single producer
had been very interested in the subject. The Mafia and
Colombians with machine guns were still the superstars
of crime, according to the media; and there wasn't much
demand for stories about people like One-Lung Curran
and Sadie the Goat and Stumpy Malarky.

Her feet were aching by the time she got to her neighborhood. She stopped outside the houseboat, looked at
the dark windows for a moment, then walked inside.
Rune dropped her bag by the door and stood listening,
her head cocked sideways. A car horn, a helicopter, a
backfire. . . . All the sounds were distant. None of what
she heard was coming from inside the houseboat, nothing
except her own heartbeat and the creak of boards beneath her feet.

She reached for the lamp, but slowly lowered her hand,
and instead felt her way to the couch and lay down on it,
staring up at the ceiling, at the psychedelic swirls of
lights reflecting off the turbulent surface of the Hudson.
She lay that way for a long time.

*   *   *

The yard was segregated.

Just like the city, Randy Boggs thought. It seemed he and Severn Washington were the exception.

The blacks were mostly young. A lot wore do-rags or stockings over their hair, or they had cornrows. They stood together. Strong, big, sleek.

Yo, homes, quit that noise.

Wassup?

Mah crib. I ever tell you 'bout mah crib?

Hells yeah.

The whites were older, crueler, humorless. They looked bad—it was the longer, unclean hair, the pale skin. They too stood together.

Black, white. Just like the city.

A lot of the men were exercising. There were weights here, though the hierarchy didn't allow for democratic use among all prisoners. Still there were always push-ups and sit-ups. Muscles develop in prison. But Boggs hadn't made a fetish of exercise. Doing that'd be an acknowledgment of where he was, and what he was. If he didn't stand in line for the thirty-pound dumbbells, then maybe he was somewhere else. Maybe he was *someone* else. He tried to cultivate a strong sense of dream.

"Amazing grace, how sweet thou art. . . ."

An a cappella black gospel group practicing in the yard. They were really good. Boggs, when he heard the low harmonies, at first wanted to cry. Now he just listened. The group wouldn't be together much longer. They'd walk in two months, four months, and thirteen months respectively.

"I once was lost but now I'm found. . . ."

The singers started a second verse, and someone nearby yelled, "Yo, shut the fuck up."

He smelled fireplace wood smoke. He tried not to think of the last time he sat in front of a fireplace.

He sat quietly. He smoked some, though since he'd been in, he'd lost his taste for smoking. He'd lost his taste for a lot of things. He sat for five minutes thinking about smoking before he realized that the prisoners he'd been sitting with were no longer next to him.

Boggs knew why, and he felt his skin crackle with fear.

Severn Washington was sick. Got the flu bad, was puking all night, and was in the infirmary.

If Boggs knew it, everybody knew it.

He looked around the yard, and saw the man immediately. He was surprised. Boggs had thought he'd be black.

Juan Ascipio wore a red headband and fatigue jacket over his jumpsuit. Two other prisoners walked beside him. Boggs didn't know Ascipio. He'd never said a word to him. He had no idea why Ascipio wanted to kill him. He was a newcomer, a dealer who'd been convicted of the assassination of two rivals. He wasn't a big man and he had a face that when it smiled might make children comfortable. A kind face, the sort you want to please. But the eyes, Boggs had noticed, were grinny-mean and chill.

The three of them stopped about fifteen feet from where Boggs sat, next to a tall wall of red brick.

"Yo, man. Here. Now."

Boggs looked at him, but didn't get up.

Ascipio pointed to a small shaded area out of sight of the towers. The prisoners called it Lover's Lane.

Ascipio stepped into the nook and unzipped his fly. "Yo, man, I'm talking you. You deaf, or what?"

His friend said, "Yo, man, on your fucking knees. Gone turn you out, man, turn you out."

The other: "Come on, man. Now!"

No one else in the yard noticed. Or rather, no one let himself be seen noticing.

No guards nearby, no Severn Washington.

Boggs looked back at them. He said, "Don't believe I will."

Ascipio spit out, "Don't *believe* you will? Motherfucker say he don't believe he will?"

Then Boggs's eyes lowered to his right hand, which rested on his knee. He glanced down at it. Ascipio followed his gaze.

A long fingernail.

It kept growing. One inch, two, three, four, six. Boggs looked back into their eyes. One by one, his head swiveling.

It was the first thing he'd made here, this piece of double-strength glass, a clear stiletto honed on one side so sharp it would shave hair. The handle was taped. Metal-detector-proof.

The fingernail could do the most damage glass could ever do.

Ascipio laughed. "Put that 'way, man. Get yo pretty white mouth over here, man."

The protocol was you put up with it. You accepted it for a while, then when it came your turn, you could do it or not. Anyway, it eventually stopped, unless you got to be a maytag for somebody, a wife. Only Boggs knew that the sex was just a set-up. They'd get him on his knees, then the other two would hold him and Ascipio would beat him to death. They thought he'd fall for it? Boggs was always surprised how stupid people could be.

Boggs shook his head.

Ascipio said, "Three of us, man. More, I want. That—" He nodded at the knife. "That do you shit. Nex week, nex month, we find you. You be here for a long time, man."

"Man," one of the others growled at the insubordination.

Boggs didn't move. The blade blasted light off its point.

Ascipio walked close. Slowly. "You want to die?"

And he looked into Boggs's eyes. He stopped. He stood for a long moment, they stared at each other. Slowly, Ascipio zipped up his fly. He smiled and shook his head. "Okay, man. You got balls. I like that."

Boggs didn't move.

"You okay, my friend," Ascipio said, and there was admiration in his voice. "Nobody else ever try that shit with me. But I like you, man. You fucking all right."

He extended his hand.

Boggs looked down at it.

A bird swooping in.

Boggs half turned, as the fist of a fourth man, who'd come up behind him silently, caught him under the ear. A loud thwock as it bounced off bone, and he felt Ascipio's hand grabbing his own right wrist with fingers that wanted to pierce the skin.

The knife fell to the ground and Boggs saw it tumble, appearing and disappearing as it fell.

Then it was in Ascipio's hand.

"No!" The word didn't come out as a shout, though. It was muffled by the meaty forearm of the man who'd hit him.

There were no guards, there were no Aryan Brotherhood protectors, no Severn Washington, there was no one except the five men in Lover's Lane. Five men and a glass knife.

Ascipio leaned forward. Boggs smelled garlic on his breath—garlic from his private stocks of food. Tobacco from the endless supply of cigarettes.

"Yo, man, you a stupid motherfucker."

As the knife went in, Boggs (thinking those were the last words he'd ever hear) felt much less pain than he'd expected. The knife retreated and returned, and he felt a loosening inside him.

Then there were other shouts, from a dozen yards

away, or hundred. But Boggs didn't pay any attention; they didn't mean anything to him. All he was aware of was Ascipio's face: the grinny-mean eyes that never flinched or narrowed, and the smile, one that might please children.

Rune sat in the overheated subway car as it stammered along the tracks and did an inventory of the tools of the trade—a claw hammer, a canister of military tear gas, two screwdrivers (Phillips head and straight), masking tape, and cotton gloves (Sam had told her one time that you could lift prints off latex gloves). She wondered if the crime was less if it wasn't breaking and entering but just entering—walking right in, even if you weren't supposed to.

It was the kind of question that Sam could've answered real fast, but of course he was the last person in the world she would raise the topic with.

She imagined, though, that it was a distinction somebody'd thought of already, and just because you didn't jimmy any locks or crack any plate glass, the crime wasn't going to be a hell of a lot less, though the sentence might be. Maybe the judge would just tell her one year instead of three. Or ten instead of twenty.

The longer term probably. It wasn't going to help the case that this was government property she had her eyes on.

The building was only a few doors from the subway stop. She climbed out and paused next to the art deco pole with a green glowing ball on top. A cop walked past, his walkie-talkie sputtering with a hiss. She pressed her face against the post, which was covered with layers and layers of paint, and she wondered what color it had been in earlier years. Maybe some Gophers or Hudson Dusters had paused under this very same post scoping out a job. Did they have subways back then?

The street was empty and she strolled casually into the old government-issue building.

In twenty minutes she was out, a bulky manila folder in her bag, cheap sunglasses hiding her pleased eyes.

Gottcha, boys. Didn't even know what hit you, huh?

She paused at a phone stand and pretended to make a call while she flipped through the file. She found the address she was looking for and she walked quickly back to the subway. After a ten-minute wait, she got on board an old Number Four train heading toward Brooklyn.

Rune liked the outer boroughs, Brooklyn especially. She thought of it as caught in a time warp, with the Dodgers always playing, and muscular boys in T-shirts flirting with tough girls who snapped gum and answered them back in a sexy, lazy drawl. Mafioso and immigrants and families with five or six kids, eating huge mounds of steaming food in the kitchen of their yellow-lit, narrow tenements.

The neighborhood that she now slipped into with the exiting crowd was quiet, residential. She paused, getting her bearings, and saw an old woman sitting in a tall-backed, overstuffed green chair draped with doilies, looking outside, past still, lace curtains.

She had to walk only three blocks until she found the row house. Red brick with yellow trim, two story, a narrow moat of anemic lawn. Bursts of red covered the front of the building. Geraniums. Sprouting everywhere. Out of flower pots, terra-cotta statues in the shape of donkeys and fat Mexican peasants. Out of green plastic window boxes. Out of milk containers. Dots of concentrated color holding their own against the monotonous street.

They bothered her, the flowers. Someone who'd grow flowers like that was probably a very nice person. Which meant Rune was going to feel pretty guilty about what she was about to do.

Which didn't stop her, however, from walking onto the front porch, dropping a paper bag on the concrete and setting fire to it.

She rang the doorbell and ran into the alley behind the house.

"Oh, hell. . . . What? . . . The boys again. . . . That's it! This time I call the cops. . . . Don't call the fire department. It's just. . . ."

Rune was walking quickly through the kitchen, which was dark and stacked high with dirty dishes. She saw the husband leaping forward fiercely stomping on the burning bag, sparks flying, smoke pouring. His roly wife held a long-spouted watering can, ready to douse his feet. Then she was past them, unnoticed, taking the carpeted stairs two at a time. Upstairs she found herself in a small hallway.

First room, nobody.

Second, nobody.

Third—chaos. The six children were staring out the window at the excitement below them, squealing.

Several of them turned as Rune walked into the room and flipped the light switch on.

And one of those was a three-year-old who said, "Rune!"

"Hi, honey," she said to Ophelia. The little girl ran toward her.

A chubby boy of about ten looked at her. "What'sis? Jailbreak?"

"Shh, don't tell anybody."

"Yeah, right, like I'm a snitch. Got a cigarette?"

Rune gave him five dollars. "Forget you—"

"Yeah, right. I didn't see nothing."

Rune said to Ophelia, "Come on, let's go home."

She pulled the girl's jacket off a hook and slipped it on her.

"Are we playing a game?" the little girl asked.

"No," Rune said, "we're playing kidnapping."

CHAPTER THIRTEEN

She heard the news on another station. Not even a Network O&O, but one of the locals. The one that broadcast *M*A*S*H* reruns and whose best-seller was a talk show that did stories about sexual surrogates and discrimination against overweight women.

The Network News hadn't thought Randy Boggs's stabbing was worth mentioning.

Rune sweet-talked Sam into taking Ophelia for a few hours. She figured this was a major abuse of the relationship, but Sam looked so happy she'd gotten the girl back (she was a little skimpy on *how* exactly) that he didn't complain at all, even though it meant he'd have to explain to his sort-of-ex that he'd be late picking up Adam because he had to baby-sit his girlfriend's kid.

A half hour later she was on the train to Attica, wondering if maybe she should buy a monthly commutation pass.

The infirmary surprised her. She expected it to be more Big House, more Edward G. Robinson, but this was just a hospital ward. A guard accompanied her, a large black man with a broad chest. His uniform didn't fit well. The glossy blue collar buttons, one a D, one a C, came just to the level of her eyes. He was silent.

Randy Boggs didn't look good at all. He was shell white, and the spray or cream that he used on his hair glued it out in all directions. The eyes were what bothered Rune the most, though. They were unfocused and still. God, eerie. All they needed was a glazing to turn him completely into a corpse.

"It's you, miss." He nodded. "Look what happened to me."

"You going to be all right?"

"Got me a pretty nice looking scar. But the knife missed everything important."

"What happened?"

"Don't rightly know. I was in the yard, and I get pulled over backwards and somebody stuck me."

"You must have seen him."

"Nope. Not a glimpse."

"Was it daytime?"

"Yep."

"How could somebody stab you, and you not see it?"

Boggs tried a smile, but it didn't take. "People get invisible here."

She said, "But—"

"Look . . ." His eyes came to life for a moment, then faded back to lifeless. ". . . this is prison. This isn't the real world. We got ourselves a whole different set of rules."

He lifted his hand to his stomach and touched a large white pad under his tattered, overlaundered dressing gown. He leaned his head back into his pillows and pressed his thin, sinewy forearm over his eyes. "Damn," he whispered.

She watched him in this still pose for a long minute, wishing at first she'd brought the camera. But then decided that no, it was better for him to keep this private. He was the sort of man who'd never want to be seen crying.

"I brought you something."

She opened her bag and took out an old book, flaky and scabbed. She held it out. The pages were edged in gold.

Boggs lowered his arm and looked at it uneasily, as if

no one had ever given him a present before, and he wondered what would be expected in return.

"It's a book," she said.

"Figured that out."

She had a moment's panic; what if he couldn't read?

He opened it. "Looks like an old one."

He flipped open to the copyright page. "Nineteen oh four. Yep that goes back a ways. Year my grandmother was born."

"It's not like it's worth a lot of money, or anything."

"What is it, like fairy tales?"

"Greek and Roman myths."

At least his eyes were reviving. He even had a slight smile on his face as he turned the pages, pausing at the plates, which were protected with tissue. The smile of somebody who receives a present he likes but doesn't know what to do with.

Rune said, "There's a story I want you to read. One in particular." She flipped through the pages. "Here."

He looked at it. "Prometheus. Wasn't he the guy made the wings out of wax or something?"

"Uh, nope. That was another dude."

Boggs squinted. "Hey, lookit there."

She followed his eyes to the old plate. "Yeah," she laughed, sitting forward. Prometheus chained to a rock, a huge bird swooping down and tearing at his side. "Just like you—getting stabbed. Isn't that crazy wild?"

He closed the book and picked a couple chips of spine off the thin blanket, which was imprinted with fuzzy lettering, NYDC. "So tell me, miss, you a college girl?"

"Me? Nope."

"How come you know this kind of stuff?" He held up the book.

She shrugged. "I don't know. I like to read."

"I kind of regretted I never was smart enough to go."

"Naw, I wouldn't feel that way, I was you," she said. "You go to college, get a real job, get married, what happens is you don't ever get a chance to play chicken with life. That's the fun part."

He nodded. "Never could sit still long enough to go to school anyway." He looked at her for a moment, eyes roving up and down. "Tell me 'bout yourself."

"Me?" She was suddenly embarrassed.

"Sure. I told you 'bout me. Remind me what life's like on the Outside. Been a while."

"I don't know. . . ." She thought: So this is what the people I interview feel like.

Boggs asked, "Where you live?"

Houseboats took a lot of explaining. "In Manhattan," she said.

"You can stand it?"

"I can't stand many places else."

"Never spent much time there. Never could get a handle on it."

"Why would you want to live somewhere you can get a handle on?" she asked.

"Maybe you've got a point there. But you're talking to somebody who's a little prejudiced. I come to town for the first time in maybe ten years, and what happens? I get myself arrested for murder. . . ." He smiled, then looked at her closely. "So, you're a reporter. Is that what you want to do?"

"I have this thing about films. I think I want to make documentaries. Right now I'm working for this TV program. I'll do it for as long as it excites me. The day I wake up and say I'd rather go have a picnic on the top of the Chrysler Building than go to work, that's the day I quit, and do something else."

Boggs said, "You and me're kind of alike. I've done me

a lot of different things too. I keep looking. Always been looking for that nest egg, just to get a leg up."

"Hey, before this job, I spent six months at a bagel restaurant. And before that I was a store-window dresser. Most of my close friends are people I met at the unemployment office."

"Pretty girl like you I think'd be considering settling down. You have a boyfriend?"

"He's not exactly like the marrying kind."

"You're young."

"I'm not in any hurry. I think my mother's got this bridal shop in Shaker Heights on call. In case I tell her I'm engaged, she'll be like SAC, you know, Red Alert. But I have trouble seeing me married. Like some things you can imagine, and some you can't. That's one that doesn't compute."

"Where's Shaker Heights?"

"Outside Cleveland."

"You're from Ohio. I spent some time in Indiana."

She blinked, he laughed. "Maybe I shouldn't put it that way. Not like I was *doing* time. I lived about a year there, working. A real job. As real as day labor can be. Steel mills in Gary."

"Miss," the guard said, "I let you stay a little longer than you should."

She stood up and said to Boggs, "I'm working really, really hard on the story. I'm going to get you out of here."

Boggs was running his finger along the edge of his book, touching it in awe, like it was solid gold. "I'll keep this." He said it as if that was the best thing he could think of to thank her.

As Rune and the guard walked back to the prison exit, the guard, without looking at her, said, "Miss, word been around about what you're trying to do."

She looked up at him. Her eyes didn't get much past the huge biceps.

"About you maybe getting him a new trial."

"Yeah?"

"I like Randy. He keeps to himself, and doesn't give us any grief. But there're some people here don't like him much."

"Other prisoners?"

He didn't answer, but said instead, "I'm not supposed to be telling you this, and I'm hoping it won't go any further than here. . . ."

"Sure."

"But if you don't get him out soon, he's not going to live to parole."

"The people who did that?" She nodded back to the infirmary.

"There's nothing we can do to stop them. If they decide they want somebody dead, he's dead."

They arrived at the gate, and the guard stopped.

"But what did he do?"

"What did he do?" The guard didn't understand her.

"I mean, why did somebody stab him?"

The guard's face snapped into a brief frown. "He ended up here, miss. That's what he did. That's all he had to do."

The place was pretty easy to get into.

Like a sieve, Jack Nestor thought. Then laughed, thinking that probably wasn't the best word to describe a houseboat. The only problem had been there was a parking lot nearby and a booth with a security guard in it, and he'd glance at the boat every so often, like he was keeping an eye on it. But Nestor waited only five minutes, until the man made a phone call, then walked past him and jogged up the yellow gangplank.

Once he was inside, he pulled on brown cotton gloves and started at the back. He took his time. He'd never been on a houseboat before.

He was pretty curious about the boat. He'd done some charters and been on more party boats than he could count, and of course had done time in LSTs and landing craft. But this wasn't like anything else he'd ever seen.

The decor sucked, for one thing. It looked like his nutzo stepmother's place. But he admired the pilot house, if that's what you'd call it, which had beautiful brass fixtures and levers and grainy oak all yellow with old varnish. Beautiful. All the controls except the wheel were frozen, and he guessed the motor was kaput. He resisted a temptation to pull the horn rope.

Downstairs, he carefully went through the bookshelves and the cheap, sprung-fiberboard desk that was a sea of papers and pictures (mostly of dragons and knights and fairies, that sort of shit). There were a couple dozen videocassettes. They were mostly that make-believe stuff too. Fairy stories, dragonslayers, the stuff he never watched. A couple dirty films, it looked like. *Lusty Cousins* and *Epitaph for a Blue Movie Star.* So, she had a kinky side to her. Too bad she didn't have the figure to go with it.

Then the closets and drawers in the bedroom and in the little supply room that had another dresser in it. He went through the kitchen and the refrigerator, which was the first place that most people who thought they were clever hid things and was the first place most professional thieves looked.

After an hour, he was convinced she didn't have anything here on the Hopper killing or on Randy Boggs. At least nowhere that he could get to without tearing the place apart. But it wouldn't make sense for her to hide things away too secretively. She was working on the story, she'd keep things close at hand.

Which meant the files would be at her office, and that was a pain in the ass.

Nestor looked around and sat down on the couch. He had a decision to make. He could wait here until she came back, and just waste her. Get it over with, make it look like a robbery. The cops would probably buy that. He was always surprised how people craved to accept the most obvious explanations. Easier all the way around. Robbery and murder.

Or rape and murder.

On the other hand, that would leave a lot of material about Boggs and Hopper floating around somewhere.

Well, whether he did her now or later, there was always a chance that somebody else would take over on the story.

Still . . .

A car door slammed. He was up quickly and glancing out the window, and saw her—not a bad looking girl, if she didn't wear those stupid clothes, like the striped black-and-yellow tights and a red miniskirt she wore now. It turned him off, and made him resent her. . . .

Oh, he knew that emotion. The feeling that he'd get looking at a wiry brown-skinned man in a khaki uniform, looking at him through a telescopic sight, feeling hatred, working up a wild, spiraling fury (maybe because Nestor was sweating like a steam pipe in the heat or because bugs were digging into his skin, or because he had a glossy, star-shaped scar on his belly). Resent, hate. He needed those feelings—to help him pull the trigger, or press the knife in as deeply as he could.

Boots scraped on the asphalt outside.

Nestor felt a low itching, and rubbed his scar. He felt the weight of the Steyr in his pocket.

But he left it where it was, and climbed out onto the deck.

He watched her open the door, clumsy, burdened, tilting against the weight of a movie camera and cassettes and a leather belt of batteries or whatever, which looked like a bandolier of M16 clips. She stacked it all by the door and disappeared into the bedroom. He waited a few minutes to see if he'd get a glimpse of skin, but when she came out in a work shirt (buttoned to the neck) and stretch pants, he silently left the boat and disappeared into the West Village.

CHAPTER FOURTEEN

A genius, but always controversial . . .
Click.
A genius, but always controversial, Hopper . . .
Click.
Rune hit the rewind button again. It was a good shot of
him: Lance Hopper. Or a good shot of his mortal remains,
at any rate—the gurney holding his body as it was
wheeled out of the deadly courtyard three years before.
She wished she could use the footage. Unfortunately, it
had been filmed by another station.

*. . . controversial, Hopper was disliked by co-workers
and competitors alike. Although under his brief leader-
ship, the seven P.M. national news program rose to number one in the ratings, he managed to embroil the network in several major scandals. Among them was an
uproar caused by numerous firings of staff members,
massive and—his critics said—arbitrary budgetary cut-
backs, and intense scrutiny of the network's news programs and their content.*

*Perhaps the incident that gave his network the black-
est eye, however, was an Equal Employment Opportunity
suit brought by five women employees who claimed that
Hopper's hiring and promotion practices discriminated
against them. Hopper denied the charges, and the suit
was settled out of court. Associates of the late executive,
though, admitted that he preferred men in executive posi-
tions, and felt that a woman had no business in the
higher echelons of network news. His flamboyant personal life belied that reputed prejudice, however, and he*

was often seen in the company of attractive women from society and the entertainment industry. His penchant was for tall blondes. . . .

Click.

Tall blondes. Why is it always tall blondes? Rune was at her desk, surrounded by piles of newspapers, magazines, computer printouts, videocassettes, and the refuse from a dozen fast-food meals. It was four-thirty in the afternoon, and everyone was gearing up for the news at seven. She felt that she was in the eye of a hurricane. Motion everywhere. Frantic, crazed motion.

The fuck do we need that story for?

No, no, no, no! Put it on at eleven. It's bullshit. It's an eleven o'clock story is all it is.

So I call Channel Eight, right, and pretend I'm the pub info officer. I told 'em we were moving the press conference to the Bronx. They goddamn believed me!

Rune watched the tape of Hopper's body rolling out into the spring night, the snakes of afterimage etched into the screen by the revolving lights on the EMS vans and police cars, the crowds—pale in the video camera's radiance of light—that looked both curious and bored at the same time.

So, he was a ladies' man and a son of a bitch and a genius. We still don't know a lot about Lance Hopper. But one thing we do know. That Randy Boggs didn't kill—

"Rune."

A calm voice, a woman's voice.

"Oh, hi."

Piper Sutton.

Should've cleaned up my desk. That was her first thought. Remembering how neat the anchorwoman's was. And seeing how neat she looked now, standing here in a dark red suit with black velvet tabs on the collar, and a white high-necked blouse and hair toasted with highlights and dark fleshy stockings disappearing into the slickest patent leather shoes Rune'd ever seen. Shoes with one red stripe along the side. High, tapping heels.

Shoes that'd put me on my ass I tried to wear them.

But, boy, they looked cool.

"You're busy." Sutton's eyes scanned the desk.

"I was just working on the story."

Rune casually picked up several of the closest paper bags—one Kentucky Fried and two Burger Kings—and dropped them into well, *onto* an overflowing wastebasket.

"You want to, like, sit down."

Sutton looked at a ketchup packet that rested on the one unoccupied chair. She picked it up and tossed it to Rune. "No. I don't." Sutton leaned forward and ejected the tape that was in the Sony player. She read the label. "Brand X," she said. "You can't use this footage, you know. I'm not putting a super in any of my news programs that says courtesy of another network." She handed the tape back to Rune.

"I know. I'm doing background is all."

"Background." Sutton said the word softly. "I want to talk to you. But not here. Are you doing anything for dinner?"

"I was going to John's for pizza. They're like real generous with their anchovies."

Sutton walked away. "No. You'll have dinner with me."

"The thing is, there's someone—"

"I want to talk to you in private."

"Anything you can say to me, you can say in front of her. She's, you know, discreet."

Sutton shrugged, took one last look at the desk, and didn't seem to like what she saw. "Whatever." Then she looked at Rune's pink T-shirt and miniskirt and fishnet stockings and ankle boots, and she said, "You do have a dress, don't you?"

Rune said defensively, "I've got two, as a matter of fact."

And wondered what she was missing when Sutton laughed. The anchorwoman wrote out an address and handed it to Rune. "That's between Madison and Fifth. Be there at six-thirty. We'll do the pretheater. Don't want to spend more than we need to, do we?"

"That's okay. My friend likes to eat early."

You couldn't call it a tip. What it was, was a bribe.

Jacques, the maitre d', took the bill Sutton offered him and slipped it into the pocket of his perfectly black tuxedo. However much it was—Rune didn't see—the money maybe bought them access to the dining room, but it did nothing to cheer up the poor, sullen man. He led them to a table off to the side, then said, "Maybe, a phone book."

Rune said, "Yellow *and* White Pages."

Jacques looked one more time at Ophelia, pursed his unhappy Gallic lips, and went to find the best child-seating device New York Telephone could offer.

Rune was having a little trouble herself. Her sunglass peeper-keeper cord had gotten tangled in her Walkman headset wire. Sutton watched, her face a visual sigh, as Rune did her best to untie the knots, while the tenor notes of Kitaro's *Silk Road* chugged out of the tiny earpieces. Sutton said in a steely voice, "Want some help?"

Rune grinned and said, "Nope. Happens all the time."

When she was finally unhooked, she looked around the room. "This is like really, really crucial. I could get into it. Living this way, I mean."

"Uhm."

The theme seemed to be flowers, and probably like the food, excess was in. The center of the room was dominated by a twisty vined centerpiece, sprouting orchids and roses and baby's breath. The walls held huge paintings of flowers. Rune liked them. They were what Monet would have done if all he'd had to work with were electric-colored Crayolas. Rune matched the decor. She'd raced home to change into one of the two dresses, a purple and white Laura Ashley, which was her spring and summer dress. It was several years old, but had very little mileage on it. She'd located it in an old refrigerator she used as an armoire, still sealed in a plastic laundry bag from the last time it had been cleaned, which was, as near as she could remember, July of last year.

"Wow," she said, "you pinned me up against that wallpaper, and all you'd see was my feet and hands and face."

Sutton smiled, and seemed to be thinking: *Don't tempt me, dear.*

On the table in front of them was a bird-of-paradise in a tall glass vase, and some kinky-looking green thing like a pinecone, which, if you saw it in *National Geographic,* you couldn't tell whether it was a plant or fish or huge insect. Rune pointed at the bird-of-paradise. "I love these dudes." She petted it. "I don't think it looks like a bird at all. I think it looks like a dragon."

Ophelia said, "I like dragons."

Sutton stared at them blankly. "Dragons."

The little girl added, "I'm going to be a knight. But I wouldn't kill any dragons. I'd have them for pets. Rune's going to take me to the zoo, and we're going to look at dragons."

Through teeth that never separated more than a quarter inch, Sutton said, "How wonderful."

Jacques returned with two bulky phone directories and set them on the third chair at the table. Ophelia smiled and giggled as he lifted her up, and the stern facade cracked for a moment.

He turned to Sutton. "This really cannot be, uh, *habituel, non?*"

"Jacques, have someone bring the little girl some . . ." She looked at Rune.

"She loves pizza."

"We are a French restaurant, miss."

"Not a problem," Rune said. "She also likes pickles, clam chowder, smoked oysters, rice, anchovies—"

"*Huîtres,*" Jacques said. "They are poached and served with pesto and *beurre blanc.*"

Sutton said, "Fine. Just have somebody cut them up into little pieces. I don't want to watch her mauling food. And have the sommelier bring me a Pouligny Montrachet." She looked at Rune. "Do you drink wine?"

"I'm over twenty-one."

"I'm not asking for a driver's license. I want to know if an eighty-dollar bottle of wine will be wasted on you."

"Maybe a white Russian would be more my speed."

Sutton nodded to the maitre d' and said, "Find me a half bottle, Jacques. A Mersault, if there's no Pouligny."

"*Oui,* Miss Sutton."

Huge menus appeared. Sutton scanned hers. "I don't think we want anything too adventurous. We'll have scallops to start—" She asked Rune, "Do you swell up, or turn red, when you eat seafood?"

"No, I get fish sticks all the time at this Korean deli. I like them when they're frozen—"

Sutton waved an abrupt hand. "And then the pigeon."

Rune's eyes went wide. Pigeon?

Jacques said, "*Salades,* after?"

"Please."

Rune's eyes danced around the room, then settled on the arsenal of silverware and empty plates in front of her.

The procedures here seemed as complicated as Catholic liturgy, and the down side if you blew it seemed worse.

Be cool, now. This is your boss, and she already thinks you're a dweebette. Don't keep giving her proof that it's true, even if it is most of the time. She resisted the impulse to adjust her bra.

The first course arrived, along with the oysters.

"Gross dudes," Ophelia said, but began to eat anyway. "Can we buy these for breakfast? I like them."

"Maybe we can get some to go," Rune said before she could stop herself. Sutton glanced at her, and Rune added quickly, "Like some other time, I meant."

Rune was thankful Ophelia was with them; the girl gave her something to do beside feeling uncomfortable. Picking spoons up off the floor, wiping oyster off her face, keeping the vase vertical.

Sutton watched them, curious. "So that's what it's like."

"What?" Rune asked. She tried an oyster herself. Whatever burr blank was, it was all right.

"Kids."

"You don't have children?"

"Yep; they're called ex-husbands. Three of them."

"I'm sorry."

Sutton blinked and stared at Rune for a minute. "Yes, I believe you are." She laughed. "But that's one thing I regret. Children. I—"

"It's not too late."

"No, I think it is. Maybe in my next life."

"That's the worst phrase ever made."

Sutton said, "You'll do anything, won't you?"

"Pretty much, I guess."

Sutton's eyes settled on Ophelia for a minute, then she reached forward and, with a napkin as big as the girl's dress, wiped her cheek. "Messy little things, aren't they?"

"Yeah, that's kind of a drag. And she isn't really into being sloppy tonight. I told her to behave. For lunch the other day, okay? We're eating bananas and hamburger, all kind of mashed up—"

Sutton's hand swept across the table. "Enough."

Two waiters brought the main courses. Rune blinked. Oh, God. Little birds.

Sutton saw her face and said, "They're not your kind of pigeons. . . ."

My kind?

"They're more like quail."

"Oh." Rune stared. No, what they were like was little hostages, their hands tied behind their backs. She decided not to tell Sutton this, but couldn't get the image to go away.

Ophelia squealed happily. "Birdies, birdies!" A half-dozen diners turned.

Rune picked up the least offensive knife, which weighed close to a pound, and started in.

They ate in silence for a few moments. The birdies weren't too bad actually. The problem was that they still had the bones in them, and using a knife as big as a sword meant there was a lot of meat you couldn't get to. Rune surveyed the room, but didn't see a single person sucking on a drumstick.

There was a pause, and Sutton looked at her and said, "Where are you with the story?"

Rune had figured it was on the agenda, and she'd already planned in her head what she was going to say. The words didn't come out as organized as she hoped, but she kept the *like*'s and the *sort of*'s to a minimum. She told Sutton about the interview with Megler and with Boggs, and with the friends and family members, and told her about getting all the background footage. "And," she said, "I've sort of put in a request to get the police file on the case."

Sutton laughed. "You'll never get a police file. No journalist can get a police file."

"It's like a special request."

But Sutton just shook her head, then asked, "Have you found anything that proves he's innocent?"

"Not like real evidence, but—"

"Have you or haven't you?"

"No."

"All right." Sutton sat back. Half her food was uneaten, but when the busboy appeared she gave him a subtle nod of the head and the plate vanished. "Let me tell you why I asked you here. I need some help."

"From me?"

"Look," Sutton was frowning. "I'll be frank. You're not my first choice. But there just isn't anybody else."

"Like, what are you talking about?"

"I want to offer you a promotion."

Rune poked at a white square of vegetable—some kind she'd never run into before. Then she looked up at Sutton, who continued, "Sometimes we have to do things for the good of the news. We have to put our own interests aside. When I started out, I was a crime reporter. They didn't want women in the newsroom. Food reporting, society, those were fine, but for hard news? Nope. So the chief gave me the shit jobs." Sutton glanced at Ophelia, then said, "I covered autopsies, I chased ambulances like a lawyer, I did arraignments, I walked through pools of blood at a mass shooting to get pictures when the photographer was kneeling behind the press car puking. I did all of that crap, and it worked out. For the stations I worked for, and for me. But at the time, it was a sacrifice."

Something in the flatness of Sutton's voice was thrilling. Apart from the words—the tone, it seemed, was what she would use to talk to another executive at the Network, an equal. People in the know. Sutton and Maisel would talk this way—in low voices, surrounded by people wearing huge geometric shapes of jewelry, sitting over the tiny bones of hostage birds and drinking eighty-dollar-a-bottle wine.

"Like you want me to be a crime reporter? I don't—"

Sutton said, "Let me finish."

Rune sat back. Her plate was cleared away, and a young man in a white jacket cleaned the crumbs off the table with a little thing that looked like a miniature carpet sweeper. Most of the mess was on Rune's side.

"I like you, Rune. You're smart and you got balls. That's something I don't see enough of in reporters nowadays. It's one or the other, and usually more ego than either of them. Here's my problem: We've just lost the associate producer of the London bureau—he quit to work for Reuters—and they were in the midst of production on three programs. I need someone over there now."

"Wow." Her skin bristled. Like a wave of painless flame passed over her. "Associate producer?"

"The bureaus in London, Paris, Rome, Berlin, and Moscow'll feed you leads, and you and the executive producer make your decisions on what you want to go after."

"What does Lee think?"

"He's given me the job of filling the spot. I haven't mentioned you to him, but he'll go with whoever I recommend."

"This is pretty wild. I mean, this is like too much. How long?"

"A year minimum. If you like it, something more permanent might be arranged. That would be up to Lee. But usually we like to shift people around. It could be Paris or Rome after that. You'd have to learn the language."

"Oh, I took French in high school. *Voulez-vous couchez. . . .*"

Sutton said, "I get the idea."

Rune asked a passing waiter for a glass of milk for Ophelia. "And a straw? The kind with the bend in them." He didn't seem to grasp the concept and Rune let it drop.

She said to Sutton, "I don't want you to think . . . I mean, I'm grateful and all, but what about Randy Boggs?"

"You said yourself you don't have any evidence."

"I still know he's innocent."

Wrinkles of frustration burst into Sutton's face for a moment.

Rune said, "Somebody tried to kill him. They stabbed him. If we don't get him out, they'll try again."

Sutton wasn't listening. "I'll assign a local reporter to pick up for you."

"You would?"

"Uh-huh. . . . So how 'bout it?"

"Uh, like would you mind if I thought about it?"

Sutton blinked and seemed about to ask, with her trademarked impatience, *What the fuck is there to think about?*, but she just smiled and said, "It's a big decision. Maybe you should sleep on it. I won't ask the other people I'm considering until tomorrow."

Sutton motioned for the last of her wine. A young waiter scurried over and with alternate glances at her freckled chest and at the crystal glass in front of her, emptied the bottle. She looked at her watch, then added, "And the check, please."

Outside the restaurant, the three of them paused.

"Wow, that is totally fresh," Rune said, as a glossy midnight-blue stretch Lincoln Town Car turned the corner and slowed. "Don't you wonder who rides in those things?"

Sutton didn't answer.

The car eased to a stop in front of them. The driver hopped out and ran to the door, opened it, waiting.

Rune's head swiveled. She said to Ophelia, "Hey, honey, there's somebody famous around here."

Sutton said, "You'll give me your answer tomorrow?"

"Oh, you bet." Rune was looking at the restaurant door, wondering if she'd just had dinner with Tom Cruise, or, no, no . . . Kevin Costner! Oh, she hoped it was him.

"Piper, we're late," a man's voice called from the limo.

"Good night," the anchorwoman said briskly to Rune and started toward the Lincoln.

Oh.

A man leaned forward to help her in. It was Dan Semple himself, in a beautiful gray double-breasted suit (which she thought would've looked even better on Kevin Costner). He glanced at Rune, then kissed Sutton on the cheek. They disappeared into the blackness of the car.

"Night," Rune said. Ophelia waved.

The door closed, and the two of them were left looking at their dark mirrored images for the few seconds it took for the driver to get back inside and speed the limo away from the curb.

CHAPTER FIFTEEN

London was the problem.

Ever since she'd read *Lord of the Rings* (the first of four times), Rune'd wanted to go to the country of pubs and hedgerows and shires and hobbits and dragons.

And Loch Ness!

She'd thought about it all day long, and every way she sliced it, there wasn't much debate: a European producer for *Current Events,* more money in one year than she'd made in her life, chances to go to Paris, Rome, Berlin. And the Loch Ness Monster. . . . Who could say no?

She wondered, then, why she was dropping Ophelia at one of the loyal, expensive baby-sitters and then giving the cab driver an address on the Upper East Side.

It was an old apartment building, dark brick with lion bas-reliefs in dirty limestone trim. She walked into the immaculate lobby and hit the intercom. She announced herself and the door opened. She took the elevator to the fourteenth floor. When she stepped into a tiny corridor, she realized there were only four apartments on the whole floor.

Lee Maisel opened the door and let her into a rambling, dark-paneled apartment. He kissed her cheek, but didn't hug her; he was dripping wet.

"Come on in."

She followed, noticing an elephant's foot in the corner; inside were a half-dozen umbrellas and canes. Several of them ended in carved faces: a lion, an old man (Rune thought he was a wizard), some kind of bird.

Maisel had been doing dishes. Encased in a blue denim

apron, water-stained with Rorschach patterns, taut over his belly.

"When I called, well, I hope I didn't interrupt anything."

"I'd have told you I didn't want to be interrupted. You ought to know I don't mince words." Maisel returned to the cumulonimbus of suds. "Come on in. The bar's over there." He nodded. "Food?"

"Uhm, I just ate."

Maisel dove into the dishwater again. Surrounded by implements—scrapers, sponges, metallic scrubbers like tiny steel wigs. A typhoon, the surf crashed over the granite countertop. A pan surfaced and beached itself on the Rubbermaid, as he examined it carefully. His face was pure contentment. She envied him; this was a love that Rune knew she would never cultivate.

In the living room, a projection TV set was showing an old movie, the sound low. Bette Davis. Who was the other dude? Tyrone Power maybe. What a name. What a face. Whoa, men looked good back then. She could watch that boy for hours.

Rune looked at the stack of dripping dishes and chose a metal platter over a glass bowl to dry. It was heavy and seemed to be pure silver; she handled it carefully as if it would shatter like crystal if she dropped it. She wondered why he didn't have butlers and maids.

He took the platter out of her hand and set it in the dish drain. "Let nature do the work."

They walked into the living room.

Rune paused, looking at a framed newspaper article on the wall. From the *Times*. The headline was: "TV Correspondent Wins Pulitzer."

"Wholly excellent!" Rune said. "That's like the Academy Award, right?"

Maisel gave her a laughing scowl. "Not exactly."

"What was it for?"

"A story in Beirut a few years ago."

She asked, "A *Current Events* segment?"

"No. It was before we developed the show. I was just a correspondent." He looked at the article for a moment. "What a beautiful city that used to be. That's one of the crimes of the century, what's happened there."

Rune skimmed the article. "It says you got an exclusive. . . . Wow, that's fantastic. What was it about?"

He didn't answer, and his face was troubled. Whatever had happened in Beirut, it brought back sad memories. Maybe he'd loved a beautiful Arab girl, who'd been killed. Or maybe one of his friends had been shot or taken hostage. . . .

"Come here," Maisel said, his face brightening. He led Rune down a long corridor, lit by overhead spotlights. It was like an art gallery.

"Hey, this is pretty crucial."

There were dozens of framed maps, most of them antique. Maisel paused at each one, told her where he'd found it, in what countries, how he'd dickered with the booksellers and vendors. How he'd been taken by some, and gypped others.

She liked the New York maps best. And Maisel pointed to a couple, describing what buildings were now on the spots that the maps showed as just fields or hills.

Her favorite was a map of Greenwich Village in the 1700s. "That is super fantastic. I love old New York. Doesn't it just do something to you? Okay, you're out on the street eating a Nedick's with onions, I really love those pickled onions, and you suddenly think, wow, maybe I'm standing right on the very spot where they rubbed out a gangster or where two hundred years ago there was an Indian war or something."

"I don't eat hotdogs," Maisel said, but absently, and

she caught him glancing at his watch. They walked into a low-lit den, filled with leather furniture and more maps and framed photos of Maisel on assignment. They sat. He asked, "So what's up?"

Rune said, "I got an offer for something, and I don't know what to do about it."

"Publisher's Clearing House?"

"Better than that." She told him what Piper Sutton had said.

Maisel listened. She got almost all the way through before she realized that his face was growing a frown. "So she offered you the Brit spot, huh?"

"I was kind of surprised."

She could see in his face he was searching for tact. "Rune, I want to be honest with you. . . . No reflection on you, but it's a tough assignment. I had a couple people more senior in mind. I'm not saying you couldn't get up to speed, but your experience is. . . ."

"Like pretty much not there."

Maisel didn't agree or disagree. He said, "I asked Piper to fill the spot. It's her call. If she wants you, it's yours."

Maisel looked across the room. More antique maps. She wondered what country he was focusing on.

"I'm pretty tempted," she said.

"Wonder why. Couldn't be more than ten, fifteen thousand reporters in the country that'd kill to have that assignment." Maisel stretched his feet out straight, then curled one up under him. He wore bright yellow socks.

"But," he said, "you're worried about the Boggs story."

"That's the problem."

"How's it coming?"

"Slow. I don't really have any leads. Nothing solid."

"But you still think he's innocent?"

"Yeah, I guess I do. The story'd still get done. Piper said she'd assign someone local to finish it."

"Did she?"

"Yeah, she promised me."

Maisel nodded.

Rune said, "She doesn't want me to do this story, does she?"

"She's afraid."

"Afraid? Piper Sutton?"

"It's not as funny as it seems. Her job is her whole life. She's had a couple disastrous marriages. There's nothing else she can do professionally, or wants to. If this story goes south on us, she and I, and Dan Semple to some extent, will take the flak. You know how fickle audiences are. Dan and I are worried about news; Piper's also got public image to sweat."

"I can't imagine her being afraid of anything. I mean, I'm terrified of her."

"She's not going to have you rubbed out if you tell her you're going to stay and do the story."

"But she's my boss. . . ."

Maisel laughed. "You're too young to know that bosses, like wives, aren't necessarily matched to us in Heaven."

"Okay, but she is Piper Sutton."

"That's a different issue, and I don't envy you having to call her up—if this's what you decide to do—and tell her that you're declining her offer. But, so what if she makes your life miserable?"

"I don't know what to do, Lee. What's your totally, totally honest opinion about my story?"

Maisel was considering. A gold clock began pinging off the hours to ten P.M. When it hit eight, he sighed and said, "I'm not going to do you any favors by being delicate. The story? You take it way too personally. And that's very unprofessional. I get the impression that you're on some kind of holy quest. You—"

"But he's innocent, and nobody else—"

"Rune," he said, harsh. "You asked my opinion. Let me finish."

"Sorry."

"You're not looking at the whole picture. You've got to understand that journalism has a responsibility to be totally unbiased. You're not. You're the most goddamn biased reporter I've ever worked with."

"True," she said.

"That makes for a noble person maybe, but it's not journalism."

"That's sort of what Piper told me too."

"There's government corruption and incompetence everywhere, there're human rights violations in South America, Africa and China, there's homelessness, there's child abuse in day-care centers . . . there are so many important issues that media has to choose from, and so few minutes of broadcast news or newspaper columns to talk about them in. What you've done is pick a very small story. It's not a bad story, it's just an insignificant one."

She looked off, scanning Maisel's wall absently. She wondered if she'd find an omen—an old map of England, maybe. She didn't.

A minute passed.

She said, "I know. You're right. Piper's right."

He said, "It's got to be your decision. I think the best advice I can give you is, sleep on it."

"You mean, stay up all night tossing and turning and stewing about it."

"That might work too."

The Twentieth Precinct, on the Upper West Side, was considered a plum by a lot of cops. The Hispanic gangs had been squeezed north, the Black Panthers were nothing more than a bit of nostalgia, and no man's land—Central Park—had its own precinct to take care of the muggings and drug dealers. What you had in the Twentieth mostly was domestic disputes, shopliftings, an occasional rape. The piles of auto glass, like tiny green-blue ice cubes, marked what was maybe the most common crime: perpetrating Blaupunkts or Panasonics. Two yuppies who'd scrunched Honda Accord or BMW fenders might get into a shoving match in front of Zabar's. But things didn't get much worse than that.

There was a lot of traffic in and out of the low, 1960s decor brick-and-glass building. Community relations was a priority here, and more people came through the doors of the Twentieth to attend meetings or just hang out with the cops than to report muggings.

So the desk sergeant—a beefy, moustachioed blond cop—didn't think twice about her, this young, miniskirted mother, about twenty, who had a cute-as-a-button three- or four-year-old in tow. She walked right up to him and said she had a complaint about the quality of police protection in the neighborhood.

The cop didn't give a shit, of course. He liked concerned citizens about as much as he liked his hemorrhoids, and almost felt sorry for the piss-ant street dealers and hangers-out and drunks who got run around by these wild-eyed, lecturing, upstanding, taxpaying citizens.

But he'd studied community relations at the Police Academy, and so now, though he couldn't bring himself to smile pleasantly at this short woman, he nodded as if he were interested in what she had to say.

"You guys aren't like doing a good job patrolling. My little girl and I were out on the street, just taking a walk—"

"Yes, miss. Did someone hassle you?"

She gave him a glare. "We were taking a walk and do you know what we found on the street?"

"Nade," the little girl said.

The cop infinitely preferred to talk to the little girl. He may have hated intense, short, concerned citizens, but he loved kids.

He leaned forward, grinning like a department-store Santa the first day on the job. "Honey, what's your name?"

" 'Phelia."

"Uh-huh, that's a pretty name."

Oh, she was so goddamn cute, he couldn't believe it. The way she was digging in her patent leather purse, trying to look grown up. He didn't like the lime-green miniskirt she was wearing, and he was thinking maybe the sunglasses around her neck, on that yellow strap, might be dangerous. Her mother oughtn't to be dressing her in that crap. Little girls should be wearing that frilly stuff like his wife bought for their nieces.

The good citizen mother said, "Show him what we found, baby."

The cop talked the sing-songy language that adults think children respond to. "My brother's little girl has a purse like that. What do you have in there, honey?"

"Nade."

"Who's Nade? Is that your dolly?"

It wasn't. It was a U.S. Army–issue hand grenade. A classic olive-drab segmented fragmentation model. She held it out. "Nade."

The mother said, "There. Look at that, just lying on the street. . . ."

"Holy Mary."

He hit the fire alarm, and grabbed the phone, calling NYPD Central and reporting a 10-33 IED and a 10-59.

It occurred to him that the fire alarm wasn't such a good idea because the forty or fifty officers in the building could get out only one of three ways—a back exit, a side exit and the front door, and most were choosing the front door, not eight feet from a three-year-old with a pound of TNT in her hands.

What happened next was kind of a blur. A couple detectives got the thing away from the girl and onto the floor in the far corner of the lobby. But then nobody knew exactly what to do. Six cops stood thirty feet away gawking at it. But the pin hadn't been pulled, and they got to talking about whether there was a hole drilled in the bottom of the grenade, and if there was that meant it was a dummy like they sold at Army-Navy stores and in ads in the back of *Field and Stream.* But whoever had put the thing in the corner had left it so that you couldn't see the butt end, and since the Bomb Squad got paid extra money to do that sort of thing, they decided just to wait.

But then somebody noticed it was in the sun and they thought that maybe that might set it off. They got into an argument because one of the cops had been in Nam, where it was a hundred and ten fucking degrees in the sun and their grenades never went off, but, yeah, this might be an old one and unstable. . . .

And if it did go, they'd lose all their windows and the trophy case, and somebody was bound to get fragged. . . .

Finally, the desk sergeant had the idea to cover the thing with a half dozen Kevlar bulletproof vests. And they made a great project out of dancing up and carefully dropping vests on the grenade one by one, each cop making a run, not knowing whether to cover his eyes or ears or balls with his free hand.

Then there they stood, these large cops, staring at a pile of vests until the Bomb Squad detectives arrived fifteen minutes later.

It was about that time that the concerned mother and the little girl, who nobody had noticed walk inside the precinct, slipped out through the back door. Holding her daughter's hand, she walked through the small parking lot full of blue-and-whites and past the cop car gas pump, then turned toward Columbus Avenue. A few cops and passersby glanced at them, but no one paid her much attention. There was still too much fun and excitement going on at the station house itself.

CHAPTER SIXTEEN

Rune filled Sam Healy's kitchen basin with water and gave Ophelia a bath. Then she dried the girl and put on the diaper she wore to bed. By now she'd gotten the routine down pretty well, and, though she didn't admit it to anybody, she liked the smell of baby powder. It'd make a crazy perfume.

The little girl asked, "Story?"

Rune said, "I've got a good one we can read. Come on over here." They were in Healy's family room, sitting on an old musty couch with tired springs. She sank down into it. Ophelia climbed into her lap.

"Ducks?" Ophelia asked. "The duck story is really crucial."

"This is even better," Rune said. "It's a police report."

The girl nodded as Rune began to read through Xeroxed sheets of paper. There were some photos, but they weren't pleasant, and Rune slipped them to the back before Ophelia saw them. She read until her throat ached from keeping her voice in a child-entertaining low register. She'd pause occasionally and watch Ophelia's eyes scan the cheap white paper. The meaning of the words was totally lost on the child, of course, but she was fascinated, catching some secret delight in the abstract designs of the black letters.

After twenty minutes, Ophelia closed her eyes and lay heavily against Rune's shoulder.

The subject of the reading matter apparently didn't matter much to Ophelia; ducks and police procedures lulled her to sleep equally quickly. Rune put her into bed, pulled the blankets around her. She looked at the U2 poster that Adam had bought for Sam for his birthday (Sam, a great father, had immediately framed and mounted it in a nice prominent location). She decided to sink some money into a Maxfield Parrish or Wyeth reproduction for Ophelia's room on the houseboat. That's what kids needed: giants in the clouds or magic castles. Maybe one of Rackham's illustrations from *A Midsummer Night's Dream*—one of her all-time favorites.

Rune returned to the report.

I'd just come back from Zabars. I walked past my living room window. I see these two men standing there. Then one pulls out this gun. . . . There was a flash and one of the men fell over. I ran to the phone to dial 911, but I'll admit I hesitated—I was worried it might be a Mafia thing. All these witnesses you hear about getting killed. Or a drug shooting. I go back to the window to see if they were just kidding around. Maybe it was young people, you know, but by then there's a police car. . . .

The report contained the names of three people interviewed by the police. All three lived on the first floor of the building. The first two hadn't been home. The third was this woman, a clerk at Bloomies, who lived on the first floor of Hopper's building, overlooking the courtyard.

That was all? The cops had talked to only three people?

Thirty or forty apartments would open onto the courtyard. Why hadn't they interviewed any others? For the same reason Fred Megler, the mercenary lawyer, hadn't? Too much trouble?

Cover-up, she thought. Conspiracy. Grassy knolls, and the Warren Commission. Rune liked conspiracies. They meant something was going on beneath the surface. Mysteries. She liked that.

That would be a good twist to the story. Payoffs to the police . . .

She finished the report. There wasn't much else helpful to her. Rune heard Healy's car pull into the driveway and hid the file. She looked in on Ophelia. Kissed her forehead.

The girl woke up for a moment and said, "Love you."

Rune blinked and didn't move for a moment. "Like, sure. Me too." But Ophelia was sleeping again by the time she said it.

"Funny thing," Sam Healy was saying the next morning.

"Funny."

"It disappeared from the Bomb Squad and next thing there's a report of a grenade in the Twentieth."

They were in his house in Queens. He'd just come in from mowing the lawn. She smelled grass and gasoline. It reminded her of her childhood in the suburbs of Cleveland, Saturday morning, when her father would trim the boxwood and mow and spread mulch around the dogwoods.

"Wow, a grenade," Rune said. "Did it go off?"

"What do you think?"

"Don't think I heard anything about it on the radio."

"It was a practice grenade. The report said a young woman and a baby found it. You were in the Squad the other day, weren't you? You and Ophelia?"

"Sort of I was, yeah. I think. I'm not too clear."

Healy said, "You're sounding like those defendants, 'Yeah, I was standing over the body with the gun, but I don't remember how I got there.' "

"You don't think I had anything to do with it?"

"Occurred to me."

"You want my solemn word?"

"Will you swear on the Grimms Brothers?"

"Absolutely." She raised her hand.

"Rune. . . . What if it wasn't a practice?"

"What?"

"The grenade."

"I don't know anything about a grenade."

"You could get me fired. And you could get arrested."
She tried to look miserable and contrite and unjustly
accused at the same time.

He popped open two Pabsts.

He was stern when he said, "Just don't forget. You've
got more to think about than yourself."

Which gave her a little thrill, like he was saying, *Remember me? I'm in your life too.* But he tromped on that
pretty fast by nodding toward the bedroom and saying,
"Think about her. You don't want her to lose two mothers
in one month, do you?"

"No."

They sipped the beers in silence for a minute. Then she
asked, "Sam, I got a question. You ever do any homicide?"

"Investigations? No. When I was ESU, we were on
crime scenes a lot, but I never did the legwork. Boring."

"But you know something about them?"

"A little maybe. What's up?"

"Say there's somebody killed, okay?"

"Hypothetical?"

"Yeah, this guy is like hypothetically killed. And there's
an eyewitness? Would the cops just stop there, and not
interview anybody else?"

"Sure, why not? If it's a solid witness."

"Real solid."

"Sure. Detectives've got more work than they know
what to do with. An eyewitness—which you hardly ever
get in a homicide—sure, they'd take the statement and

turn 'em over to the prosecutor. Then on to another murder."

"Geez, I'd just think they'd do a better job."

"Finding an eyewitness is a good job. It don't get any better than that."

The sites of tragedy.

The killing had been three years ago, but as she placed each foot on the worn crest of a cobblestone—slowly, a mourner's hopscotch—Rune felt the macabre, queasy pull of the killing. It was eight P.M. on an overcast Tuesday. She and Ophelia stood at the bottom of the huge box made up of the four sides of the building. A square of city-lit sky was above her.

Where exactly had he died? In the dim triangle of light falling through the courtyard from the leaded-glass lamp by the canopied doorway?

Or had it been in the negative space—the shadows?

Had he crawled toward the light? Had he shouted out?

Rune found it bothered her, not knowing where Lance Hopper had lain as he died. She thought there should be some kind of marker, some indication of where that moment had occurred—the instant between life and no life. But there was nothing under her Reeboks other than grit, oil film, a wet coupon for Chex cereal pasted to the cobblestones.

No reminder at all.

Hopper would have to be content with whatever his gravestone said. He'd been rich; she was sure it was an eloquent sentiment.

She looked at the windows surrounding her, at the circumstantial evidence of the building's residents—shadows falling on windows and shades, and the ghostly borealis of unseen TV sets. There was no noise whatsoever.

Rune led Ophelia into the stuccoed lobby. An entry-
way of a medieval castle. She expected at least a suit of
armor, a collection of pikes and broadswords and maces.
But she saw only a bulletin board with a faded sign,
CO-OP NEWS, and a stack of take-out menus from a Chinese restaurant ("Free wine accompanyed dinner if entre
ordered if requested").
    She pressed a button.

    "What a cute little girl. You're young to be a mother."
Rune said, "You know how it is."
    The woman said, "I had Andrew when I was twenty-
six. Beth when I was twenty-nine. That was old for then.
For that generation. Let me show you the pictures."
    The apartment was irritating. It reminded Rune of a
movie she'd seen one time about these laser beams that
crisscrossed the control room in a spaceship and if you
broke one of them you'd set off this alarm. Here, though,
no laser beams, but instead: little china dishes, animal
figurines, cups, commemorative plates, a Franklin Mint
ceramic thimble collection, vases, and a thousand other
artifacts, most of them flowery and ugly, all poised on the
edges of fake teak shelves waiting to fall to the floor and
shatter.
    Ophelia's eyes glinted at it all, and Rune kept a death
grip on the belt of the little girl's jumpsuit, like she was a
walking suitcase.
    The woman's name was Miss Breckman. She was
handsome. A born salesclerk. Trimmed, helpful, organized, polite. Rune remembered she was in her late fifties,
though she looked younger. She was stocky, with a
double chin (handsome though it was) and a cylindrical
frame.
    "Have a seat, please."
    They maneuvered through the ceramic land mines and

sat on doily-covered chairs. Rune tamped down her pride and complimented Miss Breckman on her fine collection of things.

The woman glowed. "I got them mostly from my mother. We had the same thoughts about decoration. Isn't that a coincidence? Genetic, I suppose."

From there they talked about children, about boyfriends and husbands (Miss Breckman's had left her ten years before; she was, she said, "in the market").

Mostly what Miss Breckman wanted to talk about, though, was the news.

"So you're a real reporter?" Her eyes focused on Rune like a scientist discovering a new kind of bug.

"More of a producer, really. Not like a newspaper reporter. It's different in TV news."

"Oh, I know. I watch every program. I always try to work the day shift, so I can be home in time to watch *Live at Five.* It's a bit gossipy, but aren't we all? I don't care for the six P.M. report, that's mostly business, so I fix my dinner then, and I watch the *World News at Seven* while I eat." She frowned. "I hope you won't be offended if I tell you your network's nightly news isn't all that good. Jim Eustice, the anchorman, I think he's funny looking, and sometimes doesn't pronounce those Polish and Japanese names right. But *Current Events* is simply the best. Do you know Piper Sutton? Sure you do, of course. Is she as charming as she seems? What a woman she must be."

If you only knew, honey. . . .

Rune began steering toward the story, not quite sure how honest to be. If Rune was right about Boggs's innocence, of course, she was pretty much calling Ms. Figurine here a liar, and—come to think of it—a perjurer too. She opted for the indirect approach. "I'm doing a follow-up on the Hopper killing, and I'd like to ask you a few questions."

"I'd be happy to help. It was one of the most exciting times of my life. I was in that courtroom, and there was this killer right there, and he was looking at me." Miss Breckman closed her eyes for a moment. "I was pretty darn scared. But I did my duty. I was kind of hoping that after I came out of the courtroom, there'd be all these reporters there shoving microphones at me—you know, I love those microphones with the names of the stations on them?"

"Uh-huh. Maybe I could set up my equipment?"

While Rune did, Miss Breckman hoisted Ophelia into her lap and rattled on nonstop. Bringing the little girl was a great idea—she was like a pacifier for adults.

When the portable lights clicked on, and the red dot on the Ikegami flashed, Miss Breckman's eyes shone in a way they would never do ringing up an American Express charge in Junior Sportswear.

Rune said, "Could you move over there." Nodding at a Queen Anne chair upholstered in forest-green needle-point.

"I'll set wherever you like, honey." Miss Breckman composed herself for a moment.

"Now, could you tell me exactly what happened?"

"Sure." Then she talked in rehearsed terms about the murder. Coming home from shopping, seeing the men argue. The gun appearing. The muffled shot. Hopper falling. Running to the phone. Hesitating . . .

"You saw him pull the trigger?"

"Well, I saw this flash, and the gun was right up against the poor man's body."

"Could you see what kind of gun it was?"

"No, it was too dark."

"And you couldn't hear what they were saying."

"No," her head turned, eyes gazing into the courtyard. "You can see . . ."

Beautiful. Rune zoomed past her and focused on the cobblestones.

". . . it's pretty far away."

Rune dug into her purse and pulled a piece of paper out. She looked at it, then asked, "In the police report, it said you weren't interviewed until the day after the shooting. Is that right?"

"Uh-huh. The next night, two men showed up. Detectives. But they didn't look like Kojak or anything, though. I was kind of disappointed."

"You didn't contact them right away, though?"

"No. Like I told you, I was pretty shaken by the whole thing. I was scared. What if it was a drug killing? You know what you see on the news? Practically every day, mothers and children are being murdered because they're witnesses. But the next morning I saw a news report on *Wake Up With the News* that said they'd arrested this drifter. You know, so when the detectives came to me, I didn't hesitate to tell them what I saw."

"It says here, the police asked you if you'd seen anything, and you said, 'I'm sorry I didn't talk to you sooner, but I did see it. I mean, I saw the shooting.' And the detective asked, 'Did you see the man who did it?' And you answered, 'Sure I did. It was Randy Boggs.' Was that pretty much what you said?"

"Nope, not pretty much at all. That's exactly what I said."

Rune just smiled and resisted an urge to say, *No further questions.*

What she suddenly felt wasn't so much a shadow over her as an aura of some kind. She didn't like the vibrations. Rune looked sideways to see what angel of death was hovering over her in the newsroom and found she was staring into Piper Sutton's eyes.

"Hi," Rune said.

Sutton didn't answer.

Rune's eyes skipped around the room, wondering why exactly the woman was frowning so intensely.

Rune said, "Guess what I've got." She touched the tape. "I talked to the witness, and—"

The flash of anger was like a fast shutter on a camera. So fast, Rune wasn't sure she saw it at all. Then Piper Sutton's face was neutral again, in control, cold. "You've got a little bit to learn about life." She seemed to swallow something at the end of the sentence, probably: *young lady.*

Rune began, "What did I—?"

Then it was occurring to her. Oh, shit . . .

"Nobody's forcing you to work for a network like ours." Now, the temper was on the move. The patented Sutton temper. It was rolling downhill, an avalanche, and Rune was about to get buried. "You have your choice. But if you're going to work here, goddammit, you've got to behave like an adult, or—"

"I was going to tell you. I'm sorry. I just got—"

"Or you can go pick up paychecks at some independent company, or at a fucking restaurant!" The voice dropped threateningly. "I take you out to dinner, where you and that urchin of yours embarrass the hell out of me, and I make you an offer that no one your age has ever been offered before . . ." Now the screeching began. Rune blinked and sat back, her eyes wide. She felt a jolt of physical fear. Would Sutton stab her to death? "And do you even give me the courtesy of an answer?"

Heads perked. Throughout the studio, no one dared look, and no one did anything but listen.

"I'm sorry."

But Sutton cranked up a few more decibels. "Do you even show me the respect you'd show a cab driver? Did you say, 'Thank you, but I've decided not to accept your offer'? Did you say, 'Piper, could you please give me a few days to think about it some more?' No, you goddamn well didn't. What you did was say . . . zip, and go about your merry way."

"I'm sorry," Rune heard herself whining, and didn't like it. She cleared her throat. "I got caught up in the story. I was going to tell you—"

Sutton waved her hand. "I hate apologies. It's a sign of weakness."

Rune decided she couldn't do anything right. She wanted to cry, but sat hard on the tears.

Sutton was speaking to a monitor. "Everything about this story has been wrong. I knew it was a mistake. Stupid of me. Stupid, stupid."

Rune swallowed. She touched the file. "Just let me explain, please. What happened was I talked to the witness."

Sutton smiled coldly and shook her head, exaggerating her lack of comprehension. "What witness?"

"The one who convicted Randy."

"Oh, sure, that explains your behavior." Sutton's sarcasm was thick.

"No, like I can prove that she didn't see Randy Boggs."

"How?"

"She's a real, like, newshound."

"A newshound? What the fuck is that?"

"She watches all the news programs every day. She didn't give any description of Boggs until *after* she'd seen him arrested. When the—"

Sutton's hands raised like a martyr's. "What exactly are you getting at?"

"This is really, really good. Listen. When the police

showed up to interview her, she said, 'I saw who did it, and it was Randy Boggs.' "

Silence. Pin-resounding silence. Sutton gave a short bark of a laugh. "That's your proof?"

Rune's face burned from the sting. "You can't see into the courtyard clearly. Miss Breckman saw Randy on the *news*. She saw him being arrested. *That's* where she got the description. Otherwise how would she know his name? She didn't describe him first. She said, right off, 'It was Randy Boggs.' "

The laugh continued. "Keep at it, honey. You've got a long way to go."

"But doesn't this prove that she's a bad witness?"

"A piece in the puzzle. That's all it is. Keep digging."

"I thought—"

"That we'd go with it?"

"I guess."

"You guess." A brittle nail leveled at Rune's face like a bright red dagger. "This is the big time. You keep forgetting that." She clattered through the newsroom on her medium-height heels, while the employees moved silently and unobviously as far out of her way as they could get.

CHAPTER SEVENTEEN

Downstairs, in the lobby, she surveyed the job, and didn't like what she saw.

A directory of residents, containing one hundred and eleven names.

"Help you?" The accent was Russian. But then Rune decided she didn't know what a Russian accent sounded like; the doorman—wearing an old gray uniform shiny on the butt—might have been Czech or Rumanian or Yugoslavian or even Greek or Argentine. Whatever his ethnic origin, he was big and snide and unfriendly.

"I was just looking at the directory."

"Who you wanna see?"

"Nobody really. I was just—"

He smiled slyly as if he'd just caught on that three-card monte games were rigged. "I know. They done that before."

"I'm a student."

"Yeah, student." He worked a spot on the inside of his mouth with his tongue.

"How long you worked here?" she asked.

"Six months. I just came over here. This country. Lived with my cousin for a while."

"Who worked here before you?"

He shrugged. "I dunno. How would I know? You make good money where you are? You know what I'm saying?"

"I'm a student."

"I've heard it all. You think that's new? You think I haven't heard it?"

"I'm an art student. Architecture. I—?"

"Yeah." The smile was staying put. The tongue foraged. "What you make?"

"Make?" Rune asked.

"How much you sell them for?"

"What?"

"I understand. I been around."

"What I'm doing is I'd like to talk to some people who live here. About the design of their apartments."

A nod joined the smile.

There was nothing worse than being accused of something you hadn't done—even if you were doing something you ought to be accused of doing.

She rummaged for a minute in the dark recesses of her bag until she came up with a stiff bill. A twenty. Hot out of the ATM. She handed it to him. He glanced down as if he'd just caught *her* trying to make off with it.

Zip. It vanished into his pocket.

"How much you make?"

Another twenty joined its friend.

"I'm a student."

"Ah." He walked off, pressing his hand to the pocket that held the crisp, nonreimbursable bills.

The smart thing would have been to find out which rows of apartments looked out over the courtyard, but she didn't know how soon the Slavic Latin American capitalist would be back to suck up another bribe. So she started at the top left of the directory. From Myron Zuckerman in 1B speed-writing straight down to Mr., or Ms., L. Peters in 8K.

Twenty minutes later, the doorman returned, just as she finished (and just as her hand was beginning to cramp).

"Still studying?"

"I just finished."

"So tell me, yeah, which one you with? One of the big ones?"

"Schools?"

"No. You know what I mean. The company?"

"It's a big one," Rune said.

"Is in Jersey, right?"

"How'd you guess?"

"I've been around. I seen a lot. You can't fool me."

"I wouldn't even try."

Seven hours, forty-three minutes.

Scorching pain roamed around in her back. The inside of her ear was sweating. Her voice had gone alto, and she'd have to clear it with a stinging snap every few minutes. Rune had been sitting in her cubicle at the studio, speaking into a phone, for nearly eight hours straight.

Hello I'm a producer for Current Events *the news program Mr. Zuckerman Norris Williams Roth Gelinker we're doing a segment about the Lance Hopper killing I'm hoping you can help me what I'm looking for is.* . . .

It was late, edging past eight o'clock. After bedtime for Ophelia. The little girl sat at Rune's feet, tearing scheduling sheets into the shape of Easter bunnies.

. . . *How long have you lived in apartment 3B, 3C, 3D, 3E, 3F.* . . .

"Rune, bunny."

Whispering, hand over mouthpiece: "Beautiful, honey. I'm on the phone. Make a momma Easter bunny now."

"That is the mommy."

"Then make a daddy."

Rune's poll of the tenants so far:

One was Miss Breckman. Eight had unlisted numbers. Twenty weren't home when she called. Thirty-three had moved into their apartments after Hopper's death. Eighteen hadn't been home the night of the killing (or said

they hadn't). Nineteen were home, but didn't see anything related to the murder (or said they didn't).

That left twelve others on her list.

A bad number. If there'd been three, she would've
called them. Twenty, she'd have given up and gone home
to sleep. But twelve . . .

Rune sighed and stretched, hearing some remote bone
protest with a pop.

Ophelia squirmed and tore a bunny in half.

Quitting time, Rune thought. I'm going home. Then
thought of Sutton's raspy, bitchy voice and fuming eyes,
and she picked up the phone.

Which was fortunate, because what she heard, when
she asked Mr. Frost, 6B, if he knew anything about the
Lance Hopper killing, was a moment's pause, then: "Actually, I saw it happen."

"You put that in a bottle and you've got yourself something," she said.

Rune had walked into the apartment, right past the el-
derly man who'd opened the door, and stepped up to a
glass case. Inside was an elaborate model of a ship—not
a rigged clipper ship or man-of-war, but a modern cargo
ship. It was four feet long. She said, "Audacious."

"Thank you. I've never made ships in bottles. To tell
you the truth, I don't like hobbies."

She introduced herself.

"Bennett Frost," he said. He was about seventy-five
years old. He wore a cardigan sweater and pants worn
shiny. He was balding and had dark moles on his face
and head. He leaned forward, a vestigial bow, as he
shook her hand. He held it for a moment longer than one
normally would have, as if he were taking her pulse. Yet
he kept his distance. His visual forays along her body

were not sexual. He was appraising. He looked mostly at her jaw and shoulders. He nodded at the glass case.

"The *Minnesota Princess*. Odd name, don't you think for a ship that spent most of her time in the Mediterranean and the Atlantic? My very first ship. No, I shouldn't say that. My very first *profitable* ship. Which is, I suppose, better than my first ship. I named her Minnesota because I was born there."

He walked into the large apartment. Rune studied the squarish ship. The deck was covered with tiny boxes. Then she followed him. In the cluttered living room she noticed suitcases.

"You going on a trip?"

"I have a place in Bermuda. Haiti was my favorite. Used to be superb. Isn't any longer. But it was the spot to be. The Oloffson, what a hotel that was. I never used to go to British colonies, but you know how things are elsewhere." He looked at her with slits of eyes, a shared secret. She nodded.

His eyes fell on her camera.

"You have a press pass or something?"

She showed him her Network ID. He scanned her up and down again, critically. A CAT scan of her soul. "You're young."

"Younger than some. Older than others."

He gave that a curly smile and said, "I was young when I got started in business."

"What did you do?"

He gazed at the model. "That was my contribution to the shipping industry and the aesthetics of the sea. She isn't beautiful, she isn't a stately ship."

"I think she looks pretty nifty."

Frost said, " 'And the stately ships go on/To their haven under the hill/But O for the touch of a vanished hand/And the sound of a voice that is still.' Tennyson. Nobody knows poetry anymore."

Rune knew some nursery rhymes, and some Shakespeare, but she didn't volunteer anything.

He lifted a heavy decanter and started pouring two glasses of purple liquor, as he asked, "Would you like some port?"

Which Rune thought was wonderful—that a drink was called port. Something old sailors drank. As in: Any port in a storm.

It was cloying as honey and tasted like cough medicine. She'd rather have had a beer. Or grog. She wasn't sure what grog was, but it had to be better than this Formula 44 stuff.

"Do you know what a ship's chandler is?"

"A candle maker?" Rune shrugged.

"No, a provisioner. A supplier. Anything a captain wanted, from a ratchet to a side of beef, I would get it. I started when I was seventeen, rowing out to the ships as soon as they dropped anchor, even before the agents arrived or they'd started off-loading. I gave them cut prices, demanded half as a deposit, gave them fancy-looking receipts for the cash, and always returned with what they wanted, or a substitute that was better or cheaper. Some chandlers were pimps. I wasn't. By the time I was eighteen and learned about pimps, I was so successful I didn't need to be one."

"What I'd like to do—" she began.

Frost said, "During the thirties I moved into shipping. I worked out of a little office downtown, John Street. I had a desk, chairs, secretary, lithos of some old ships. That was it. Nothing else. No hoopla, no luxury. I took my lunch in a pail, just like the masons and carpenters building skyscrapers. I poured every dime back into the business. Then, World War Two. I saw what was going to happen and started doing charter-party leases for the co-coa and coffee trade. I kept my ships running north to south. Nowhere near the torpedoes."

A half hour later, he was talking about ship propellers he'd designed himself. "They called them Frost Efficiency Screws. I got such a kick out of that! Efficiency Screws! So my ships could make the run from the Straights of Hormuz around the horn to the Abrose Light in thirty-three days. Of course, I was wrong about the Suez Canal, but I still had the fastest oil carriers in the world. Thirty-three days."

Rune said, "If I could ask you a few questions. About the Hopper killing."

"There's a point I'm trying to make."

"Sorry."

"I got out of shipping. I could see what would happen to oil, I could see the balance of trade shifts. I didn't want to leave my ships; oh, that hurt me. But you must think ahead. Did you hear about the buggy whip manufacturers who went out of business when autos were developed? You know what their problem was? They didn't think of themselves as being in the accelerator business. Ha!" He loved the story he would have told a thousand times. "So what did I go into?"

"Airlines?"

Frost laughed derisively. *"Public* transportation? Regulation ad nauseam. I thought about it, but I knew that it would take one Democrat, two at the most, to ruin the industry. No, I diversified—financial services, mining, manufacturing. And I became the fourth richest man in the world. . . . Ah, you're skeptical, I can see that. You've never heard of me. Some old crackpot, I can see you thinking, who's lured me in here for who knows what nefarious prospects. But it's true. In the seventies I had three billion dollars." He paused. "And those were the days when a billion meant something."

Rune sensed he was getting to his point.

"But what could I do with it? Provide for my wife and children. Buy comfortable shoes, a good set of golf clubs, a warm coat, an apartment where the plumbing worked. I don't smoke, rich food makes me ill. Mistresses? I was contentedly married for forty-one years. I put my children through school, set up trust funds for the grandchildren, though not very fat ones, and . . ." He smiled, significantly. "I gave most of the rest away. Hence, you."

"Me?"

"I could go on and on."

That worried her. She asked, "What exactly does all that have to do with the Hopper killing?"

Frost considered this for a moment. "I'm confessing."

She blinked.

"But," he said, "it didn't make any difference, you know."

"Uh, like, how exactly do you mean?"

"They had the other witness. You can't blame me really?"

"Nobody's blaming you."

"At the time, three or four years ago. I had my fortune. You people in the media, you never feel a man has any privacy."

He pronounced it with a short *i*, privacy. Like *privileged.*

He continued. "Sometimes the words we create and then lose control of can do a lot of damage. I was, in short, scared. I was afraid to tell the police that I'd seen Hopper killed. I'd be on news programs. I'd be in court. There'd be stories about my wealth. Kidnappers might come after my family or me. Development people would start hounding me for money for their causes. I felt guilty at first, but then I heard that that Breckman woman . . ." His voice seemed to sneer. ". . . downstairs saw the whole thing. It took the pressure off me."

"But now you don't mind telling me what you saw?"

Frost walked to the window and looked into the gloomy courtyard. "I'm a different man than I was three years ago. All that's important to me are my charities," Frost said, "I have a different attitude toward life."

Oh, please, Rune was thinking, do it now. Tell me what you saw. And, please, make it good.

The lights clicked on. The camera hummed. She aimed it at Frost's long face.

"It's odd," he said wistfully, "what giving away your fortune does. It's a marvelous thing. I don't know why it hasn't caught on." He looked at her seriously. "Let me ask you, you know anybody else giving away a billion dollars?"

"None of my friends," Rune said. "Unfortunately."

CHAPTER EIGHTEEN

Rune and Piper Sutton sat in front of her desk, watching the monitor. Out of it came two tinny voices.

"Mr. Frost, did you see the shooting?"

"Plain as the nose on my face. Or your face. However that expression goes. . . . It was horrible. I saw this man come up to Mr. Hopper and pull out this little gun and shoot him, just push the pistol at him. It reminded me of the pictures of Ruby. You know, when he shot Oswald. Mr. Hopper held his hands out, like he was trying to catch the bullet. . . ."

Sutton stirred, but didn't say anything.

"Could you describe him?"

"He was a fat man. Not fat all over, but with a beer belly. Like a timpani—"

"A what?"

"A drum. Dark blondish hair. A moustache. . . . What's that? Sure, I'm positive about the moustache. And sideburns. A light jacket. Powder-blue."

Rune said to Sutton, "That's Jimmy. The man who picked up Randy and drove him to New York."

Sutton frowned and waved her silent.

"Why didn't you go to the police?"

"I told you."

"If you could tell me again. Please."

"I was afraid. Of retaliation. Of publicity. I was very wealthy. I was . . . scared. Anyway, he was identified. That woman downstairs identified the man, and I read that the police caught him practically red-handed. Why would they need me . . . ?"

"I'm going to show you a picture of someone. Could you tell me if this is the man you saw in the courtyard?"

"Who? This skinny fellow? No, that wasn't him at all."

"You'd swear to it?"

"Sure I would."

Click.

Rune kept staring at the monitor, a proud schoolkid waiting for the teacher's praise.

But Sutton's only comment was: "You're a lousy interviewer." She looked at her watch, then added, "I'm late for a meeting with Lee. Did you make a dupe of that tape?"

"Sure," Rune said, putting as much hurt into her voice as she could. "I always make dupes. It's locked in my credenza."

Sutton said, "We've got a story conference on Friday. Bring your proposed script. You'll present to both of us, and be prepared to defend every goddamn line. Got it?"

"I—"

"Anything else?" Sutton snapped.

"No." Rune's hurt eyes were sweeping the desk.

Sutton looked at her for a minute and said, "We'll pat each other on the back after we air. Now get some sleep. You look awful."

This is the story of a man convicted of a crime he didn't commit unjustly. . . .

Uh, no.

. . . of a man unjustly convicted of a crime he didn't commit. . . .

Well, sure, if he didn't commit it, it's unjust.

. . . of a man convicted of a crime he didn't commit. . . .

Words were definitely the hard part.

Rune spun around in her desk chair and let go a soft,

anguished scream of frustration. Words, she hated words.
Rune *saw* things. She *liked* seeing things. She remem-
bered things she saw, and forgot things she was told.
Words were real tricky little dudes.

*This is the story of a man convicted of a crime he
didn't commit, a man who lost two years of his life because . . .*

Why? Why?

*. . . because the system of justice in this country is
like a big old dog, chasing . . .*

A dog? Justice is like a dog?

"Crap!" she shouted. "Crap, crap, crap!" Half the newsroom looked at her.

What is Lee Maisel going to say, he hears this stuff?
What's Piper going to say? I'm gonna be the dweeb queen
of the year. . . .

*. . . because the system of, no, because the justice sys-
tem in this country, no, because the American justice
system is like a bird with an injured wing. . . .*

Crap, crap, crap.

Fred Megler was as enthusiastic as could be expected,
considering that his lunch was three Sabrett hotdogs
(with kraut and limp onions) and a Diet Pepsi, and considering too that the view while he was eating was the
Criminal Courts Building—the darkest, grimiest court in
all of Manhattan.

And considering finally that one of his clients was
about to be sentenced on a three-count conviction for
murder two.

"Stupid shmuck. He fucking put himself away. What
can I say?"

Megler, skinny and gray, was chewing, drinking, and
talking simultaneously. Rune stood back, out of the tra-
jectory of flecks of hotdog that occasionally catapulted

from behind his thick, wet lips. He said, *"Huph,* yeah, sounds like Boggs might have a shot at it. Not enough to reverse the conviction, probably. But the judge might go for a new trial. I'm not saying yes, I'm not saying no. Who knows, depends on the mood when he wakes up, his wife's on the rag, whatever, he might say fuck it, that's not new evidence. . . ."

"But it *is* new evidence."

"Huph, there's new evidence, then there's new *evidence.* What you're telling me, this was evidence that could have been discovered at the time of the trial."

"I was sort of wondering about that. How come you didn't find Frost?"

"Hey, I was making minimum wage on that case. I don't have an expense account like you news people do. I don't sit around at five o'clock drinking manhattans in the Algonquin. . . ."

"What's a manhattan?"

"Huph. You know, rye and vermouth and bitters."

"Sounds romantic. Like Nick and Nora. Nineteen thirties New York. Neat."

"Romantic. Neat. *Huph.* Look, the Boggs trial, I did what I could. I had limited resources. That's his problem, he doesn't have any money."

The tail of the last hotdog disappeared. Rune had an image of a big fish eating a small fish.

"Doesn't sound like justice to me."

"Justice?" Megler asked. "You want to know what justice is?"

Rune sure did, and as she pressed the record button on the little JVC camcorder hidden in her leopard-skin bag, Megler—who could probably cite all kinds of laws on being taped surreptitiously—was polite enough to finish chewing, and look reflective for a few seconds before he spoke again. "Justice in this country is luck and fate and circumstance and expedience. And as long as that's true, people like Randy Boggs're going to serve time they shouldn't ought to."

"Will you handle the case?"

"We were talking about compensation?"

"Come on. He's innocent. Don't you want to help him out?"

"Not particularly. I don't give money to homeless people. Why should I be more generous with my time?"

"I don't believe you." Rune's voice went high. "You—"

"Would your network pay my bill?"

Something sounded wrong about it. She said, "I don't think that'd be ethical. . . ."

"What, ethical? I wouldn't get into hot water for that."

"I meant journalists' ethics."

"Oh, *your* ethics." He swilled the last of the Pepsi. He glanced down and noticed a spot on his navy-blue tie. He took a pen from his pocket and marked back and forth on it until it disappeared. He looked up at her. "Well, that's the net-net. *Huph.* I work, I get paid. That's carved in stone. But you got some options. There's Legal Aid. Or ACLU—those dips get orgasmic they get a case like this. One of those three-piece do-gooders from Yale or Columbia or Hahvahd might get wind of it, and pick up the case. . . . So you run your story, I'll guarantee you, some scrawny little NYU graduate'll be banging on your door begging to get Boggs's phone number."

"But that could take months. He's got to get out now. His life's in danger."

"Look, I've got to walk back into that hellhole in twenty minutes and stand next to a man who—it is alleged—machine-gunned three rival gang members while he told Polack jokes to one of his mistresses. I have to stand next to this man and listen to the judge explain to him that he's going to spend at least fifteen years in a ten-by-twenty cell. When he came to me, he said, 'Fred, I hear good things boutchu. You get me off. You do that? You get me off.' "

He laughed and slapped his chest. "Hey, I didn't get him off. He's not happy. . . . What I'm saying is, Boggs's in danger, I'm in danger. *Huph.* Think about it. You're in danger too. *You're* the one saying the cops, the prosecutor, and your own network're a bunch of dickheads. Life is dangerous. What can I say?"

Megler looked at his watch. "Time to do my bit to beautify America, get some more garbage off the street."

"Then you won't handle the case?"

Megler grinned. "Pay to the order of. . . ." He walked toward the steps.

"Hey, you want to know an interesting fact?" Rune called.

Megler looked over his shoulder. "Make it fast. You don't keep drug lords waiting."

She said, "You know how many people watch *Current Events*?"

"No, and I don't know the average rainfall in the Amazon. Do I care?"

"Depends on whether or not you want ten million people to see your name and face and hear what kind of work you do. And figure out what a great lawyer you must be to handle a case like this for free."

Fred Megler stopped.

Rune repeated, "Ten million."

Megler glanced at the courthouse door. He muttered something, and walked back down the steps.

Me, okay. I was born in Atlanta, and we lived there for ten years before our daddy decided he was going to the land of greater opportunity, which was what he said, and I can still remember him saying that. . . .

From inside a thirteen-inch Japanese television monitor, the color unbalanced and too heavy in red, Randy Boggs was telling his life story.

Greater opportunity. First off, I was scared, because I thought we were going to die because I got "greater opportunity" confused with "Promised Land," which I remembered from Day of the Ascension Baptist Church meant heaven. At the time I was close to eleven, and religious. Okay, I got myself into some pretty fair scrapes at school. Somebody, some older kid'd say, "Jesus Christ," and I'd get madder'n a damp cat and make him say he was sorry, and what happened was I got the hell beat out of me more times'n I can recall, or care to. . . .

Editing videotape was a hundred times easier than film. It was electronic, not mechanical, and Rune thought that this represented some incredible advancement in civilization—going from things that you could see how they worked to things that worked but you couldn't pull them apart and figure them out. Rune liked it because that was similar to magic, which she believed in, the only difference being that with magic you didn't need batteries. The ease of editing, though, didn't solve the problem that she had so much good tape. Thousands and thousands of feet. This footage was from the first time she'd interviewed Boggs, and she had no idea what to cut.

. . . Anyway, it wasn't heaven we ended up in but was Miami, and some opportunity that turned out to be. . . . Just like Daddy. This was right after Batista, and the place was lousy with Cubans. For years I didn't like, you know, Spanish people. But that was stupid 'cause a few years ago I went down to Central America—the only time I was ever out of the country—and I loved it. Anyway, I was talking about before, when I was a kid, and I saw these wealthy Cubans who were no longer wealthy, and that's the saddest kind of man there is. You can see

*that loss in his walk, and the way he looks at the car he's
driving now, which isn't nearly so nice as the kind he
used to have. But what happened was they begun sucking up the jobs us white folks oughta've been having. Not
that I mean it in a racial way. I mean American, when I
say white, but I mean it for Negroes too. American Negroes. But these Cubans worked for nothing. They had to
—the size of the families! I've never seen so many little
shitters in one family. I thought my daddy was bad. He'd
practically roll over on Momma and bang, she was carrying. Home, I had six sisters and two brothers, and I lost
a brother in Nam, and a sister to ovarian cancer. . . .*

*. . . Daddy had a head for mechanics and he never
applied himself. I'm just the opposite. You pay me and I'll
sweat for you. I like the feel of working. My muscles get
all nervous when I don't work. But I have problems with
calculating. My daddy was out of work many days running. My eldest brother signed up, Marines, and I was
coming up on sixteen so naturally I considered doing the
same, but started working instead. . . .*

The careers of Randy Boggs: carny hawker, then ride
operator, then sweeper at a Piggly Wiggly, then selling
hotdogs on the highway near Cape Kennedy where he
saw the Apollo moon launching and thought he might like
to be a pilot, then a stock boy, then fisherman, then
janitor, then cook.

Then thief.

*I was to Clearwater once, with Boonie, that was my
brother, what I called him, and a friend from the service.
And we went to this drive-in, and they were talking
about the money they were making and how Boonie was
going to buy himself a Bulltaco motorcycle, the kind with
the low handlebars, and here I was—oh, heavens—I was
nineteen, and my brother had to pay my way into the
theater? So that night they went to a, well, you know,*

whorehouse—which wasn't all that easy to find in Clear-
water, and they let me keep the car for a couple hours.
What I did, I was feeling so bad about the money, I drove
back to the drive-in, which was just closing up and I did
this distraction—I set fire to some brush near the screen,
and when everybody ran out to see what was going on, I
ran into the booth, and was going to grab the money, only
what happened was there was no money. It'd been
packed up and taken somewhere already, probably the
night deposit at the bank. I run out, right into one of the
owners. I'm a thin man now, and I was a thin boy then
and he saw what was happening and laid me right out.
. . . You know what they got me for? I have to laugh
now. They couldn't arrest me for stealing, and they
couldn't arrest me for burglary. They arrested me for ar-
son. For burning a plant that wasn't more'n a weed. You
believe that?

The format of the *Current Events* stories made Rune's
job tough. Piper Sutton insisted that she be on camera in
each segment. Most of the story would be the interviews
Rune was now editing. But every three minutes or so
would be a cut back to Piper Sutton who would continue
with the story, reading off a teleprompter. Then, back to
more tapes—the crime scene, atmosphere footage, interviews. Coordinating everything—the voice-over and the
dialogue on the tape segments, and Piper Sutton's script
—was overwhelming.

("And," Lee had warned her. "While you're juggling,
don't ever forget about the most important Indian Club of
all." Which was Sutton's ego. "Give her full two minute
segments in front of the camera, and bear in mind, if you
put a mixed metaphor or string of sibilants into her
mouth, not even God can help you.")

But so what if it was tough? Rune was ecstatic. Here
she was—three in the morning, Ophelia (and a stuffed

bear) dozing in a sleeping bag near her feet—editing tape
into what was going to be a sensational news story on
the number-one-rated prime-time news magazine on network television. Best of all, the story would get seen by
ten million people, who unless they made a snack or john
run immediately after the FADE OUT would also see her
name.

And, she considered for a moment, maybe there was a
better best of all: She'd be responsible for getting an innocent man released from prison—a man whose muscles
got nervous when he couldn't move. Prometheus, about to
be unbound. . . .

. . . *Most of the money I gave to Momma. She did
something not too nice. I didn't catch on to it till I was
older, but she'd manage to take the money only in front
of Daddy. To point up him not keeping a job. Poor man.
. . . Poor man. He never raised a hand to her, and the
complaints he made about her he never dared aim close
to the mark, though I'm thinking he could have. And
probably should have. But the taking the money thing,
that was harsh. Oh, she was shrill and mean. . . .*

Randy Boggs spoke in quiet static, the monitor
hummed, the tape player gave off satisfying snaps and
clicks as Rune punched the buttons to edit the choicest
segments. She paused for a moment and found that despite the exhaustion and the pressure of a looming deadline and the aching that had split into pieces and bled
into her back and eyes and temple, she could stay up all
night doing what she was doing. She felt like she'd never
need to sleep again.

CHAPTER NINETEEN

The conference room.

The legendary conference room.

Here was where the Network News execs planned the special coverage for Martin Luther King's assassination, and Bobby Kennedy's, and Nixon's resignation, and the taking of the hostages in Iran, and the *Challenger* explosion. It didn't look very impressive—yellow-painted walls, a chipped and stained oval table, and ten swivel chairs whose upholstery had faded to baby-blue from the parent company cerulean. But the shabbiness didn't detract from the fact that this was the room where the chronicle of history—and sometimes even that history itself—had been made.

Rune paused outside the teak door, looking inside. Lee Maisel and Piper Sutton sat at the table. Behind them was a map of the world with red stickers showing where the Network had permanent bureaus. No more than a couple inches of space separated any of the red dots, except in the oceans and at the North and South Poles.

This was a room Rune never thought she'd be in. When she'd applied at the Network for a job as assistant cameraman, they'd told her there was no chance to move into news. All she could hope for was an engineer or technician in the production department, since she didn't have an M.A. in journalism (she'd been somewhat vague about her bachelor's degree, which she'd pretty much had to be because she only had eight hours of credits toward a bachelor's, and they were from one lit course in fairy tales and two in mythology). Techie was the best Human Resources told her she could hope for.

And now here she was, a line producer working for Lee Maisel, and holding in her nervous hands a draft script, one she'd actually written for Piper Sutton.

Ohmygod . . . Piper Sutton! Rune fought down the assault of anxiety.

She shifted the huge stacks of notes and tapes from one arm to the other. Her heart was beating wildly, and her palms left sweaty stains on the black cassettes she held. Sutton noticed her, and nodded her in. "Come on," she said abruptly. "What're you waiting for?"

Maisel gave her a fast distracted glance.

"Let's get on with it," Sutton said. She was speaking to her Rolex. But since the watch seemed to be working fine, Rune figured she was the one Sutton was barking at. "Let's see the script. Come on."

Rune distributed them, and they both read in silence, except for the tapping of Piper Sutton's gold Cross pen, impatient, on the table. Stone-faced, they skimmed the fifteen pages. First Sutton, then Maisel, slid the sheets into the center of the table.

"All right," Sutton said. "Why is it so important that you do this story?"

Right out of left field. Rune swallowed. Maisel didn't offer anything. He too sat like an Inquisitor. She thought for a moment, and began to speak. She *knew* better than she could *say* (words, goddamn words again). As she talked, a lot of *uhm*'s and *what I mean is*'s slipped in. She corrected herself, she said the same things twice. She sounded defensive. She tried to look into Sutton's eyes as she spoke, but that just turned her mind to jam. Words came out, some nonsense about justice and journalism's responsibility.

And all the while she never once responded to Sutton's

question with an honest answer. She never once said, *Why am I dying to do this story? Because I want to be* you. *I want to be tall and have crisp blonde hair that stays where I put it, and walk on high heels and not look like a klutz. I want presidents of networks and corporations to look at me with envy and lust. I want a mind that's as cool and sharp as a black-belt's body. I want your kind of power, not mine. Not like magic in fairy stories, but the power to cast the strongest kind of spells —the ones that make it seem like you know exactly what to do every minute, exactly what to say. . . .*

But she talked about the press, about innocence, about Boggs. Rune finished and sat back. Sutton must have been satisfied with the response. She said, not too abruptly, "All right, let me ask you a few specific questions."

These were even worse, though, because they were about things Rune should have thought of herself. *Did you interview the original crime scene team? . . . Did you talk to any of Boggs's earlier lawyers?* (Rune didn't know he'd had any.) *Did he ever see a shrink about his criminal tendencies?* (Shit, why didn't I think of that?)

The three of them debated for ten minutes and in the end both Maisel and Sutton seemed satisfied. They felt the program should go forward, as long as the show didn't claim Boggs was innocent, only that there were some serious questions about his guilt.

That left only the question of when the story should air.

They asked her opinion.

Rune cleared her throat, shuffled papers, then said, "Like next week's show."

Maisel snorted, "Be serious."

And the battle began.

"The thing is," Rune said, "he's got to get out of prison

as soon as possible. They don't like him in there. They've already tried to kill him. I told you that."

Sutton said, " 'They'? Who's 'they'?"

"Other prisoners."

Maisel asked, "Why?"

"I don't know. A guard told me he isn't popular. He's a loner. He—"

"Today's Friday," Maisel barked. "Rune, to air next Tuesday, the whole program should have been shot and edited by now. It has to be in the computer by Monday. That just can't be done."

"I don't think he'll last another week. They tried to kill him once, and they could try again."

Sutton and Maisel looked at each other. Sutton looked back to her and said, "Our job is to report the news, not save anybody's ass. Boggs gets killed, the story's still valid. We could—"

"That's a horrible thing to say!"

"Oh, come off it," Sutton said.

Maisel said, "Piper's right, Rune. The story is the important thing. And I don't see how we can do it. There just isn't time."

"The script's all written," she said. "And I've spent the last three nights editing. I've got everything timed to the second. . . ."

"The second," Sutton said in a tired sigh.

Maisel said, "Piper'd have to tape on Sunday night or Monday morning."

In a soft, spiny voice, Rune said, "I want the story to air next week." She folded her hands and put them in her lap.

They both looked at her.

Rune continued. "What's going to happen if somebody finds out that we could have saved his life and we just didn't get around to doing the story in time?"

Silence, as Sutton and Maisel exchanged glances.

Maisel broke the tension asking the anchorwoman, "What do you think?"

Rune felt her teeth squeeze together with tension. Sutton responded by asking, "What else was scheduled for that show?"

"The Arabs in Queens," Maisel said. "It's half edited."

"I never liked it," Rune said.

Sutton shrugged. "It's soft news. I hate soft news." She was frowning, apparently because she found herself agreeing with Rune.

"My story isn't," Rune said. "It's hard news."

Sutton said, "I suppose you'll want a credit."

For ten million people to see.

The anchorwoman continued, "But that name of yours . . . You'll have to—"

"Not to worry," Rune said. "I have a professional name."

"A professional name?" Maisel was fighting to keep down the smile.

"Irene Dodd Simons."

"Is that your real name?" the anchorwoman asked.

"It's sort of real."

Sutton said, "Sort of." And shook her head, then she added, "At least it sounds like the name of somebody who knows what she's doing. . . ." She pulled her personal calendar out of her purse; the scents of perfume and suede followed it. "Okay, honey, first we'll get together and do a script—"

Rune blinked. "But it's all finished."

Sutton laughed. "No, dear, I mean a *real* script. We'll meet at six-thirty tomorrow morning in the *C.E.* newsroom."

Rune's first thought was: Shit, a baby-sitter. Where'm I

going to get a sitter? She smiled and said, "Six, if you want."

"Six-thirty'll be fine."

You don't have a right to talk on the phone, but they usually let you. *A privilege, not a right.* (One day, Boggs'd heard some prisoner yelling, "Gimme the phone! We got rights, you asshole. We got rights." A guard had answered, pretty politely under the circumstances, "You got what we give you, asshole.")

But maybe because Boggs had been knifed, or maybe because he wasn't a punk, or just maybe because it was a nice warm day, the guard in charge of the mail and telephone room sent somebody to find him so he could take the call.

"Randy, how you feeling?" Rune asked.

"That you, miss?"

"You out of the infirmary?"

"Kicked my butt out yesterday. I feel good as a cow after milking. No pain to speak of, unless I stretch. I read that story. In the book you give me. I like it. Don't think I look much like him, and if I ever stole fire from the gods, I sure don't know a fence'd handle it. . . ." He paused, and she laughed, like she knew she was supposed to, thinking he'd probably spent a good amount of time thinking up the joke.

"Guess what?" she asked.

"Don't know."

"I found a new witness."

"New witness?"

"Sure did."

"Well, my, tell me about it."

She did, from start to finish, all about Bennett Frost, and Randy Boggs didn't utter a single word the entire time she was speaking. In fact, not a single syllable or grunt or even, it seemed, a breath.

When she was through, there was silence for a long moment.

"Well," she said, "you're not saying anything."

"I'm grinning, though, I'll tell you that. Damn, I can't believe it. You done yourself something, miss."

"What's going to happen now is I'm going to try to get the program on the air next week. Megler said that if he gets his name and picture on the air he'll do the motion for you for free. . . ."

"Mr. Megler said that?"

"It hurt him. I could see the pain, but he said he would. He said if the judge buys it, and grants the motion for a new trial, you could be out in two weeks."

"The judge might not grant it, though, I suppose."

"Fred said that having the program on *Current Events* would really help. The judge'd be like more inclined to release you, especially if he was up for reelection."

"Well, damn. Goddamn. Am I going to be . . . out?"

"Fred didn't say exactly what was going to happen. I don't think he was sure himself. He said we'd have to wait till the program ran, then he'd get the papers together."

"What do I do now?"

"You just take care of yourself for the next couple weeks. Don't go getting knifed any more."

"No, ma'am. . . . Uh, one thing. . . . What you did. . . ."

Silence.

"I guess I'm trying to say thank you."

"I guess you just did."

*   *   *

After they hung up, Randy Boggs, the grin still on his face, left the administration building to go find Severn Washington and tell him the news.

He was walking slowly. What he'd told Rune wasn't quite true. His side hurt like a son of a bitch, the stitches as much as anything, and every time he set his right foot down, pain shot through his bones up to his jaw. He didn't notice it so much now. As Boggs left the building, another prisoner, a short Colombian, followed, then overtook him. Prisoners like this were what used to be called trustees in the prisons of the forties and fifties and were now generally known as pricks or assholes or scum. He'd just had a short conversation with the guard he worked for, the guard who randomly monitored prisoner's phone conversations. The prisoner smiled at Boggs, said, *Buenos dias,* and walked ahead, not hearing what Boggs said in reply. He didn't particularly care what the response was. He was in a hurry. He wanted to get to Juan Ascipio as soon as he could.

CHAPTER TWENTY

Rune decided she'd found a great new drug, one that was completely legal and cheap. It was called *awake*, and you didn't even take it. All you did was not sleep for thirty hours straight, and it sent you right on the most crucial trips you could imagine. Tim Leary, get outa here; this stuff is totally fresh.

Gremlins climbed out of the Sony, dragons swooped down from Redhead lights, and trolls had abandoned bridges and were fox-trotting on the misty dance floor of her desk. And all kinds of psychedelic amoeba were squooshing through the studio.

Truly existential.

It was six P.M. on Tuesday, and the reason for the hallucinations was a small plastic cassette containing a one-inch videotape master of a news story called "Easy Justice." The voice-overs were mixed, the leads and countdown added, the "live" portions of Piper Sutton's commentary (and primping) had been added. The tape, which ran the exact time allocated for the segment, rested somewhere in the bowels of the Network's computer system, which acted like a brilliant, never-sleeping stage manager, and would start the segment rolling exactly on time, at 8:04:36 P.M. The system would then automatically broadcast the Randy Boggs story for its precise length of eleven minutes, fourteen seconds, which was the Network's version of a quarter hour—a bit shorter than in Edward R. Murrow's time, but back then each additional minute of advertising didn't mean another half-million dollars in revenue the way it did today. Following which, the IBM would treat the viewers to a stream of noisy commercials.

Rune squinted away a few squooshy apparitions and sat back in her chair.

The last two days had been a nightmare.

Piper Sutton had been satisfaction-proof. "What's this? What do you call this?" she'd shouted, pacing back and forth behind Rune, who sat terrified, willing her hands not to shake as she typed. "Is this supposed to be poetry? Is it supposed to be art?"

Sutton would walk another ten feet, leaving behind a wake of cigarette smoke and Chanel.

Nothing she'd write could please Sutton. "Is that a *fact?* Is it supported? Who's your attribution? . . . What the fuck is this? A figure of speech? You think that's a figure of speech. 'Justice is like a lumbering bear'? Sure, I know a lot of lumbering bears. Our audience is really going to relate to lumbering bears. Just look out on Broadway, Rune, you see many bears? Come on, get with it. . . ."

Rune would write some more, then Sutton would lean over and look at the screen, focusing on the words like a sniper.

"Here, let me . . . ," Sutton would say.

Tap, tap, tap . . . The delete code would chop another dozen sentences. Sutton's nails never chipped. They were like red Kevlar.

Then, at last, it was over.

The final script, completed Monday night (no, make that Tuesday morning at five-thirty) was the twenty-eighth draft. As Sutton was leaving, Rune asked her, "You like always spend this kind of time with producers?"

"No, I don't *like* spend this kind of time. Most producers can spell."

"Oh."

But it got done. Rune had caught an hour's sleep, phoned the now-much-wealthier baby-sitter and asked her to take Ophelia to the day-care center. Then, at eleven, Piper Sutton, wearing a crimson suit and looking as if she'd just had a thirteen-hour beauty sleep, sat for the taping of her sequences—the ones that to the audience appear live. She did everything in one take, and left for lunch at Lutece. At noon, everything had been dumped in Rune's lap for final mixing, then delivery to the computer.

Now, though, it was finished, and she had nothing to do but try to stay awake and watch the show, while she fought the sensation that she was levitating. There were a couple options. Her first choice: She wanted to be home watching it with Sam. But he'd gone to investigate a package sitting in front of an abortion clinic in Brooklyn. Another possibility: There was a bar not far from the houseboat, where Rune was a regular, and everybody there would be glad to watch her program (this being Tuesday, and no games scheduled).

But that involved standing up and walking somewhere. Which at the moment was an effort Rune believed she was incapable of.

So, she sat. There was a nice color monitor in front of her, and maybe—just maybe—Piper and Lee would come and join her, and they'd all watch the show together and tell her what a good job she'd done, then take her out for a drink at some fancy bar afterwards. *(You owe me a pat on the back, Piper. . . .)*

Then her thoughts shifted and she found she was thinking of Randy Boggs. She had a clear image of him, and she hoped they were letting him watch *Current Events.* That thought sounded funny—*letting* him watch—like when she was a kid and she'd begged her parents to let her stay up to read more fairy stories or watch TV.

The room got fuzzy, then it got black.

"Hey, Rune."

She opened her eyes and found her head resting on the word processor keyboard. The monitor screen was completely filled with the letter *g*. She rubbed her cheek and glanced at the clock. It was seven-ten. Well, she'd gotten an hour's sleep. Not bad. She wondered how many *g*'s she'd programmed into the computer. There could be billions of them. She started to backspace.

The man's voice repeated, "Rune. . . ."

She looked up, thinking the hallucinations were getting stranger: Some heavyset guy was disattaching himself from a camera and coming toward her. How did he do that? Like the monster in *Alien*. Rune squinted. He should be disappearing now, or at least turning into a troll. But no, he kept walking toward her. Rune sat and stared, dazed as a Bowery drunk.

"Rune." It knew her name. She squinted. Morrie Weinberg, the chief engineer of the show. He did tend toward being troll-like: pear-shaped and with thick, bushy hair that always slanted sideways. He wore engineer clothes —blue jeans and a black shirt and a tweed jacket.

"Morrie," she said. He was frowning—the first time she'd ever seen him try it. Engineers are usually Rolaids-poppers, but Morrie didn't understand the concept of stress. She had an image of him as a lumbering bear, and she wanted to giggle.

"What's up?"

"Your segment."

She giggled. "Uh-huh."

"What happened?" His voice fluttered.

The humor was leaving quickly. "Happened?"

"How come you didn't get your segment in? It should've gone into the computer by three. It was already a day late. We had to have it there by three. You know that."

Her eyes swept around the studio. Was he saying what she was hearing? That was always an issue with exhaustion. "No, I did. I gave it to Charles. It must have been around four. It was late because . . ."

Morrie looked at a clipboard. "It ain't in there now. We got eleven minutes of blank air time starting at eight-oh-four-thirty-six."

"Check again." Her voice was edged with panic.

"I just did check. Five minutes ago."

"Check again, check again!" No giggling, no lumbering bears or amoeba. Adrenaline had wakened her completely.

Morrie shrugged and made a call. He held his hand over the mouthpiece, and said to her, "Zip."

"How did it happen?"

"The way it usually happens is the producer doesn't get the tape in on time."

"But I *got* it in." She ran through her vague memory. She didn't think she'd screwed up. It was too major a mistake even for her. It was like the pilot forgetting to lower the airplane's wheels before landing.

Anyway, there were other tapes. She had a dupe of the final cut.

An inconvenience was all, not a tragedy.

Her hands were shaking. Morrie listened into the phone again. He looked up and said to her, "All right, your butt is safe so far. Charlie says he remembers you delivering it. Somehow, it's vanished. He's looking, but do you have a dupe?"

"Sure."

He said into the phone, "We'll get another one up to you in five minutes." He hung up. "This's never happened before. Thank you, my sweet Lord, for dupes."

The prayer was premature. The dupe was missing too.
Rune's voice was shrill in panic. "I put it there. On my
desk." She pointed frantically to an empty corner.
"Oh-oh."
"I put it right there." He stared skeptically at the bald
spot. She said, "I'm not making this up."
"Rough cuts?" Morrie was looking at his watch. "Shit,
we don't have time. But we maybe—"
She opened a drawer. The look on her face told him
that mastering a rough cut wasn't going to be an issue.
No longer a convenience matter; tragedy had arrived.
He said, "They're gone too?"
Rune was nodding. She couldn't speak.
"Oh, boy. Oh, shit. Eleven minutes of blank air. This's
never happened before. This's never happened."
Then, she thought of something else, and ripped open
her credenza.
The original tape she'd done of Bennett Frost, the new
witness, and the dupe of that, were also gone. All that
remained of the story about Randy Boggs were scripts
and notes and background interview tapes.
"We've been robbed," Rune whispered. She looked
around in panic, feeling a terrible sense of violation.
"Who was it?" She looked at Morrie. "Who'd you see on
the set today?"
"Who'd I see?" he echoed shrilly. "A dozen reporters, a
hundred staffers. Piper was here, Jim Eustice, Dan Semple . . . I mean, half the Network walked through here
today."
Morrie looked at the phone, and she knew what he was
thinking: Somebody had to call Piper Sutton. The large
quartz wall clock—timed, for all Rune knew, to the vibrations of the universe—showed that they had forty-four
minutes until *Current Events* was going to air. Forty-four
minutes until it became the first prime-time television

program in history to air eleven minutes and fourteen seconds of blank space.

The only thing that kept Sutton from exploding through the double doors into the newsroom was the live broadcast of *Nighttime News With Jim Eustice,* the Network's flagship world news show. But she was suddenly there, storming up to Rune's desk. During the broadcast the veteran anchorman was so damn reassuring and smooth that even the crew enjoyed watching him. Tonight, though, only the head engineer and the producer kept their eyes on his craggy, square face. Everyone else in the huge studio followed Sutton and Maisel, as they hurried toward the *Current Events* desks like surgeons answering a code blue.

"What the fuck happened?" Sutton asked in a shrill whisper.

"I don't know." Rune felt the tears start. She dug her short nails into her palms furiously, and with the pain, the urge to cry lessened.

Maisel looked at the clock above the control booth. "We've got nothing? Nothing at all?"

"I don't know what happened. I turned the tape in—"

Morrie said delicately, "She did. Charles got it. He programmed it in. Some time after four it disappeared."

"Son of a bitch. How long was that segment?"

Morrie consulted his clipboard, but Rune answered from memory. "Eleven minutes, fourteen."

Sutton whispered furiously, "You should always make backups, you should—"

"I did. They were stolen too. Everything. Even the original tapes. . . ."

"Fuck," Sutton spat out. Then she turned to Maisel, whose mind must have been in the same place and known what she was thinking. He said, "None of the other stories are even half finished, Piper. We'll have to cancel the show."

"Can we go with Arabs in Queens?" she asked.

He said, "We never finished editing. We stopped all post-pro for the Boggs story."

"What about the former mayor profile?"

"Mostly unshot, and a lot of unattributed quotes. It's hot stuff. Legal's still got to go through it."

Sutton was leaning forward, her hands on Rune's desk, staring at the empty spot. Rune wondered if she knew that the Boggs dupe had occupied that space on the Formica. "The Guardian Angels piece?"

"We've got footage, but there's no script."

"It's outlined?"

"Well, in general. But—"

She waved her hand. "We'll do that."

Maisel's voice rasped, "Piper, we'll have to cancel. We can slot a rerun." He turned to Morrie. But she said, "Lee, a rerun of a news show? We'll go with the Angels."

"I don't understand what you're saying, Piper. We don't have a script. We don't have footage of you. We—"

"We'll go live," she said.

"Live?"

"Yep."

Maisel looked at Morrie. "It's too late, isn't it?"

He answered calmly. "We can't do half and half. We can shut off the computer and queue everything by hand, using a stopwatch. But that means commercials too, and you know how many fifteen-second buys there are during *Current Events*?"

"I didn't say it was going to be easy," Sutton snapped. "Okay, let's do it."

No one moved. Morrie looked at Maisel.

Sutton's voice screeched, "I said, let's do it. Get me the Guardian Angels tapes. *Now!*"

Maisel nodded just in time to save Morrie's job. The engineer hurried off.

"Piper—" Rune began.

Sutton ignored her and turned to Maisel. "Who's the producer of the piece?"

Maisel told her. A young woman with PBS experience. Sutton said to an assistant, "Page her. I want her here in ten minutes, you've gotta get a police escort."

She and Maisel cleared a place at the *Current Events* central desk.

Rune, uninvited, stayed in her cubicle. She sat in her office chair. She drew her legs up and huddled, rocking back, thinking of all the work she'd have to do over again. She felt like somebody had died. Numb, stunned.

Uh-uh, she thought. Like someone was *about* to die.

Randy Boggs.

At eight o'clock that evening *Current Events* was broadcast live for the first time ever.

Maisel oversaw the control booth, three times its normal staff (most of whom were from the Jim Eustice crew and had experience with the delicacies of live production). Maisel hadn't done live producing for years, and he stood like a captain of a torpedoed ship, holding an inexpensive digital stopwatch in his sweaty hand, gripping it tightly, prepared to walk Sutton through the program.

With the producer, Maisel and Sutton had managed to write half the Guardian Angels piece and get it, handwritten, into the teleprompter, but at 7:58, they had to break off. So Sutton said, "I'll ad-lib."

Maisel voted again to cancel the whole program. "We'll just run a technical problems announcement."

"Yeah? And fuck up a couple million in ad revenues? Can't do it, Lee."

"Technical difficulties. It's no stigma."

"Not on my show."

Maisel could have reminded her that it wasn't exactly *her* show, and that he, as executive producer, could decide to pull the program that night or any other. It would take only a fast call up to the parent company for pro forma approval.

But this was Piper Sutton, so Lee Maisel, whose million-dollar-a-year job depended exclusively on the quality of these next sixty minutes, nodded and said, "You got a ten-second countdown, and a five second cheat. . . . Break a leg."

She gave him a fast smile, and sat down in the black leather chair, clipping the lavaliere mike into her collar and inserting the small earphone into her left ear, the one hidden under the flop of hair (where it was less visible and no one would absently think she was wearing a hearing aid). Makeup did a fast dusting.

She took a deep breath.

In the control booth, Maisel was speaking into the dot of the microphone in front of his lips, "Seven, six, five, four, three, two, one. . . . Graphics up, now. . . . Theme running. . . ."

Exactly four seconds later, he said, "Graphics dissolve, camera one fade in. . . . Theme down. . . . Okay, honey, this is it, you're . . . on!"

Snap. Sutton's eyes locked directly into twenty million others around the country. "Good evening. Welcome to *Current Events* for Tuesday, April twentieth. I'm Piper Sutton. . . ."

Exactly fifty-six minutes later, the computer-generated credits rolling at a breakneck pace, viewers stood or stretched, arguing about some of the stories, or critiquing Piper Sutton's fashion selection of the week, or wondering which sitcom to turn to next, all unaware that they'd just seen TV history.

Morrie oversaw the passing of the scepter back to the computer, and the fifty-million-dollar system began sending the spurious art of television advertising into American households.

As soon as the studio mikes were shut off, the newsroom applauded. Sutton was too diplomatic to ignore it, and she gave a brief smile and fast wave to the crew, then bowed theatrically.

Maisel left the booth and walked straight up to her, hugging her and kissing her on the cheek.

Somehow, both Dan Semple and Jim Eustice had heard about the broadcast and had been watching from the control room. They now joined her. Eustice shook her hand formally and complimented her, then left with Maisel. Semple kissed Sutton quickly, and the two of them walked into the corridor. None of them glanced at Rune, who sat in her desk chair and stared at the monitor where her program would have run.

The next morning, Ophelia woke her up by climbing into bed.

"Can we go to the zoo?"

Rune had collected the girl just after the program was over the night before. They'd gone home, had tuna sandwiches for dinner, and Raisin Bran for dessert. They both went to bed at ten.

Rune rolled over and sat up. "The what?"

"The zoo."

"First, coffee, then we'll think about the zoo."

"I want some juice."

Rune was feeling better now that she'd gotten some sleep. True, the tapes had been stolen, but there were advantages to what'd happened. For one thing, it was clear proof that somebody else had killed Hopper. Randy obviously hadn't stolen the tapes; the real killer must have. Also, there was now another dimension to the story. Somebody breaking into a major television network studio and stealing a news program—that was a story in itself.

Anyway, the damage wasn't that bad. All that was missing was the master tape and the tape of Frost. Everything else remained. The background tapes, her notes. The program could be remixed from that material, although she would have to retape Bennett Frost.

What worried her the most was that Randy was still in danger. But then she decided that maybe the story didn't have to run to get his release started. True, the impact wouldn't be so neat—her story actually getting him released. But what had been her goal anyway? To get him out.

She thought about it. Did her story have to run first?

No. She could do the story after he was released. That might be a nice touch. She'd add footage of him wandering around New York, a free man. Super.

In the galley, Rune poured cranberry juice for Ophelia and made her some instant oatmeal.

"I want to go to the zoo."

"Okay, honey, we'll try. But there's something I have to do first. We're going to go visit somebody. A man."

"Who is he? Is he a nice man?"

"Not really," Rune said, and looked up Fred Megler's address in her book.

"Huph," Megler said, "I thought there was that show running last night. What happened? I missed poker to stay home. I really hate to miss poker." He lifted up a series of soda cans, looking for one that was full.

"It got stolen."

"Stolen? Somebody stole a TV show?"

"The tape, they lifted it."

"No shit?" He glanced at Ophelia and winced.

"Shit," the little girl said.

Rune said, "I'm going to do the story over again. But I was thinking maybe you could start the—the what do you call it? To get Randy out?"

"The motion papers."

"I thought you could get Mr. Frost to go into court, or—"

Megler's face was blank for a moment. *"Huph,* you didn't hear?"

"Hear what?"

"The accident?" His voice, thin as his body, rose, sounding as if everybody in the city were supposed to know.

Oh, no. She closed her eyes. "What happened?"

"Frost slipped in the bathtub. He drowned."

"What? Oh, God. . . . When did it happen?"

"A couple days ago." Megler found a nearly full can of Diet Pepsi. His face brightened at the discovery. "Sure is a good thing you made that tape of him. Otherwise we'd be up . . ." He glanced at Ophelia. ". . . you know which creek without a paddle."

CHAPTER TWENTY-ONE

Allah tells us: *Those who do good, will find the best reward in heaven, and more. Neither dust nor ignominy touch their faces. Such are the rightful owners of the Garden, and they will abide therein.*

Late Thursday morning, Severn Washington was waiting for Randy Boggs to come out of the library. He sat on a concrete step and read the Koran. He frequently did this. Like praying five times a day and ritual washing and forsaking liquor and pork, reading the holy book gave him great personal satisfaction. He kept it with him at all times.

The typeface of the copy he owned was dense. Under the repeated touch of his huge, nubby fingers, the delicate onionskin paper of the small volume had become even more translucent than when it was new. He liked that. He had an image of Allah reaching down and making the book more and more invisible every time Washington read it. Eventually it would become transparent, would become just a spirit, vanished and gone to heaven.

And then Washington would follow, and his sins—all of them (the liquor store in particular)—would be forgiven; his new life would begin.

Washington didn't want to go too fast, however. There were certain aspects of his present life that he'd come to enjoy. Even here, in Attica. At first he'd thought that was strange, but then he realized that prison life wasn't much different from that in his prior residence. Instead of a brick project, he had a stone cell-block to live in (a building that wasn't graffiti'd and didn't smell of shit). Instead of his common-law wife's bland macaroni and chicken and potatoes, he had the Department of Correction's bland macaroni and hamburger and potatoes. Instead of hanging out on the street and doing occasional construction work, he hung out in the yard and worked in the machine shop. Instead of getting dissed and illed by dealers and gangs, who had MAC-10s, he got dissed and illed by the Aryan Brotherhood, who had clubs and shivs.

On the whole, it was *better* inside. Maybe you didn't get paychecks, but you didn't *need* paychecks like you did doing straight time.

He had friends, like Randy Boggs.

He had his Koran.

No, couldn't complain ayetall. He glanced down at the book.

. . . *If Allah afflict thee with some hurt, there is none who can remove it save Him, if He desireth good for thee, there is none who can repel His bounty. He—*

The sentiment in that passage was the last thought Severn Washington ever had.

And the last sound he ever heard was the hiss of the steel barbell pole that swung into the back of his head. He didn't hear the sound of contact, as the metal met bone, and one gave way. He didn't even live long enough to hear the delicate flutter of his Koran as it pitched from his convulsing fingers and lay open on dirt, the book which it turned out wasn't going to precede Washington into heaven after all.

The conversation was hushed.

"Whatever you thinking, man, fuck it," said Juan Ascipio. "We had to do the nigger. I tole you . . ." He was talking rapidly to one of his Hispanic brothers in an area beside the library. They'd just dragged Washington's body here. ". . . we move on Boggs, put the bar in his hand and knife in the nigger's. Looks like the nigger wanted to fuck Boggs and Boggs moved on him, and then the nigger did Boggs."

"I know, man," the second man said. "Hey, I'm not saying nothing."

"You just don't look happy, man, but it had to be that way."

"Yeah. It's just, man, they know it's us. They gotta know it, man."

"Fuck," Ascipio spat out. "What they know ain't what they can prove."

"After the first time, man. You know."

"Motherfucker didn't talk then. He coulda said who it was did him. He didn't say nothing."

"Yeah."

"Pussy, man. He's a pussy." Ascipio laughed.

A third man loped back to them. "He in there by hisself."

Ascipio laughed again.

Randy Boggs liked the library. That was one of those things you don't think anything of until you actually do it. Reading, he meant. When he was Outside, there were some things he'd do for the peace of it. Like sitting with a quart of beer for the evening, listening to cicada and owls and the surf of leaves and the click of branches. That was something he could do practically forever. Which seemed like doing nothing, but was actually the most important way a man could spend time. Like the saying his daddy told him, St. Peter don't count the hours you spend fishing.

That was how he now looked at reading.

Most of the books here were pretty bad. Somebody, a school someplace, he guessed, had donated a lot of textbooks. Sociology and psychology and statistics and economics. Boring as dry toast. If that was what people learned in college, no wonder nobody seemed to have any smarts.

And some of the novels were a bit much. The older ones—and the library here seemed to have mostly nineteen twenties and thirties books—were pretty dense. Man, he couldn't make heads or tails out of them. Word after word. He had to slug his way through, just like the way he'd clean a floor, scrape, then sweep, then mop, then rinse. Slow. Inch by inch. Then he found some newer ones. *Catch 22*, which he thought was a real pisser. He grinned for five minutes straight after finishing that one. Then somebody mentioned Kurt Vonnegut, and although there were none in the prison library, a guard he'd become friendly with gave him a copy of *Cat's Cradle* and a couple other Vonneguts, as well. Whenever he saw the guard, he'd wink and say, "So it goes." Boggs loved Paul Theroux's travel writing and tried John Cheever. He didn't like the short stories, but the novel about prison really struck home. Sure, it was about prison, but it was about something bigger than prison. He wasn't sure what, but that seemed to be the sign of a good book. To be about something, then about something more too, even if you didn't know exactly what.

The book that girl reporter had given him wasn't so good. The writing was old-fashioned, and he had to read some sentences three, four times in order to figure out what was going on. But he kept at it, and would pull it out occasionally and read some more. He wanted to finish it, but the reason was for her, so he could talk about it with her.

That got him thinking about the girl again, and he wondered why her program hadn't run on Tuesday. Rune hadn't called to say anything about it. But then he wasn't sure what day she'd said. Maybe she'd meant a week from Tuesday. She'd probably said *next* Tuesday, instead of *this* Tuesday; Boggs always got confused with *next* and *this*.

Damn, she was something else. Here, he'd spent months and months trying to figure out how to get out of prison, thinking of escaping, thinking of getting sick, thinking of appealing, and then here she comes and does it for him, and it doesn't cost him anything in grief or money.

He—

And that was when he felt the first hum of fear.

The prison itself was old, but the library was a newer addition, away from the cell-blocks. It looked and smelled like a suburban school. There was only one door in and out. (That was one thing about prisons. Fire codes weren't the same as on the Outside.)

Boggs heard slow footsteps of several men coming up the corridor toward that one door.

He noticed for the first time that he was alone. No other prisoners, no guards. No clerk behind the desk. He'd been reading away, and hadn't noticed everybody else leaving.

He knew Severn Washington was outside, and he knew too that the big black man was as loyal as a friend could be in prison.

But that was a big qualifier. *In prison.*

Inside, anybody can be bought.

And, it comes right down to it, anybody can be killed.

Boggs still had no idea why Ascipio wanted to move on him. The man had plenty of maytags around him to keep him in blowjobs for months. But it was clear he was marked. No doubt in his mind. And right now, hearing footsteps come closer to the door, he knew—not a premonition or anything like, he *knew*—something was going down.

He stood up instinctively. The possibilities for weapons were: a book or a chair.

He laughed.

Hardly mattered. From the sounds of the footsteps there were three of them, or four. And they'd have glass knives. And clubs.

Oh, he didn't want the knife again. That terrible feeling as flesh separated. Terrible . . .

He looked at the chair. He couldn't pull it apart. And when he tried to lift it, a searing pain from the first knifing swept through his back and side.

He tried again and managed to get the chair off the ground, holding it in both hands.

Then part of his mind said, Why bother?

They'd burst in, they'd circle around him. They'd take him. What could he do? Swing a chair at them? Knock one of them off balance while the others easily stepped behind him and swung for his neck and kidneys with baseball bats?

Randall Boggs, failed son of a failed father, simply sat down in the chair, sat at a fiberboard table in a shoddy prison library, thinking for some reason, suddenly and obsessively, about Atlanta and the Sunday dinner menu of his childhood.

From his pocket he took out the book the reporter girl had given him and put his hands on it as if it were a Bible, then he thought that was funny because probably to the old-time people, the old Greeks or Romans, or whatever, this myth book probably *was* a bible.

Prometheus.

He got freed.

But it didn't seem like that there was going to be a replay of that story. Not here, not now.

The footsteps stopped, and he heard voices.

Randy Boggs swallowed and tried to remember a prayer.

He couldn't, so he just swallowed again, and tried not to think about the pain.

The door swung open.

"Hey, Boggs."

He blinked, staring.

"Boggs, come on. Haul ass."

He stood up and walked toward the guard. He opened his mouth to say something, but nothing came out, which was just as well because he didn't know what to say anyway.

"Let's move it along, Boggs."

"What's up?"

The guard had drowsy eyes and a voice to match. "The warden wants to see you. Hustle it."

"Huph, whatever, you got yourself a pretty little girl," Fred Megler said to Randy Boggs. Megler was trooping around the office. He couldn't sit still, and was on some kind of energy trip.

Randy Boggs was sitting forward in a chair in Megler's office, his hands pressed tightly together as if they'd been manacled. He wore blue jeans and a blue denim work shirt, clothing he'd worn when he'd entered the prison three years before. The clothes smelled of mothballs. Rune wished he'd worn a suit into prison; in what he was now wearing, he still looked like a prisoner.

"Little girl, yessir." Boggs was nodding a lot, agreeing with what everybody said. But at the little girl part, he looked questioningly at Rune, who launched Ophelia toward him. Boggs's hands reached out and she gave him a shy hug.

"Daddy," she said, and looked at Rune to see if she'd gotten the line right. Rune nodded, then said to Boggs,

"Mr. Megler didn't know that you had a little girl. That was one of the reasons he was so nice to help you."

"Yeah," Boggs said, squinting to see if that helped him understand things any better. It didn't seem to. "Sure appreciate it."

Megler couldn't sit still. He was pacing. His polyester tie with the Bic repair job flopped up and down on the baggy shirt where his belly would have been if he weighed forty pounds more. His hair jutted out behind his thin skull as if he were facing into a gale. He said, "So, here's the deal: The young lady here had some pretty good evidence that would've gotten you out but seems some asshole . . ." He looked at Ophelia, but she was playing with Daddy's shoelaces and missed the word. ". . . some person got into the studio and destroyed it. That was strike one. Then—"

"Oh, you should've seen it!" Rune leapt to her feet. "It was a really great story, Randy. It would've gotten you out in a minute. I did the fades just perfect. The sound was mixed, oh, it was like a symphony. And I had a really, really super shot of your mother—"

"Mom? You did?" He grinned. "What kind of stuff'd she say?"

"Didn't make a lot of sense, I have to tell you. But she looked real motherish."

"Yeah, that's one thing she does good."

Megler said, *"Huph,* you guys mind?" Ophelia pointed her tiny index finger at him like a pistol and fired. It was a game she decided they should play. He smiled grudgingly at her and shot back. She clutched her chest and fell to the floor. He looked like he hoped she'd be dead for a long time.

Rune preempted Megler. "You know who did it? You know who the killer was?"

"Uhm. If I knew that . . ." Boggs shrugged.

"It was the guy who picked you up who did it. Jimmy."

Boggs was shaking his head. "I don't know about that."

"Wait, wait, wait," Rune bounced in the chair. "I'll tell you why I know in a minute. But, see, everything got stolen by Jimmy—he somehow found out about the story. I kind of told a reporter about it, and there was this newspaper story, so I think he read it and came to town to stop the program. . . ."

Ophelia revived and climbed up into her lap. She started sniping at Megler.

"Anyway, I came here to tell Fred that the evidence had been stolen. We felt awful, didn't we 'Phelia?"

"Awbul, yeah."

Megler said, "And I told this young lady that not having the tape or the second witness—"

Rune interrupted to explain about Bennett Frost's death.

Boggs was frowning. "Got himself killed?"

"ME says it was an accident, *huph*, but who knows?" Megler said, wanting to take the stage again. "Anyway, with him dead, it wasn't looking too good. But what with you having a cute little girl you have to support—"

Megler missed the glance Boggs shot Rune, and the sweep of her eyes across the grimed ceiling.

"—I thought we could make a good case in court. I got a deposition from the first witness, who admitted that most of her ID was based on seeing you on TV *after* you'd been arrested. Then . . ." He paused dramatically. "I got a special ex parte hearing and presented my new secret witness."

Boggs cocked his head. "You found yourself *another* witness?"

Rune bowed. "Me!"

"*Huph,* I put Rune on the stand for Frost's testimony. Frost told her what he saw, about this other guy killing

Hopper. Normally, that's hearsay, and wouldn't be admissible, but since Frost is dead, Rune could testify about what Frost said."

She said, "Oh, you should've seen me! I was great. 'Do you solemnly swear. . . .' Oh, it was like totally audacious! Just like *L.A. Law,* only real."

Megler said, "I also let slip the fact that she was a reporter for *Current Events.* I think the judge liked that part the most. I mean, justice is one thing, but media? Forget about it. . . . He practically asked her to get the spelling of his name right."

Rune said, "And, poof, he released you."

"From the bench," Megler said solemnly. "Don't happen too often that way."

"I'm free?"

"Pending the prosecutor's decision for a new trial. They'll probably just let it drop. But you have to stay in New York City until they decide. You can travel, if you tell the DA's office, but you can't leave the state."

"My dear Lord," Boggs said. "I don't know what to say." He leaned forward and shyly kissed Rune's cheek. Then he stood up and walked to the window. "You mean I can just walk out there, just like that?"

Megler said, *"Huph,* you earned yourself the right to walk through the slime of New York just like anybody else. . . . Now, you got any money?"

"They give me some when I came out. Not a lot."

Megler was opening up his wallet. A wad of twenties appeared. A couple hundred bucks' worth. He aimed it toward Boggs, who shook his head. "No, sir, thank you anyway."

"It's a loan is all it is. *Huph,* come on. Pay me back when you can. Ha, you don't I'll sue your butt."

Boggs seemed to be blushing as he took the money, and he put it into his pocket as quickly as possible.

Megler was giving him advice about getting jobs, what sort of work to look for.

Boggs looked solemn for a moment. "Something I'd like to do. A friend of mine got himself killed in prison. I'd like to go see his family. Up in Harlem."

"You look like you're asking permission," Megler said. "You want to go, just go."

"Yeah, I could, I guess. Sure."

Then Boggs was saying he had to look for a hotel room. . . . No, first some food, then a room. No, first, he wanted to walk down, what was that street there? Boggs pointed out the window.

"Over there? Broadway," Megler answered.

"I want to walk down Broadway."

Rune corrected, "Actually, you'd be walking *up* Broadway from here."

"Up Broadway, and I want to stop and go into some stores."

"Plenty to choose from," the lawyer offered. "Shitty merchandise, overpriced."

"Shitty," Ophelia echoed.

"And check out some other streets too. And nobody's going to tell me not to."

"Not a soul in the world."

Boggs was grinning.

Rune said, "I have to start my story all over again. That man stole everything. Will you help me?"

Boggs laughed. "Well, you don't hardly have to even ask. There's only one thing I'd ask first."

"Sure."

"You think we might rustle up some beer? It's been a while, and I've really got me a taste."

CHAPTER TWENTY-TWO

The plastic bag rang like sleigh bells. It contained: a Heineken, a Moosehead, a Grolsch, two Budweisers ("Was my first, you know."), a Tecate, and a six-pack of Corona. Rune had also bought some Amstel, but Randy Boggs had never drunk light beer in his life. "Don't believe I'd like to celebrate my freedom with something like that."

They turned onto Christopher Street and aimed themselves at the Hudson, waiting for the stoplight to change. When it did, they crossed the wide West Side Highway, Ophelia holding tight to Rune's hand and looking left and right the way she'd been taught.

Boggs asked, "Uh, where'd we be going?"

Rune felt Southern when she was with Boggs, and she answered, "Yonder."

He looked at where she was nodding and laughed.

They walked up the yellow gangplank to the houseboat, Boggs grinning and looking around him. "You don't need me to comment, I suppose. You live on one of these, you must hear pretty much everything from people."

Inside, Boggs walked from room to room, shyly inspecting. He'd touch the stuffed animals, the scraps of lace Rune draped over lamps, the rosy and blue magic crystals, her books. He'd laugh occasionally as he tried to figure out something—an eyelash curler or a broken antique apple parer that Rune bought because she thought it was a medieval weapon, a tear gas canister.

In the kitchen, she put the beers away and fixed the food they'd bought—crispy-fried Cheetos and cans of refried bean dip and little shrimp cocktails in jars with pry-off lids. "I love these things. And you can use the jars for juice glasses later."

"Juice," said Ophelia. Rune poured Ocean Spray, then filled a Winnie-the-Pooh dish with bean dip and handed her a spoon.

"This is ugly," the girl said, looking into it. "Yes, it is." But she took the utensil and began to pick up bits of dip and wad it onto the spoon.

"She's showing off for guests," Rune said to Boggs. " 'Phelia. You know how."

"Ugly food." She scrunched her nose up, but began to eat properly.

"Napkin," Rune reminded her, and Ophelia picked a paper napkin out of a stack in the center of the table and placed it on her lap. She resumed eating.

Boggs watched them. "Where'd you come by the little one?"

Rune didn't answer. She said, "What kind of beer you like to start with?"

"Believe I'll start with a Bud. Buy American. When I went Inside, three years ago, that's what everybody was saying. Buy American. But nobody makes beer like Mexicans. I'll save that Corona for dessert."

"Oh, I've got dessert. Twinkies. They're the best. You freeze them." Rune led him out to the deck, where they could stand, and she could still watch Ophelia.

"I didn't want to say anything in there. In front of her." She told him how Claire had abandoned the girl.

Boggs shook his head. "I don't think I ever met anybody who'd do something like that."

"Claire's like hyper-immature."

"I never had me any, kids." He grinned. "Not that I know of, anyway. Not so there was a paternity suit."

Rune said, "Me with a kid." She shook her head. "You don't know me that well, but it's kind of a role reversal."

"But looks to me like you two get along pretty good."

Rune's eyes were dancing. "Oh, she's the best. I always thought kids were, like, completely obnoxious. You know, they go through this phase where they can't talk, they have to screech. And they don't eat, they just barf. But what it is, I've figured this out, they're just like adults. Some days they're in good moods, some days they're in bitchy moods. Just like me. And can we talk! We walk all over the place and I tell her things, she understands. Our minds kind of work alike." Rune glanced at Ophelia. "She's going to be just like me when she grows up."

"I know mothers don't sound that happy with their kids."

Boggs was tasting the Bud like it was vintage wine. Rune offered him the bag of Cheetos. He shook his head. He said, "Must be nice having someone to live with. I had me a couple girlfriends, various times, but I was never married. I don't know, it'd be pretty strange for me, I think. Living with somebody when you don't have to. Inside, you don't have much choice, of course."

"Inside?"

"In prison."

"Oh, sure. . . . Well, I usually have roommates. They're sort of a necessary evil in New York. But I've lived by myself a lot. I've gotten used to it. It's like a skill you work on. I remember when I first moved to New York. I was living in this walk-up in the East Village. It was pretty icky. I got the place with another girl, only she decided she wanted to be a model in Europe. Or what it was really was she met this rich, fat guy who wanted to take her to Europe and make her a model, yeah, right. Although who'm I to comment? I'd send in my resume for that job in about five seconds flat. Anyway, so she moved out, and I was there by myself for six months. Didn't know a soul in the city, except the people I met waitressing. I didn't have any money. I'd go home at night and read my fairy tales. It was tough."

"Lonely, huh?"

"I remember some nights I'd be sitting there, watching *Gilligan's Island* reruns on this old black-and-white TV, it was so groady, you know, the kind with a coat hanger for an antenna? And I'd be watching this show, and I'd hear a piece of paper slide under the door. And I'd start to get up, but then I wouldn't. Because I knew it was only a menu from a Chinese restaurant a delivery guy was slipping under doors in the building. But if I didn't go see, maybe it would be a note from someone. Maybe it would say, 'There's a party, in three-G. Plenty of men. Come in costume.' Or maybe it would be mysterious. 'Meet me on the corner of Avenue A and Ninth Street at midnight on the night of the full moon.'"

Boggs was looking at her, trying to figure this all out.

"But, naw, it was always just a menu. And I'd go back to sitcoms and commercials. But ups and downs, that's what makes life what it is." She thumped her chest. "I'm from Ohio peasant stock."

Boggs said, "There's one thing I'd like to say. . . ."

Rune had been wondering if he'd bring up the sleeping arrangements, and figured that was the next item on the agenda. But just then Ophelia called, "Juice."

Rune called, "One minute, honey." To Boggs, she said, "I'm hungry. I've got a couple leftover Whoppers in the fridge. You interested?"

"Sure. Heat me one up too."

"Oh, you want it heated? There's an idea."

Rune started into the houseboat. Suddenly Boggs stopped. He turned and twisted his head, like a dog hear-

ing an ultrasonic whistle. He lifted his face to the sky. His
nostrils flared wide as he inhaled. "How 'bout that?"

"What?"

"The smells," he said.

"Yeah, we aren't exactly talking perfume in New York."

"No, I don't mean that. What I mean is there are so
many of them. A thousand smells."

She sniffed, then shook her head. "Can't tell too many."

Boggs inhaled again. "When you're Inside, there are
only a couple smells you smell. Disinfectant. Onions or
grease from the kitchen. Cold spring air. Hot summer air.
. . . It's like you get used to them. But here—What do I
smell?"

"Rotten fish and dog do and garbage and car exhaust."

"Nope. What I smell is freedom."

One potato, two potato, three potato four. . . .

Jack Nestor was thinking: In Florida, people *ought* to be
on boats. Especially in South Florida, you get close to the
'Glades, you realize that even on land there's water everywhere and it's a part of your life. Houses are raised up
on stilts and everybody's got a boat of some kind in the
yard.

But in New York, it seemed pretty weird.

Five potato, six potato, seven potato, more. . . .

Nestor had parked on Tenth Street, not far from West.
He'd rented the car, which he didn't like doing because
that left a record. But he knew that after what was about
to happen, there was a pretty good chance his description
would go out citywide, including to the Port Authority
police at the airports and bus and train stations. Nobody
could ever stop you from driving out of New York.

The sun was down by now and the sky was a blue the
shade it never was in Florida. It was a gray-blue, metal-
blue, junkyard blue. Nestor was thirsty, but didn't want

to wander until he found a deli—that many more people
to see him. So he sat on a bench facing the city and
waited for more darkness. He stubbed out his cigarette,
after taking one long final drag, thinking the menthol
made him less thirsty.

Eight potato, nine potato, no cops any more. . . .

The blue-and-white that had been parked on the highway near the houseboat, the cops eating sandwiches,
drinking coffee, pulled away, made a lazy U-turn, then
headed north.

Time to go to work.

"I learned a lot of law for one thing. They had a mess
of law books there. Some of the fellows write their own
appeals. They do pretty good at it."

Rune nodded. Boggs was working on his Corona—he
still wasn't drunk, or even tired, it seemed—and Rune
was sipping herbal tea and eating Twinkies. She'd
wanted to tape him and ask him more questions about
what life was like in prison. But he'd begged off. He was
tired. Tomorrow, he said. Shoot me all you want tomorrow.

Ophelia had gotten cranky; it was a little early, but
she'd had a busy day being dragged around town and
playing the role of a convict's daughter, so Rune gave her
a bath (Boggs blushing and looking away from the naked
girl), then put her to bed. She fell asleep almost at once.
Rune bounded back into the living room portion of the
cabin, and saw Boggs sitting back on the couch, looking
uneasy, nervous.

He cleared his throat and looked at her for a long moment, then away.

Something was on his mind, and she wondered if this
was the moment when he was going to try something.

As in, a man and a woman.

As in, a man who's been behind bars for three years suddenly alone with a woman.

She wondered if she could have sex with a convict (well, an unjustly convicted convict). She didn't think so. She was also pretty certain she'd never have sex with anyone who used Brylcream and meant it.

She sat down on the couch.

They talked about life in the city for a few minutes, about Atlanta, about politics and Washington (he knew a lot more than she did). Rune, expecting the line at any minute: *You know, I was thinking I might have me some trouble getting a room. . . .* But just as that was going through her head, Boggs yawned and looked at his watch. He said, "I ought to be finding a room for the night."

And she surprised herself by saying, "You want, you can sleep in the living room. Ophelia's got the futon, but we could fix up something."

Then wishing she hadn't, then glad she had, because by saying *in the living room,* instead of *you can sleep here* or something vaguer, she was making it clear what her position was.

But he was shaking his head. "No, it's funny, I can't explain it, but I'd really be inclined to spend the night by myself, you know?"

"Sure." Not understanding, but feeling relieved.

"Let me pack up the rest of the beers. And I'll give you some pizza for breakfast."

"Uh, no thanks. I'm pretty partial to oatmeal."

"I got some packets of instant," she said. "You want a couple?"

Which was a question that never got answered.

With a huge crack, the front door burst open, hitting a table and knocking over a pile of Rune's books.

She looked at the man stepping quickly into the house-boat, then saw the gun, and before she did anything else, she leapt in front of the storeroom, where Ophelia was asleep, and shut the door, standing defiantly in front of it. Staring back at the man she knew without a bit of doubt had killed Lance Hopper and Bennett Frost.

Boggs stood up fast, knocking over the beer, which chugged onto the floor.

The man closed the front door slowly, calmly, as if he'd been invited in.

He stood with his arms hanging awkwardly at his side. Cautious, but confident, squinting, checking out the room and its inhabitants. Nothing he saw scared him.

Randy Boggs, his eyes wide with shock, faced the man. The way Boggs stood made him look like a soldier. No, more like a boxer—one foot forward, turned sideways. Which was crazy because even without the gun, no way could he have taken this fat guy, who outweighed him by fifty pounds and looked like a ball-kicker and eye-gouger. A dirty fighter.

"What do you want?" Rune whispered.

He ignored her, though, and stepped right up to Boggs. Five seconds of complete silence passed as the men seemed locked in a staring contest.

No one moved.

It was Randy Boggs who grinned first, then said, "Jack, you son of a bitch. Wasn't expecting you for a couple days or so."

Nestor laughed and let out a whoop. He slipped the gun into his belt, and the two men embraced like long-lost cossack brothers suddenly reunited.

CHAPTER TWENTY-THREE

The one question on her mind: Could Ophelia swim?

Rune could, pretty much. About as well as any Midwest girl who never saw a body of water with waves until she was ten.

Hell, she could just hold on to Ophelia—picturing her now, screaming and waving her arms in panic—and kick to the far pier. How many yards was that? Maybe thirty or forty?

God, was the Hudson gross and yucky. . . .

But, it didn't matter much. If they didn't get out now, they'd be dead in three minutes.

She tore the door to the storeroom open and lunged through, vaguely aware of a sudden rush of activity behind her in the living room. Footsteps, voices. She slammed the door, and turned the skeleton key lock. " 'Phelia, wake up."

The little girl didn't stir.

Rune pressed her back against the thick wood and began to untie her boots, which were laced up tight through dozens of eyelets. She shouted, "Ophelia."

"Juice," a weak voice said.

"Wake up!"

Maybe some of the toys would float. There was an anemic balloon tied onto the wall. Rune grabbed it and tied it around the girl's wrist. "I'm sleepy," she said.

Rune had one boot off. It flew across the room. She started on the second.

The swimming issue didn't arise, though. With a huge snap of cracking wood, the door blew inward, catching

Rune on the shoulder. She flew into the far wall and lay still. Jack Nestor stepped into the room, narrowing his eyes against the darkness. He looked around and walked toward Rune.

When he got to her, she sprung.

It wasn't much of an assault. The only damage: Her shoulder caught him in the cheek, and he jerked back, blinking in surprise, as a tooth cut into his tongue or the flesh of his mouth. She pounded with her hands, knotted into small fists. But he was resilient as hard rubber. And goddamn strong too. He just picked her up, stuffed her under his arm and carried her out into the living room.

She screamed and twisted and kicked.

Nestor was laughing hard. "Whoa, this one's a powerhouse." He dropped her into a wrought-iron butterfly chair. She kicked him in the thigh. Flinching, he said, "Settle down."

"You son of a bitch!" She leapt out of the chair, making for Boggs. Nestor roared, "Settle down!" He grabbed her like a receiver snagging a sixty-yard bomb and dropped her into the chair again. She bounced once, the breath knocked out of her. She wiped at her tears. "You bastard." Looking into Randy Boggs's evasive eyes.

Boggs said to Nestor, "You got yourself wheels?"

"Sure do. Some kind of Hertz shit. But it'll do. Damn, you look good, for somebody who ain't seen but prison sunlight for three years."

Boggs said, "You look ugly as you ever did."

Nestor laughed, and the men did a little good-natured sparring.

Boggs landed a left hook on Nestor's chest, and the fat man said, "You prick, you always were fast. You hit like a pussy but you're fast."

"You'll see a bruise the shape of my knuckles there come morning."

"Fuck that." Nestor looked around. "We gotta blow this joint."

"I'll vote for that."

Rune said to Boggs, "You did it? You really did it?"

Nestor was speaking to Boggs. "Let's take care of business, and get on our way." He pulled the gun out of his waistband and glanced at Rune as if she was a pesky raccoon.

The smile left Boggs's face. "Whatcha aiming to do?"

Nestor shrugged. "Pretty clear, wouldn't you say? Don't see we have much choice."

Boggs was looking down, avoiding both their eyes. "Well, Jack, you know, I wouldn't be too happy, you did that."

Rune stared at the gun, afraid to look into Nestor's face, as if it would set him off. He seemed to be the sort who would look you in the eye while he hurt you.

"Randy, we gotta. She's seen me. She knows now."

"I know, but, hell, I wouldn't want that to happen. It just wouldn't be right, you know."

"Right?"

Her hands were shaking. Sweat popped out on her forehead, and she felt a trickle run from under her arms to her waist.

Boggs said, "The thing is, she's got a kid. A little girl."

Nestor's face darkened. "A baby?"

"This little kid."

"In there?" Nestor looked at the storeroom. "I didn't see her."

"You can't do the kid, Jack. I just won't let you do that."

Meaning it's okay if he shoots me? Rune began to cry more seriously. Nestor was saying, and he seemed to mean it, "I wouldn't do a kid anyway. You know me better than that, Randy. After all we've been through, I hope you do."

"And what's the kid going to do without a mother? She'd starve to death, or something."

"She's pretty young to be a mother."

From somewhere Rune found the voice to say, "Please, don't hurt her. If you . . . do anything to me, please call the police or somebody and tell her that she's here. Please."

Nestor was debating. Rune stared at the gun, and at the man's taut pregnant belly.

Boggs said, "I really gotta ask, Jack. I really gotta ask you to let her be."

Nestor sighed. He nodded and put the gun into his belt. "Shit, that's the way it is, that's the way it is. Okay. For you, Randy. I don't think it's a good idea, I just want to go on the record and say that, but I owe you, so I'll do it. But . . ." He walked to the chair and took Rune's face in his onion-scented fingers. "You listen up good. I know who you are, and where you live. And I know you got yourself a little girl. If you say anything to anybody about us, I'll come back. I get to New York all the time. I'll come back and I'll kill you both."

Rune was crying—in pure fear, in pure relief.

And from the worst pain of all—betrayal.

You *believe* him? Piper Sutton had asked Rune such a long time ago, as if she was talking to a child. You *believe* it when he says he's innocent?

Nestor said brutally, "You hear me?"

She couldn't speak. She nodded her head.

They used lamp cord and tied her into the chair (which was hard enough to get out of anyway without being tied) and gagged her with an old wool scarf. With the moisture from her tears and spit, the taste reminded her of sledding back home when she was a teenager. The poignancy of that innocent time, compared with what she felt now, made her sob harder.

Boggs knelt down and tested the wires. He smiled shyly. "I suspect you're right upset, and I don't blame you. You helped me out, and I repay you this way. But sometimes in life, you've gotta do things just for yourself. You know, for your own survival. I'm sorry it worked out this way, but you saved my life. I'll always be thankful for that."

She wanted to say *Fuck you!* Or *Go to hell!* Or *Judas!* A thousand other things. But the gag would make it sound comic, and besides, no words could hold the undiluted anger she was feeling for this man. So she stared into his eyes, not blinking, not wavering a millimeter, forcing him to see that hate that welled up and overflowed between them.

Boggs squinted for an instant, and didn't speak. She prayed he understood that what she wanted was him tied up to the rock again, torn at by birds. Her anger was just as deep as Jove's.

Then they were gone.

Man, man, man, there's nothing like driving.

There's not a goddamn thing in the world like it. The way the tires make that hissing sound on asphalt. The way the car dances over beat-up pavement. The way you know the road'll always be there and that you can drive forever, and never once cover the same spot twice, you don't want to.

The Ford Tempo, Jack Nestor driving, had left Jersey way behind and was cruising down the Blue Star Memorial Highway into Maryland.

Motion, like smooth whisky. Motion, like a drug.

And the best part of all—when you're driving, you're a moving target. You're the safest you can ever be. Nothing can get you. Not bad love, not a job, not your kin, not the devil himself. . . .

"Crabs," Nestor said. "Keep an eye out for a crab place."

They couldn't find any, and instead got cheeseburgers at McDonald's, which Boggs preferred to crabs anyway.

They drank beer out of tall Double-Arches waxed cups they'd emptied of soft drink. They drove the speed limit, but at Boggs's insistence had rolled down all the windows; it seemed like they were racing at a hundred miles an hour.

Randy Boggs lowered the passenger seat and sat back, sucking the beer through a straw, and ate a double cheeseburger and thought again about freedom and moving, and realized that was why prison had been so hard for him. That there are people who have to stay put and people who have to move, and he was one who, if he didn't move, he was going to die. That's what prison was going to do to him. Kill him. His soul, if not his body.

These were thoughts he had and that he believed were true in some universal way. But they were thoughts that he didn't tell to Jack Nestor. Not that Jack was a stupid man. No, he'd probably understand, but he was somebody Boggs simply chose not to share them with. If he needed an excuse, Boggs thought, it was that he didn't want to dilute them.

"So," Jack Nestor asked, "how's it feel?"

"Feels good. Feels real good."

"How 'bout that little girl back there. She's a pistol. You get any?"

"Naw, wasn't that way."

"Didn't seem to have any tits to speak of."

"She was more like a friend, you know. Wished I could've leveled with her."

"Did what you had to, though."

"I understand that. Couldn't've stayed in for any

longer, Jack. I gave it my best. But I had to get out. Somebody was moving on me."

"Spades?"

"Got myself cut. Wasn't black, though. Was an asshole from, I don't know, Colombia or someplace. Venezuela. Drugs, you know. For some reason he didn't take to me."

"Cut huh?"

"Two weeks ago. Missed everything important. Hardly hurts anymore."

"Yeah, I was cut once. I didn't like it. Better to get shot. Kind of numb-er."

"Prefer to avoid either."

Nestor was in a good mood. He was talking about restaurants down in Florida and fishing for tarpon, and the quality of the pot they had down there, and this Cuban woman with big tits and a tattoo somebody'd given her with his teeth and a Parker pen. Talking about the heat. About a house he was buying and how he had to live in a fucking hotel until it was ready.

"Where're we headed to?" Boggs asked.

"Thought you might want to stop in Atlanta. I'm going to Florida. You interested in coming with me, you'd be welcome. You like spic women?"

"Never had me one."

"Don't know what you're missing."

"That a fact?"

"Yessir. One I's telling you 'bout? Man, she could probably do both of us at once."

Boggs thought he'd pass on that. "I don't know."

"Well, just keep 'er in mind."

"Will do."

Nestor was driving carefully, not speeding, signaling when he changed lanes. "Figured you'd be wanting to pick up that money," he said.

"Yessir."

"You got the passbook with you?"

"Got her good and safe."

Nestor said, "Funny about how that works. You just let it sit in the bank, and there she be, earning interest every day. They just throw a few more dollars into the till."

"Yeah."

"Bet you made yourself another ten thousand dollars."

"You think?"

"For sure. I think that account earns maybe five, six percent."

Boggs felt a warm feeling. He hadn't remembered about interest. He'd never had a savings account to speak of.

"You know, there's something you ought to think about. You hear about all those bank failures?"

"What's that?"

"A lot of savings and loans went under. People lose money. Well, they don't actually lose all of it, because it's insured by the government, usually. But it sometimes takes four or five years to get their money back."

"Hell you say."

"Happens a lot. Last couple years. Didn't you watch the news Inside?"

"Usually they were cartoons what we were watching."

Boggs was tired. He put the seat way back. The last car he'd owned was a big '76 Pontiac, with a bench seat that didn't recline. He liked this car. He thought he was going to buy himself a car, a new one. He lay back, he closed his eyes, and tried not to think about Rune.

Nestor said, "You might want to think about investing that money."

"I aim to."

"You have any idea what?"

"Nope. Not yet. I'm going to keep my eyes peeled for the right thing. You got money, people listen to you."

"Money talks, shit walks," Nestor said.

"That's the truth," Randy Boggs said.

Three hours later Ophelia woke and wanted some juice.

She sat up slowly and unwound herself from the cocoon of a blanket that had twisted around her as she slept. She eased forward and climbed over the edge of the rolled-up futon like Edmund Hillary taking the last step down from Everest, and then sat on the floor to put her shoes on. Laces were too much of a challenge, but the shoes didn't look right with the white dangling strings, so after staring at them for five minutes, she bent down and stuffed the plastic ends into her shoes.

She climbed carefully down the stairs, sideways, crablike, then walked up to Rune, tied into the butterfly chair. She looked at the cords, at Rune's red face. She heard hoarse, wordless sounds coming from behind the scarf.

"You're funny." Ophelia laughed and went into the galley.

The refrigerator was pretty easy to open, and she found a cardboard carton of apple juice on the second shelf. The problem was that she couldn't figure out how to open it. She looked at Rune, who was staring into the kitchen and still making those funny noises, and held up the carton in both hands, then she turned it upside down to look for the spout.

The carton, which, it turned out, had been open after all, emptied itself onto the floor in a sticky surf.

"Oh-oh." She looked at Rune guiltily, then set the empty container on top of the stove, and went back to the refrigerator.

No more juice. A lot of cold pizza, which she was tired of, but there were dozens of Twinkies, which she loved.

She started working on one and then wandered around the small kitchen to see what she could find to play with.

Not a lot, though there was a large filleting knife on the counter. She picked it up and pretended it was a sword, like in one of Rune's books, stabbing the refrigerator a few times.

Rune, watching this, was making more noise, and started jiggling around, rocking and swaying back and forth.

Ophelia walked to the doorway, carrying the knife, and stared at Rune for a few minutes. She sat on the steps and dug the blade into the banister, then practiced making Celtic letters, the way Rune was teaching her. The knife, though, was harder to hold than crayons, and it slipped from her hand, tumbling behind the TV.

"Oh-oh." Ophelia peered into the darkness behind the console. "Gone," she said to Rune, then walked back into the kitchen.

She looked into drawers and opened up some pretty-much-unused cookbooks, looking for pictures of ducks, dragons, or princesses. She found only casseroles and sponge cakes, and after five minutes she gave up on them and started playing with the knobs on the stove. They were old and heavy, glistening chrome and trimmed with red paint. Ophelia reached up and turned one all the way to the right. Way above her head was a *pop*. She couldn't see the top of the stove, and she didn't know what the sound came from, but she liked it. *Pop*.

She turned the second knob. *Pop*.

Rune hit a higher note and started moving along the floor in the chair.

Ophelia laughed and squealed. This was the most fun she'd had in days.

With the third *pop*, she got tired of the knob game. That was because something else happened. There was suddenly a red glare from above her head and a hissing sputter, then flames.

Ophelia stepped back and watched the juice carton burn. The flaming wax shot off the side of the carton like miniature fireworks. One piece of burning cardboard fell onto the table and set a week-old *New York Post* on fire. A cookbook (*A Hundred Glorious Jell-O Desserts*) went next.

Ophelia loved the flames, watching them creep slowly along the table. They reminded her of something. . . . A movie about a baby animal? A big fire in a forest? She squinted and tried to remember, but soon lost the association and stood back to watch.

She thought it was great when the flames quickly peeled away the Breeds-of-Dog contact paper Rune had painstakingly mounted on the walls with rubber cement.

Then they spread up to the ceiling and the back wall of the houseboat.

When the fire became too hot, Ophelia moved back a little further, but she was in no hurry. This was wonderful. She remembered another movie. She thought for a minute. Yeah, it was like the scene where the Wizardoz was yelling at Dorothy and her little dog. All the smoke and flames. . . . Everybody falling on the floor while the big face puffed and shouted. . . . But this was better than that. Oh, yeah, this was better than Peter Rabbit. It was even better than Saturday morning TV.

CHAPTER TWENTY-FOUR

The tourists, it turned out, were from Ohio.

They were a middle-aged couple, driving a Winnebago from Cleveland to Maine because the wife had always wanted to see the Maine coast, and because they both loved lobster. The itinerary would take them through New York, up to Newport, then on to Boston, Salem, and finally into Kennebunkport, which had been featured in *Parade* magazine a year before.

But they'd made an unplanned stop, and that was to report a fire in lower Manhattan.

Cruising up from the Holland Tunnel, they were staring at the Empire State Building, talking about King Kong, when the wife saw a column of black smoke off to their left, coming, it seemed, right out of the river. They slowed, like almost everybody else was doing, and saw an old houseboat burning furiously. Traffic was slowed to a crawl, and they eased forward, listening for the sirens. The husband looked around him to find a place to pull off when the trucks arrived.

None did.

They waited four, five minutes. Six.

She asked, "You'd think somebody'd've called by now, wouldn't you, dear?"

"Ummm."

They were astonished because easily a hundred cars had gone by, but it seemed that nobody had bothered to call 911. Maybe figuring somebody else had. Or not figuring anything at all, but just watching the houseboat burn to the ground. Well, to the water.

The husband, an ex-Marine and head of his local Chamber of Commerce, a man with no aversion to getting involved, drove the Winnebago over the curb and up onto the sidewalk. He braked to a fast halt in front of the pier where the flames roared. He took the J.C. Penney triple-class fire extinguisher from the rack beside his seat and rushed outside.

The wife ran to a pay phone while he kicked in the front door (something he'd always wanted to do). The smoke wasn't too bad inside; the hole in the rear ceiling of the houseboat acted like a chimney and was sucking most of it out. The flames, though, were fierce. Still, he stopped cold in the doorway, blinking in surprise at what he saw: two girls. One, a baby, was laughing like Nero as she watched the back half of the houseboat turn into charcoal. The other, a girl wearing a yellow miniskirt, two sleeveless men's T-shirts and low boots dotted with chrome studs, was tied in a chair! Who'd do such a thing? He'd read about Greenwich Village, but he sure wasn't ready for this.

He pulled the pin of the fire extinguisher and emptied the contents at the advancing line of flames more because this, too, was something he'd always wanted to do; it had no effect on the fire. He carried the little girl outside to his wife and then returned to the inferno, opening his Case pocketknife as he ran. He cut the wires holding the older girl. He had to help her walk to the camper; her legs had fallen asleep. Inside the Winnebago the little girl saw the older one's tears and caught on pretty fast that it was about time to start crying. She started to wail. Three minutes later, the fire department arrived, and they had the fire out in twenty. The older girl had calmed down by then and had a stoic, sorrowful look about her. The police and fire department investigators knocked on the door.

The girls stood up and went outside, and the couple followed.

A huge black cloud hung over the pier. The air smelled of sour wood and burnt rubber—from the tires that had dangled from the side of the boat to cushion it against the pier.

One of the detectives asked the girl, "Could you tell me what happened?"

She paced in a tight circle. "That goddamn son of a bitch he tricked me he lied to me I'm going to find him and have his ass thrown back in jail so goddamn fast. . . . Shit. Hell. Shit!"

"Shit," Ophelia said, and the husband and wife looked at each other.

The police asked questions for almost a half hour. The girl was telling a story about a man who was convicted wrongly of murder, then he got out, only now it was clear he'd done it after all, and there was a big fat man with a gun, who tried to kill them, and he was involved in the killing, and. . . . The couple lost a lot of the details—just like the cops must have too—but they didn't really need to hear any more. They had enough of the facts for a good traveling story, which they'd tell to friends and themselves and anybody they happened to meet on the way to Maine, and which unlike a lot of the stories they'd told didn't need much embellishment at all. Then a tall, balding man in a plaid shirt and blue jeans and with a badge on his belt arrived and the girl fell into his arms, though not sobbing and hysterical, then pushed him away and went into one of her tirades again.

"Goodness," the wife said.

Then the girl calmed down and told the cop the couple had saved her life, and he introduced himself and said thank you. Then he said that the girls could go to Bomb Squad and stay there until he was off duty, and then the little girl laughed and asked if she could have another grenade.

And that was when the couple from Ohio decided not to do what had crossed their Midwestern minds—ask the girls if they would like to stay with them in the camper that night—and figured it would probably be best if they pressed on to the alternate destination of Mystic, Connecticut, which the Triple A had plotted out for them.

At eleven that night, Jack Nestor said he needed a real drink, and he pulled off the highway at a motel somewhere in Virginia.

"I could use some real food, too," Boggs said. He wanted a steak burnt on the outside and red inside. He'd spent a lot of time thinking about steaks when he first went in. Then—like with a lot of things, most of the things he enjoyed—he forgot about them. Or it was more that they became distant. Like facts in a history book. He understood them, but they had no meaning for him.

But now he was out, and he wanted a steak. And the way Nestor had said *real drink,* Boggs was now thinking that he'd like his first shot of whisky in three years. His mouth began to water like a bird dog's when it hears a double-barrel snap shut.

They parked the car and went into the motel office. Nestor gave a fake name and car license, then asked for a room in the back, explaining to the young night clerk that he didn't sleep well. Highway noise bothered him. The young man nodded apathetically, took the cash and gave him the key. Boggs was impressed at how smoothly Nestor had handled it. Boggs himself would have been more careless, leaving the car in front. But Nestor was right. What if the girl had gotten free and turned them in? Or if someone in New York had seen the license plate? He was glad he was with somebody like Nestor, somebody who could teach him to think Outside again.

Nestor lugged his duffel bag into the room, and Boggs followed with the paper bag that was his suitcase. He was relieved to see there were two large beds. He hadn't wanted to spend his first night of freedom in bed with another man. Without commenting on the room, Nestor dropped his bag onto the bed nearest the door and said, "Food."

Boggs said, "Hold up. I want to wash." He disappeared into the bathroom, amused and feeling almost heartsick with joy at how clean it was. At all the flowery smells. At the soap and wrapped glasses and a john behind a door that closed and locked. He ran the water cold, then hot, then cold again, then hot and washed his face and hands as the steam rose up and filled the room.

"I'm hungry," Nestor bellowed over the sound of the running water.

"Minute," Boggs shouted back, and luxuriously dried himself with towels that seemed thick as down comforters.

The bar-restaurant near the hotel was a local hangout, done up in prefab Tudor—dark beams, plastic windows mimicking stained glass, beige stucco walls. The place was half filled—mostly around the bar—with contractors and plumbers and truck drivers and their girlfriends. The men were in jeans and plaid shirts. A lot of beards. The women, in slacks, high heels, and simple blouses. Almost everyone smoked. *The Honeymooners* was showing on a cockeyed TV above one end of the bar.

Nestor and Boggs sat down at a rickety table. Boggs stared at his place mat, which was printed with puzzles and word games. He could figure out the visual ones— "What's Wrong With This Picture?"—but he had trouble unscrambling letters to make words. He turned the place mat over and looked at the women at the bar.

The waitress came by and told them the kitchen was closing in ten minutes. They ordered four Black Jacks, neat, Bud chasers, and steak and fries.

"That girl," Nestor said. "Too bad you didn't fuck her."

"Who?"

"The one sprung you."

"Naw, I told you, we was mostly friends."

Nestor asked, "So?"

"Well, I only got out a few hours before you showed up."

"It was me, the first thing I woulda done was get me some poontang."

Boggs felt he was on the spot. He said, "Well, she had the baby there."

Nestor said, "I could fuck somebody in front of her kid. Be a turn-on. Think about it."

Boggs did, and didn't find it a turn-on at all.

The drinks arrived, and they poured the shots down without saying anything because neither of them could think of a toast. Boggs wheezed, and Nestor laughed, as he did his second shot right after.

"Don't get any of that Inside, do you?"

"There was stuff you could get, depending on what you did, or how much money you had. It was shit, though. Me, I didn't get any care packages, so I had to settle. Sometimes, I'd get me some watered vodka or a joint or two. Mostly, didn't get nothing."

"When I was in, we had it easy. Fucking country club. A lot of dealers from LA. There was so much shit."

Boggs, dizzy from the liquor, asked, "You did time?"

"Fuck yeah, I was in. Did eighteen months in Obispo. Fanfuckingtastic. You wanted blow, you got blow. You wanted sess, you got sess. You wanted fucking wine, you could get a good bottle of wine. . . ."

Boggs was feeling the liquor sting his lips. They must've gotten windburned from the drive. "When were you in Obispo?"

"Four, five years ago about."

"I didn't know you'd done time."

Nestor looked at him, surprised. "Hey, there's probably a thing or two we don't know about each other. Like I don't know how long your dick is."

Boggs said, "Long enough to keep a grin on *her* face for an hour or two." His eyes slipped to the bar, where a round-faced young woman, with two-tone hair—blonde returning to black—sat with her elbow on the bar and her hand up, a cigarette aiming at the ceiling like a sixth finger. In front of her was a no-nonsense martini. The way she stared vacantly at the TV, he figured the drink was the descendant of a long line of the same.

Nestor said, "You can have her. She don't have tits."

"Sure she does. She's setting hunched over."

Nestor looked carefully and agreed that she might.

The food arrived, and took both men's attention. Boggs was eating slowly, cautiously, but he'd found his appetite was gone. Maybe the steak was too rich. Maybe the burgers had filled him up, or the alcohol had burned out his taste buds. He ate mechanically. He looked at the woman, who caught his eye and held it for a minute, before she looked back at the TV. He thought a bit more, then decided to finish eating. He thought the food would sober him up.

Nestor wasn't a shoveler, which Boggs figured he'd be. He cut small bites of food and chewed very carefully, as if his mother were standing over his shoulder reminding him how to eat properly. Boggs finished while Nestor was still halfway through.

"Man," Boggs said, "that was a meal."

Nestor looked at Boggs's thin stomach. "You eat that way, how come you ain't fat?"

"Dunno. I just never gain it. Not my doing." Boggs's voice faded, as he stared again at the girl at the bar. This time she gave him a bit of a smile.

Nestor caught it. "Oh, oh." He smiled. "Prison-boy gonna get laid."

Boggs finished his beer. "You mind if I take the room for about an hour?"

"Shit, boy, it'll take you five minutes, unless you jerked off every night inside the slammer."

"Well, gimme an hour anyway. Maybe we'll wanta do it twice."

"Okeydokey," Nestor said. "But get her butt out by two. I'm tired, and I need some sleep."

Boggs stood up, and walked slowly toward the bar, trying to remember how to be cool and slick, trying to remember how to talk to women, trying to remember a lot of things.

CHAPTER TWENTY-FIVE

Boggs and the girl had been gone a half hour when Jack Nestor finished the lousy apple pie and sucked the ice cream off his fork. He took the last swallow of coffee and called for the check.

The bar was pretty empty now, and aside from the waitress, there was nobody who saw him get up and go out to the parking lot. He looked up and saw the light on in the room. He opened the trunk of the car and took out his pistol. He hid the gun under his jacket and climbed the stairs to the second floor, then moved slowly along the open walkway to the room. He'd thought about getting another key from the desk, but that would give the clerk another look at him. He decided to just knock on the door, and when Boggs opened it, shoot him in the gut. Shove it into his I-dunno-I-just-eat-and-don't-get-fat gut. Then do the girl, if she was still there.

He paused. What was that noise? The TV? They were fucking and the TV was on? Maybe she was a screamer and Boggs kept the sound up so other guests wouldn't hear. That was good. Maybe it was a cop show, and there'd be gunshots, which would help cover up the sound of the Steyr.

Nestor walked closer to the door. He pulled the slide back on the gun. He saw something flashing.

The putz.

Boggs was so horny, he'd left the key in the door, which wasn't even fully closed. All Nestor had to do was push. He made sure the safety was off, slipped his finger into the trigger guard and swung into the room.

Empty.

The bedclothes weren't even turned down.

The bathroom was dark, but he walked inside anyway, thinking that maybe they were fucking in the tub. But no, that was empty too. The only motion in the room was the flicker of the TV screen on which several *Hill Street Blues* cops were looking solemn. Nestor shut off the set.

Then he noticed that Boggs's bag was gone. Shit.

He picked up the note, which rested on the pillow. Shit.

Jack, Lynda—that's her name—and I went back to her house. Seems she is going to Atlanta tomorrow too, so we're going to be driving together for a spell, her and me, I mean. I will meet you at your place in Florida in a couple a days. Sorry, but you don't have legs like her.

Son of a bitch.

Motherfucker.

Nestor kicked the bed furiously. The mattress bounced off the springs and came to rest at an angle. He slammed the door shut violently, which brought a sleepy protesting pounding from the next room over. Nestor hoped the guest would come over because he had an incredible desire to beat the living hell out of someone. He could taste it, he was so mad.

He sat down on the bed, picturing Boggs balling the scrawny cunt from the bar, while the passbook sat in a crumpled paper bag probably five feet away from them. The anger seeped away slowly, as he decided what to do.

Well, it wasn't the end of the world. It was a change of plans was all—going back to New York tomorrow. Didn't really matter though; whether he killed Boggs first or the girl—six of one, half a dozen of another.

* * *

The way Piper Sutton found out was the *Post* headline: *TV NEWS OOPS.* Which she wouldn't have thought about, except there was a picture of Rune talking to a couple of men in suits. They didn't look happy. Rune didn't either, and now Piper Sutton joined the club.

On her way to work, staring at the story. She'd bought the *Post,* a *Daily News* and a *Times.* Ripping open each furiously, skirt and hair tousled by the wind as she stared at the smudged type. Thank God for a big assault in Central America that buried the *Daily News* story inside. The *Times* hadn't made the deadline with anything other than: *Houseboat Burns in Hudson,* and a reference to a possible convict's escape.

But they'd be on the story today. How the Fit-to-Print paper loved to take potshots at the competition!

Sutton flagged down a cab, giving up her usual mile walk to the office, and sat with the newspapers on her lap, staring out the window at people on their way to work. Staring, and not seeing a single one of them.

At her office, Sutton found her secretary juggling two calls.

"Oh, Ms. Sutton, Mr. Semple has called several times, there're calls from all the local TV stations, and somebody from the *Village Voice.*"

The fucking Voice?

"And a Mr. Weinstein, with the Attorney General's office, then—"

"Hold all my calls," Sutton hissed. "Ask Lee to come over. Get the legal department—"

"Oh, someone from there has already come. . . ."

Sutton's look silenced the woman. "Get the legal department. I want Jerry Birnbaum here in fifteen minutes. If any other reporters call, tell them we'll have a statement by noon. If any of them say they have an earlier deadline, take his or her name and let me know immediately." Sutton pulled her coat off. "And I want her. Now."

"Who, Miss Sutton?"

"That girl," Sutton said in a whisper. "I want her here now."

Rune had been fired worse, but the sad thing was, before this, she didn't care.

She'd screwed up often in the past, sure, but there's a big difference between getting fired from a video store or restaurant, and getting fired from this, a real job.

Usually she'd say, "Eh, happens," or "Them's the breaks."

This was different.

She wanted the story. Bad. She'd lived for that story. She'd breathed it and tasted it. And now not only was she getting axed, but she'd found the whole thing was a lie. The very core, the most very basic fact was false. The worst. It was like reading a fairy tale and then the writer telling you, *Oh, yeah, by the way, I was just kidding. There's no such things as dragons.*

Although she had proof there was such a thing. And his name was Randy Boggs.

Rune now stood in front of Piper Sutton's desk. Also in the room were a tall, thin middle-aged man in a gray suit and white shirt, and Lee Maisel, who leaned against the wall behind Sutton, reading the *Post* account. "Jesus Christ," he muttered. He looked at Rune with dark, impenetrable eyes and went back to the paper.

"Tell me exactly what happened," Sutton said. "Don't embellish, don't minimize, don't edit."

Rune explained about the fat man, and Boggs and what happened on the houseboat.

"So Boggs did it, after all," Maisel said. "Jesus."

"Sort of looks like it." Rune wasn't counting *like*'s, *sort of*'s and *kind of*'s. "When I saw them there, kind of hugging each other, I totally freaked. I mean . . ." Her voice faded.

Sutton closed her eyes and shook her head slowly, then asked the gray-suited man, "What's the legal assessment, Jerry?"

The lawyer said calmly, "I don't think we have any liability. We didn't fabricate evidence, and the court decision was legitimate. I wish she—" not looking at Rune "—hadn't gotten him released without telling anybody here. That adds another dimension."

For the first time since she'd known him, Maisel turned angry eyes on Rune. "Why didn't you tell me you were going to get Boggs sprung?"

"I was worried about him. I—"

Sutton couldn't keep cool any longer. "I've told you from the beginning that our job isn't to get people out of jail. It's to report the facts! That's the only job."

"I just didn't think. I didn't think it would matter."

"Didn't . . . think." Sutton stretched the words out for a vast second.

"I'm really—"

Sutton turned to Maisel. "So, what's the next step?"

"Nighttime News."

The lawyer winced. "It's a New York story. Can't we justify keeping it local?"

Maisel said, "No way. *Time* and *Newsweek*'ll cover it. You know what the other Nets are going to do, and forget about the *Times*. They'll crucify us. I mean crucify."

"We'll have to preempt them," Sutton said. "Put it on the *News at Noon,* then do a piece at five and have Eustice do it at seven."

The lawyer said, "God, that'll hurt."

Maisel sighed. "I'll have Jim bury it. No more than thirty seconds, and we can tuck it after a commercial."

The lawyer asked Rune, "You have any idea where Boggs went?"

"All I know is like he came from the South. Atlanta was where he was born, and he lived in Florida, but other than that . . ." She ended in a shrug.

The lawyer said, "I'm going over to our law firm and brief the litigators, just in case." With a fast, curious glance at Rune, he left the office. Sutton stared at the *Daily News*. Lee Maisel played with his pipe and sat in a slump. He was uncomfortable. Rune looked into his eyes, though his darted away quickly. She was glad they did. What she saw hurt her more than the hatred she felt gushing from Sutton. It took a minute to recognize it, and then she understood that she was looking at someone who was vulnerable. Lee Maisel was afraid. Afraid. Her cheeks blazed. She'd jeopardized his whole career.

Oh, how could I do it?

I believed Boggs, that's how. I believed he was innocent. I believed—

Sutton looked up at Rune. "Don't talk to the press about what happened. You've already blabbed your mouth off, I see." Waving her arm at the newspapers.

Rune said, "I didn't say anything. The police must've told the reporters."

"Well, all I'll say is, the Network is going to be in deep shit for this, and heads are probably going to roll. If you make things worse for everybody because you can't keep your mouth shut, then you'll be opening yourself up to a big fat fucking lawsuit. You understand me?"

Rune nodded.

There was a long pause, broken by Sutton saying, "Well, I guess that's it. You're out of here."

Rune stared at her, blinked. "Just like that? Today?"

Then she looked at Maisel, who she thought had a

splinter of sympathy in his eyes as he said, "Sorry, Rune. Today, yes. Now."

Sutton added, "And don't take any files or cassettes with you. That's our property."

"Do you mean I should go back to my job at the O&O?"

Sutton looked at her with a disbelieving smile.

Rune said, "You mean, I'm like totally fired."

Sutton said, "Like totally."

Sam woke up at eight the next morning, when Ophelia emptied a box of Raisin Bran in their bed. Rune didn't wake up.

"Jesus Christ," Healy muttered and shook her arm. He rolled over. Rune opened her eyes, and said, "What's that noise? That crunching?"

Ophelia stood in front of the bed and looked down at it, frowning.

Rune swung her feet over the side of the bed, her legs covered with cereal. " 'Phelia, what did you do?"

"I'm sorry," the little girl said. "Spilled."

Healy, who'd gotten home two hours before from duty watch, said, "I'm going into Adam's room."

He vanished.

Rune scooped the cereal up and brushed it off her legs, then put it back into the box. "You know better than that. Come on."

"I know better."

"Don't look so damn cute when I'm yelling at you."

"Damn cute," Ophelia said.

"Come on."

Rune showered and dressed, then went into the kitchen. She poured juice and bowls of cereal, made coffee. "Can we go to the zoo?" Ophelia asked.

"Tomorrow. I've got some errands to do first. You wanta come?"

"Yeah, I wanta come." She held up her hand. "Fi-high."

Rune sighed, then held up her hand. The little girl slapped it.

CHAPTER TWENTY-SIX

A half hour later, Rune and Ophelia got off the E train at West Fourth and started walking up Christopher to the water. Rune paused at the West Side Highway, then plunged around the corner.

The houseboat hadn't sunk, but it looked like a load of charred wood dumped onto a black barge. Irregular, glistening slabs of fluted charcoal rose above the deck. A haze of smoke still hung around the pier, and made everything—the houseboat, the debris, the trash cans, the chain-link—appear out of focus. The front of the pier was cordoned off with a yellow police tape, fifty feet in front of where the boat bobbed like a man-o'-war that had lost a sea battle. Rune walked to the tape. She remembered seeing the houseboat for the first time, riding in the Hudson, up north. Flying a Jolly Roger flag next to the FOR SALE sign.

And now, a Viking burial.

She sighed, then waved to the patrolman in the front seat of a blue-and-white. He was a friend of Sam's from the Sixth Precinct, the station where the Bomb Squad was housed. "Hey, Rune."

"Look at this," she called. "Very rude. Totally rude."

"Sorry about it, honey. Some of us'll drive by once in a while, check up on things, just till you get your stuff moved out."

"Yeah, if there's anything left."

There was, but the stink and smoke damage were so bad, she didn't have the heart to go through it. Anyway, Ophelia was restless, and kept climbing on the pilings.

Rune took her by the hand and led her up Christopher Street.

"What's that?" Ophelia asked, pointing at a storefront sign encouraging safe sex. It showed a condom.

"Balloon," said Rune.

"I want one."

"When you're older," Rune answered. The words came automatically, and she decided she was really getting into this kid bit. They continued down Christopher, then along the tail end of Greenwich and turned onto Eighth Street. It had become a lot shabbier in the past year. More graffiti, more garbage, more obnoxious kids. But, God, the shoe stores. More places to buy cheap shoes per square foot than anywhere in the world.

They walked down to University Place, past dozens of chic, black-clad NYU students. Rune made a detour. She pointed to an empty storefront. Above the door was the sign, WASHINGTON SQUARE VIDEO.

"I used to work there," she told Ophelia. The little girl peered inside.

In the window was another sign, on yellow cardboard. FOR RENT NET LEASE.

Just like my life, she thought. *For Rent Net Lease.*

They walked to Washington Square Park and bought hotdogs, then kept walking south, through SoHo, and into Chinatown.

"Hey," Rune said suddenly, "want to see something neat?"

"Yeah, neat."

"Let's go look at some octopusses."

"Yeah!"

Rune led her across the street to a huge outdoor fish market on Canal. "It's like the zoo, only the thing is the animals don't move so much."

Ophelia didn't buy it, though.

"Pukey," she said about the octopus, and she got yelled at by the owner of the stand when she poked a grouper.

Rune looked around and said, "Oh, hey, I know where we are, come on. I'll show you something totally audacious. I'll teach you some history, and when you start school you can blow everybody away with how much you already know."

"Yeah. I like history."

They walked down Centre Street past the black Family Court Building. (Rune glancing across the square at the Criminal Courts Building, and thinking of Randy Boggs. She looked away quickly.) In a few minutes they were in front of the New York Supreme Court at 60 Centre.

"This is it," Rune announced.

"Yeah." Ophelia looked around.

"Five Points. A hundred years ago, this was the worst area in all of Manhattan. This is where the Whyos hung out."

"What's a Whyo?"

"A gang, the worst gang that ever was. Worse than trolls and orcs and dragons. . . . I'll read you a bedtime story about them some night."

"I like books."

Rune remembered that her present copy of *New York Gangs* was now just a cinder, and wondered where she could get a new one. She said, "The Whyos were really tough. You couldn't join them unless you were a murderer, and they even printed up a price list, you know, like a menu, for how much it cost to stab somebody or shoot him in the leg, or kill him."

"Yuch," said Ophelia.

"Oh, and you hear all about Al Capone and Dutch Schultz, right?"

Ophelia said, "Uh-huh. Dutchells."

"But they weren't anything compared with the Whyos.

Danny Driscoll was the leader. There's this great story about him. He was in love with a girl named Beezy Garrity—isn't that a great name? I'd like to be named Beezy."

"Beezy."

"And this rival gang dude, Johnny somebody or another, fell in love with her too. Danny and him had this duel in a dance hall up the street. They pulled out guns and blasted away—" Rune fired a couple shots with her finger. "Blam, blam! And guess who got shot?"

"Beezy."

Rune was impressed. "You got it." Then she frowned. "Danny was pretty bummed by that, I'd guess, but it got worse, because they hanged *him* for killing her. Right over there," Rune pointed. "That's were the Tombs were. The old Criminal building. Hanged him right up." She dropped her head to her shoulder and stuck her tongue out, mimicking a hanged corpse.

Well, now she'd have plenty of time to do her story about gangs. She wished she'd done that story in the first place. *They* wouldn't have lied to her. Nope, Slops Connolly would no way have betrayed her. They were creeps and scum, but she bet that back then thugs were honorable.

"Come on, honey," Rune said, starting toward Mulberry Street. "I'll show you where English Charley started the last big fight the Whyos were ever in. You want to see?"

"Oh, yeah. Whyos're crazy fun."

Rune stopped and bent down and hugged the girl. Ophelia hugged back, squeezing with just the right amount of strength that Rune needed just then. The little girl broke away and ran to the corner. A woman in a business suit, maybe a lawyer on break from Housing Court, crouched down and said to Ophelia, "Aren't you a cute one?" Rune joined them, and the woman looked up and said, "She's yours?"

And as Rune started to say she was just looking after her, Ophelia said, "This's Mommy."

Rune stared at the girl for a moment, then said, "That's me."

Randy Boggs laughed out loud. The man sitting in the seat next to him, on the Atlanta-bound Greyhound bus, glanced his way, but must have been a seasoned traveler. He kept mum, knowing that some things you just didn't respond to. Not on a bus, not in north Georgia.

What Boggs was laughing at was the memory of Lynda's astonished face as they walked out of the restaurant and he handed her fifty dollars, telling her to get on home, and don't go back in that bar if Tom Cruise himself was in there offering to take her to Bermuda. "Uh-huh," she said. "Why?"

"Because," Boggs answered and kissed her forehead.

"You don't wanna?"

"Nope."

He collected his bag, and she gave him a drive to the Charlottesville bus station, which was a ways away, but not so far that fifty dollars didn't buy the trip. He thanked her and trotted off to wait at the terminal for the bus that would eventually get him to Atlanta.

It had been the Men's Colony thing.

The California State Men's Colony at San Luis Obispo.

Funny that Nestor, knowing that Boggs was Inside and all, knowing intimately *why* Boggs was Inside, funny that he'd never mentioned he'd served time. It'd be natural for him to tell Boggs what it was like. Maybe brag a little. Ex-cons always did that.

But what was stranger still was that Jack Nestor had

been in the same prison, at the same time, as Juan Ascipio.

Okay, could have been a coincidence. But if Nestor
wanted something to happen to Boggs in Attica, Ascipio
would have been a good choice for an accident.

An accident that killed Severn Washington, and was
then looking to kill Boggs.

Okay, first, the Obispo thing. Second, the way the witness, Frost, had died. And then the tape of Rume's story
disappearing. . . .

Now, no coincidence. No way.

Here he'd done right by Nestor, never said a goddamn
word the entire time he was in. Randy Boggs being a
stand-up guy, and look what happened. Betrayed.
Somvabith. . . .

The bus rocked around a turn fast and he felt less angry. Boggs smiled. It wasn't as good as a car, but it was
still movement. Movement taking him away from Attica
and toward a pile of money.

He laughed again, and said to the man, "I love buses,
don't you?"

"Be all right, I guess."

"Be damn all right," Boggs said.

Whoa, a fire.

Jack Nestor, back on Christopher Street, looked at the
charred wreckage of the houseboat. He leaned on a brick
building next to the highway and wondered what it
meant. He played with it some. Okay, if she'd been inside, still tied up when it happened, she'd be dead and
fuck it, he could leave. But it was also possible that somebody would've seen the fire and come to help her.

Or maybe she'd moved, and some asshole just torched
the place.

A lot of questions, no answers.

So Boggs the prick was gone.

And now the girl was gone too.

Damn. Jack Nestor lit a cigarette, and leaned up against the brick, wondering what to do next.

The answer, he decided, was to wait.

He hadn't slept well the night before. The pictures again, always the pictures. They'd wakened him, and he lay in bed, thinking, now that he was going to have to kill Randy, he wanted to find something to resent about him. There wasn't much. He wasn't a nigger, a fag, a spic. . . . He didn't insult you, he didn't go after your woman. . . . All he was was a loser, and that made Nestor pity him more than anything.

A drifter and a loser.

Nestor's hand went to his stomach and he squeezed the glossy scar. The imaginary itching crawled around in his belly somewhere.

Boggs wasn't like the girl, who he could do in a minute. Kid or no kid. Boggs was somebody he'd drunk with. Somebody he'd broken bread with. Somebody who hadn't snitched when he could have. That counted for something.

One hour passed, then two. Nestor was pretty comfortable. It was a mild April night, too mild for New York, and the sky was lit by this eerie glow you couldn't tell where it came from. All the streetlights, probably. And headlights from cars, and taxis, and office buildings and stores . . .

He was getting hungry. Salivating. The feel of the gun did it. It was the same sense, the weight, the presence, as if he were carrying a one-pound T-bone steak. He wanted to grab it and tear it apart, feeling the fibers give under his teeth.

And then, just as he was about to go get a burger, there she was.

He squinted. Yep, it was her, dressed in those weird clothes of hers—black miniskirt, boots, a black jacket and a weird floppy hat, silly looking, like they wore during the French Revolution. Over her shoulder was a large bag, but she was nice enough to set that down and stand with her hands on her hips looking at the boat, shaking her head. She walked forward and sifted through some of the burnt junk on the pier, kicking it absently. She walked to the yellow police DO NOT CROSS tape, and stood with her hands on it.

Nestor took the gun from his jacket pocket and looked around him. No one else was on the street. The sun was going down fast, a huge wad of orange fire, sinking, directly in front of him. He could see it disappearing, inch by inch into the Palisades behind the charred skeleton of the houseboat.

Nestor aimed. He kept both eyes open; he didn't squint. It was a seventy-five-yard shot, and he wished he had a stock and butt piece, but he leaned into the brick, crooked his arm and set the pistol in the V between his bicep and forearm. He aligned the sights and lifted it a millimeter to account for the distance. There was no wind.

He held his breath.

Complete stillness.

Then: The last streak of orange merged with the earth.

A car sped past and honked.

The girl turned.

Jack Nestor fired two fast shots, whose sharp cracks spread across the water and echoed in the Jersey-side banks of the Hudson.

He'd aimed for her back first, then her head, and was pleased when he saw two hits. The first one struck her body somewhere high, and was probably a lung shot, if not a heart. The second caught her in motion. He wasn't sure where it hit, but seemed to be the temple. He saw a puff, like smoke, around her face. Only the mist was red. She dropped to the ground like a puppet with cut strings.

One car braked to a screaming stop, and others did too.

Nestor slipped the gun into his belt and got into his car. He felt immense satisfaction. Suddenly he was no longer in a hurry to leave town. He found his mouth was filled with saliva and he rolled down the window, lifted his head back like a rearing horse, and let go a long tail of spit.

The only problem: He suddenly found that his hunger had come back double. He started the car and decided he was going to eat the biggest rib dinner he could find in this goddamn town.

CHAPTER TWENTY-SEVEN

At first, Randy Boggs thought he'd been cheated.

He'd never had a good relationship with banks. Although he'd never robbed any, several Georgia and Florida institutions (some, with the word *Trust* in the names, no less) had foreclosed on houses after his father had missed various numbers of mortgage payments. ("Son, the phone rings, you ask who it is, and he says he's from a bank, you tell him Daddy's out and'll call back soon's he gets home. You hear?")

So he was predisposed to be suspicious.

Then, when the pretty girl behind the window counted out the bills, then counted them out again, he looked at the ten tiny piles of green so crisp they looked like plastic blocks and thought in panic they'd kept most of the money for a fee or something.

She looked at his expression and asked, "Is everything all right?"

He picked up a block and riffled through one, and relaxed considerably. Each stack contained ten thousand dollars in hundreds. He held one close, staring. Looked right at Ben Franklin, who stared back with that weird Mona Lisa smile, looking calmly over Boggs's shoulder, like it was as natural for him as for anyone to be holding a fortune.

A warm feeling dropped right through Randy Boggs, a feeling that wasn't much different from when he slept with a girl for the first time.

"Kind of thought a hundred thousand'd be a bigger pile."

"Y'all got it in nickels and dahms, I bet it'd be pretty sizable then."

"Yes, ma'am."

"Y'all want an escort? Lahk a guahd or anything?"

"No, ma'am."

He left the interest he'd earned—Nestor'd been right about that—in the account, just so he didn't start a panic at the bank or arouse too much suspicion, and walked outside into the dripping heat.

He wandered around in downtown Atlanta for an hour. He was astonished at the changes. It was clean and landscaped. He laughed at the number of streets with the name Peachtree in them. He laughed at the street named Boulevard. This was a town where it seemed you could laugh at something like that and nobody would think you were crazy—as long as you eventually stopped laughing and went about your business. Boggs went into a luggage store and bought an expensive black-nylon backpack because he'd always wanted one, something made for long-distance carrying. He slipped the money and his change of shirt into the bag, which put him in mind of clothes. He passed a fancy men's store, but felt intimidated by the fancy mannequins. He walked on until he found an old-time store, where the styles were bulky and the fabrics mostly polyester and the colors mostly brown and beige. He bought a tan off-the-rack suit and a yellow shirt, two pairs of black-and-red argyle socks, and a striped tie. He thought this might be too formal for a lot of things, so he also bought a pair of double-knit brown slacks and two blue short-sleeve sport shirts. He thought about wearing the new clothes, and having the man bag his jeans and work shirt. But they'd think that was odd, and they might remember him.

Which probably wouldn't matter at all. So what if they remembered him? He hadn't done anything illegal here.

And so what if they thought he was odd? If he'd been a rich Buckhead businessman who'd decided on a whim to buy some clothes and wear them home, nobody'd think twice.

But he wasn't a businessman. He was a former convict.

Anyway, what he wanted to do was pay quickly, take the clothes in the beige bag with the store's name in small red letters on the side, and leave. And that was what he did.

He walked into the Hyatt hotel and strolled past the fountains. Boggs had always loved hotels. They were places of adventure. Where nothing was permanent. He liked the meeting rooms, where every day there was a new group of people, learning new things for their jobs or maybe learning a new skill, like real estate investing or learning to become Mary Kay pink-Buick saleswomen. Every guest in a hotel stayed there because they were traveling. And a traveling person, Randy Boggs knew, was a happy person.

He went into the washroom on one of the banquet room levels, and in a pristine stall, changed into his suit. He realized then that he was still wearing his beat-up loafers with the 1943 steel penny in the slit on the top. He wished he'd gotten some new shoes. Something fancy. Maybe alligator skin or snakeskin would have been good. He'd do that this afternoon. He looked at himself in the mirror and was pretty satisfied. He needed more color; he was pretty pale, and he didn't like his hair. He'd been watching people on the street and very few men wore it slicked back the way he did. They wore it bushier and drier. So, after lunch: a haircut too.

He walked out of the john and into the coffee shop. He was seated, and the waitress brought him an iced tea without him saying a word. He'd forgotten about this Southern custom. He ordered his second steak since he'd been Outside—a sandwich on garlic bread—and this one, along with the Michelob that went with it, was much better than the first. Boggs considered this his first real meal of freedom.

By three he'd bought his new shoes and had himself a new hairstyle, and was thinking of taking MARTA out to the airport. But the hotel held an intense, gleaming attraction (he felt like a kid who'd just found a new bone-handled hunting knife still in its tooled sheath). Boggs decided to stay the night. He checked in.

He asked for a room close to the ground.

"Yessir. Not a problem, sir."

He tried out the room, and the bed, and felt comforted by the closeness of the walls. He realized only then that he'd been uncomfortable in the spaciousness of Atlanta. With their tall, dark canyons of buildings, the streets of New York made him less vulnerable. Here, he'd felt exposed. In the darkened room, he took a nap and then went out for dinner. On the way, he passed an airline ticket office, and went inside.

He walked up to the Pan Am counter, which was the first international airline he saw. He asked the pretty ticket agent what was nice.

"Nice?"

"A nice place to go."

"Uh—"

"Outside of the country."

"Paris'd be beautiful. April in Paris, you know."

Randy Boggs shook his head. "Don't speak the language. Might be a problem."

"Interested in a vacation? We have a vacation service. Lot's of good packages."

"Actually I was thinking 'bout moving." He saw a poster. Silver sand, exquisite blue water crashing onto it. "What's the Caribbean like?"

"I love it. I was to St. Martin last year. Me and my girlfriends had us a fine time."

Man, that sand looked nice. He liked the idea. But then he frowned. "You know, my passport expired. Do you need a passport to go to any of those places?"

"Some countries you do. Some all you need is a birth certificate."

"How would I tell?"

"Maybe what you could do is buy a guidebook. There's a bookstore up the street. You make a right and it's right there."

"Now there's an idea."

He paused for a moment, then quickly asked, "You be interested in having dinner with me?"

She blushed and consulted her computer terminal. Immediately he wanted to retract his words. He'd stepped over some line, something that people on the Outside— people who stay in Hyatt hotels and buy Pan Am tickets —instinctively know all about.

She looked up shyly. "The thing is, I sort of have a boyfriend."

"Sure, yeah." He was as red as a schoolboy's back in August. "I'm sorry."

Her eyes looked startled at his apology. "Hey, nothing is harmed. Nobody ever died from being asked out." He looked at her smile and smiled back and left the office. Thinking, this was going to take a little while.

Thinking too: Man, that was the best sand he'd ever seen.

Sam Healy, sitting on his couch, looked over his lawn as he hung up the phone, and told himself to stand up, but his legs didn't respond. He stayed where he was and watched Ophelia playing with a set of plastic blocks. When Healy was a kid, blocks were made of varnished hardwood and they came in a heavy corrugated card-board box. The ones the little girl was making a castle out of were made of something like Styrofoam. They came in a big clear plastic jar.

Castles. What else would Rune's child build?

Magic castles.

Sam Healy stared at the colored squares and circles and columns, wondering not so much about the toys of his childhood as about the human capacity for violence.

People'd think a Bomb Squad detective would have a pretty tough skin when it came to things like shootings. Hell, especially NYPD, the constabulary for a city with close to two thousand homicides a year. But, Healy'd be fast to tell them, it wasn't so. One thing about bombs: You dealt with mechanics, not with people. Mostly the work was render-safe procedures or postblast investigations, and by the time you got called in, next of kin had been notified and the bodies—or the parts of them—had been wheeled out. A case like that, you were basically a fancy crime scene technician.

That was one of the reasons he'd gone into bomb work, he figured. Maybe a department shrink would be more specific—he'd say something about avoiding a direct confrontation with human tragedy.

But this was one that he couldn't avoid any more.

He stood up and heard a pop in his shoulder—a familiar reminder of a black-powder pipe bomb he'd gotten a little intimate with a couple years back. He paused, glancing at the little girl again, and walked into the rec room, the room he'd been intending to turn into a pool room but he'd never saved up enough money for the kind of table he wanted. He walked across the thick carpet, focusing on the TV, on which was playing some western. Bad color, bad acting. He shut off the set.

"Hey, that dude was about to draw on three bad guys.

Sam, you should watch this stuff. It's like continuing education for you."

He sat down on the ratty green couch and took Rune's hand.

She said, "Oh-oh, what's this? The-wife's-coming-back-to-roost speech? I can deal with it, Sam."

He glanced into the living room to check on Ophelia. After he saw she was contentedly playing, he kept his eyes turned away as he said, "I got a call from the Ops Coordinator at the Sixth. It seems there was a shooting on the pier where your boat was docked."

"Shooting?"

"A girl about your age. Shot twice. Her name was Claire Weisman."

"Claire came back?"

Two fears grabbed her simultaneously, and she hated herself for allowing them both equal time.

Her voice was a whisper as she said, "Oh, my God, no. Is she dead?" Rune's eyes were on Ophelia, playing obliviously, making the castle Rune had suggested she build.

"Critical condition. St. Vincent's. They don't expect her to make it."

"Oh, God. . . ." Rune was crying softly. Then her voice was fading, and she said, "They thought it was me, didn't they?"

"There are no suspects."

She said, "You know who did it, don't you?"

"Boggs and the other guy, the fat one?"

"It has to be them. They came back to kill me." Her eyes were red and miserable. "I—" Her hands closed on her mouth. "I never thought Claire'd come back."

Healy held her, then said, "I'll call it in to the detectives. About the two of them. For a shooting, they'll do a citywide."

"Please," she whispered, "please, please. . . ."

"Her mother's on her way. She's flying down from Boston."

"I've got to go see her."

"I'm on watch in an hour. Come on, I'll drive you there."

"I'm so sorry," Rune said and started to cry again.

The woman, must've been in her late forties, early fifties, didn't know how to respond to the grief, and did the only thing she could think of—putting her arm around Rune's shoulders and telling her to be brave.

She was heavy, with thick ankles that showed under a long blue satiny dress. Her hair was a mix of pure black strands and pure white, which made it look disorganized even though it was sprayed perfectly into place. She held a crushed bouquet, which turned out to be a thin white handkerchief, the kind Rune's grandmother called a hankie. Her face, which was probably always doughy, was now pale and even more puffy from tears.

Rune looked at the bed. It was hard to see Claire. The lights were very dim, as if the doctors were afraid that too much brightness would give her life a chance to get away. Rune leaned forward. Claire's left shoulder and arm were in a huge cast, and the left side of her face was a mass of bandages. Tubes were in her nose, and several others led from a dressing on her neck into jars on the floor. A Hewlett-Packard monitor above her head gave its alarming messages about heartbeats or pulses or breaths or who knew what. The lines were erratic. Rune wished it faced the other way.

Mrs. Weisman kept her eyes on her daughter and said, "Where's Ophelia? Claire said she was staying with you."

"I left her with the nurse. I didn't think it was a good idea for her to see Claire like this."

There was the dense silence of two people who have nothing in common except grief.

After a few minutes, Rune asked, "Do you have a place to stay?"

The woman wasn't listening. She stared at Claire, then a moment later asked, "Do you have any children?"

"Other than Ophelia, no," Rune said.

Mrs. Weisman turned her head at the answer, then looked back at Claire. "Did you tell her anything?"

Rune looked at her blankly.

"Ophelia, I mean. About what happened."

"I said her mommy was sick, and she was going to see her grandmother. She's okay. But she should get some sleep pretty soon."

Mrs. Weisman said, "I'll keep her with me."

Rune hesitated. "Sure."

"Does she have her things with her?"

The clothes *I* bought, she's got. The toys *I* gave her. Rune said, "Claire didn't leave her with much."

Mrs. Weisman didn't answer.

Rune said, "I've got some things to do. Could you like call me if she wakes up?" She wrote Healy's name, address, and phone number on the back of a restaurant receipt she'd found in her purse. "I'm staying here for a while."

She nodded, and Rune wondered if she was hearing the words.

"Who'd do such a thing?" Mrs. Weisman asked vacantly. "Robbery? She didn't look like the kind of girl who'd have a lot of money. Do you think it was like what you hear about in California? You know, where they shoot people on the highway just for the fun of it?" She

shook her head, as if the answer didn't make any difference.

"I don't know," Rune said. If Claire lived, her mother
would find out soon enough what happened. No sense in
long explanations now.

But there *was* something Rune wanted to add. She
wanted so badly to turn to this poor woman and tell her
exactly what she was thinking right now. Which was that
she didn't give a shit about the news story any more, she
didn't give a shit about the Lance Hopper murder. She
cared about one thing, and only that. Finding the two of
them—Randy Boggs and his fat friend—and putting them
both in Attica.

She'd get into the studio somehow and steal her tapes
and notes, get all the details on where Randy'd lived,
where he liked to go, what he hoped to do in the future.
Somewhere in there'd be a clue as to where he was running to right now.

She'd turn it over to the cops.

Or . . .

Maybe not. Maybe there was another answer. One that
blew her away when it occurred to her. But what was
really scary was that the thought didn't blow her away as
much as she knew it should. Didn't blow her away at all,
really, when she saw that Claire might die and her
mother might take Ophelia away to Boston. The more she
thought about it, the clearer it became. As clear as a
double-terminated crystal: She'd kill Boggs and his friend
herself.

CHAPTER TWENTY-EIGHT

The Model wasn't real pleased with the idea.

"The word is Piper wants you drawn and eighthed. Quartered isn't good enough."

"Look, I just need to get into the newsroom."

"I were you, I wouldn't be in the same *city* as Piper Sutton. The same building is a very, very, very bad idea. Very bad."

He was in a good mood. Jolly. Rosy-cheeked, Midwestern, jolly. Rune hated jolly people as much as she hated tall, busty blondes.

They were at Kelly's, a bar on the southern butt end of Columbus Avenue, around the corner from the Network. It couldn't make up its mind whether it wanted to be the home base for yuppies who traded insider information or for IRA sympathizers who argued politics. It looked shabby and smelled yeasty-beer bad.

Rune ordered the Model another martini (a *reporter's* drink).

For Christsake, what does he want? To see me beg?

She asked him again. "Please, pretty please?"

"What for? Tell me what for."

"I can't. It's just really, really important."

"Give me a clue." He speared the olive expertly. Midwesterners are good with martinis.

"You know, that might not be the best question to ask."

"Now that's an honest response. I don't like it, but it's an honest response."

"What's the worst that could happen?" she asked.

"I could get fired, then arrested and then raped by a dozen badass prisoners on Rikers Island."

"You're not going to get fired."

"Then knifed—"

"If anybody asks, I'll tell them I snuck in. I promise. I wouldn't jeopardize your career. I know what it means to you. And to the world." She'd reined in the sarcasm, but even if she'd been a little more blatant, he probably would have missed it.

"Did you see me on *Live at Eleven* the other night?"

"I missed it. My house got incinerated, remember?"

"I got a drug bust. You know, they had all those packets of coke lined up, and then they had the guns and the cash. I got an exclusive interview with the buy-and-bust cop. I talked him into doing the interview. He didn't want to, but I talked him into it as long as we scrambled his face."

"I'll catch it on tape. Did you wear your trench coat?"

"Don't be snide."

"Please, help me out. Just this once."

"You're very persuasive," he said.

"I haven't even started trying yet."

He looked at his watch. "What am I supposed to do?"

"Nothing serious."

"Just distract the guard while you slip in?"

"No, it's a lot easier than that. All you've got to do is deactivate the alarm on the fire door downstairs, open it up, and let me in. Piece of cake."

"Oh, Christ."

The Model poured down the last slug of martini. "Look at it this way," Rune said, "if you do get arrested and sent to Rikers Island, you'll be able to do a great exposé on what life's like in prison." She swallowed the last of her beer. "What an opportunity."

* * *

It didn't go quite the way she'd planned it.

She got in okay. No problem. She even managed to get to her old desk unseen.

The only problem was that someone had beat her there.

Everything about Boggs was gone.

Rune went through every drawer, every shelf of her credenza, every wadded-up Lamston's and Macy's bag under the desk. There was a lot remaining—notes to herself, names and phone numbers exchanged at parties and never followed up on, shopping lists, ideas for stories, possible names for dogs when she got one *(Radcliff, Bonus, Exterminator . . .)*, her clumsily hand-drawn doodles of wizards and fairy-tale characters (including one of Prometheus, breaking free from his rock, which made her want to scream), dozens of the forms the Network required for practically anything, and many more dozens of the memos that people churned out constantly. But there was zip about Randy Boggs. All the files, the background tapes—gone.

Who? Who? Who?

Rune sat at the desk until six P.M., when the first live Network newscast began. Everyone's attention was on the far side of the studio, and Rune walked up to a gaffer, a heavyset man in jeans and a white striped shirt. He wore a Mets cap. He was sipping coffee from a cardboard cup, watching the attractive Oriental anchorwoman deliver a story about the mayor's press conference.

"Hey, Rune," he said, then looked back to the set. "Welcome back."

"Danny, I need some help," she said.

"Help?" he asked.

"You been on set all day?"

"On set?"

"Somebody's gone through my desk. You see who it was?"

He sipped more coffee, avoiding her eyes. "I'm off shift."

"Danny."

He stared at the newscaster, whose short-cut hair shone under the lights like a blue-black jewel. He sighed. "I saw."

"Who was it?"

"Do I have to tell you?"

Rune hesitated for a moment. "Yes," she said.

Where the hell else you gonna get a bankroll like that?

Randy Boggs hadn't been on an airplane in six years, but he was surprised to find that they hadn't changed much. Seemed there were more men flight attendants, and it seemed the food was better, but maybe that was just because of what he'd been eating off metal trays for the past thirty-three months, fifteen days.

Where the hell else?

He'd dozed, and had a dream that he couldn't remember now, and then the weather got rough, and the seat belt sign came on. He didn't like to fly, never had. For one thing—the dry, close air bothered him. But also, they cheated you. Here you were moving at five hundred miles an hour! But what did the airlines do but try their best to fool you into thinking you were in a restaurant and movie theater. Randy Boggs wanted the planes to have picture windows. Man, seeing the clouds go past like they were trees on the interstate!

Randy, okay, lissen up. It's Jack. You okay? You okay? Shit, man, what happened? I was in the courtyard, and this guy comes up to me and he says I know what you're doing, and he starts shouting for the police. He thought I was a dealer, or something, I don't know. Yeah, I had a

*gun, I pulled it out just to keep him quiet, and it went off.
Shit, I couldn't believe it. I just panicked and ran. Why
the hell did you get out of the car? You should've hauled
ass. You should've got the fuck out of town and not worried about me. . . .*

The question was now what to do with the money.
Man, he'd gotten one at last. . . . A nest egg. What his
father called a stake (Randy used to think the old man
meant *steak),* and now that he had one, he was going to
do something with it. Something smart.

Eighty thousand dollars.

*You haven't told them about me? Hey, you're a fucking
okay guy, Randy. A stand-up guy. Lissen up, I've been
humping streets for a week putting something together,
and I got no right to ask, but I'd like to make you a deal,
buddy. You interested?*

Boggs was thinking maybe a clothing store. He'd really
enjoyed going into that place in Atlanta. He liked the
smell—he figured it was after-shave—and he liked the
even rows of clothes on the chrome racks. He liked the
way the men who worked there stood with their arms
folded, standing in front of the shiny counters. If it was
slow, you could wander outside into the warm weather
and pace the sidewalk. He wondered how much it would
cost to open a clothing store.

*Okay, Randy, here's what I can do for you. Shit, I wish
it were more, but you take the rap for me on this, you
forget you ever heard the name Jack Nestor, and I'll deposit a hundred thousand dollars into an account for you.
Mail you the passbook. Nobody can get it but you. What
do you say, Randy? I talked to this lawyer and he says
you'll probably walk in four years. A hundred thousand
for four years, well, it ain't a fucking fortune, but it's tax
free, and besides, where the hell else're you gonna get a
bankroll like that?*

Nowhere else.

He'd taken the offer.

He'd never told anyone, not so much because that was the promise he'd made to Nestor, but more because he just didn't know whether taking the rap for a hundred thousand bucks was another dumbass idea like lobster farming, and water filter selling, and computerized sign painting, and Boggs's other bad business ideas. The kind of thing somebody'd listen to and say, "Boy, you out of your shitkicking cracker mind? That's the dumbest thing I ever heard of." And maybe it was. Sure had come close to getting him killed, but on the other hand, he now had eighty thousand dollars in a locker at the Atlanta airport and another twenty thousand dollars in a bag in his lap. He'd even gotten out of prison early, and he'd kept his bargain to Nestor. He'd taken the rap, Nestor's name never came up. And now he was out.

The terrible doubts that tormented him the last six months Inside, those long, long months, seemed vindicated. Maybe, for once, he'd made a good decision.

Eighty thousand. Instead of a store, maybe he could invest the money in the stock market. He felt exhilarated, thinking of himself being driven to work, wearing his tan suit and alligator-skin loafers, riding in an elevator up to some penthouse office on Wall Street.

His father's advice: Lissen up, young man, you paying attention? You're not, I'll tan your hide. Come here, son, come here. Listen to your old man.

Don't work for any other man. . . .

Don't lien on the house. . . .

Don't be me. Don't be me, son. Don't be me. . . .

Eighty thousand dollars.

But there was a reason he was thinking about making good investments, versus all the times he'd made bad ones. Because he felt that he was about to make a bad one right now, and yet here he was flying right toward it, right toward his bad judgment again.

Lord, Lord, Lord, why do I do this to myself?

Because he wasn't headed toward the Bahamas, but right smack back to Manhattan.

Going to do something stupid. To give Severn Washington's family ten thousand dollars, and Rune and that little girl another ten.

Lying awake in the wonderful hotel bed the night before, a bed so wide and soft it was like a swimming pool, he kept thinking about her. About what he'd done. About using her.

He didn't think of it in terms of right or wrong. He tried to think back to the Baptist creed, but there was nothing about thou shalt not use people to get your ass out of prison. This was more something he knew instinctively he had to do. It was what kept him quiet about Nestor even before he knew the man would pay him all that money. It was what kept him quiet about Ascipio and the glass knife. You just were that way, or you weren't, and if you were, you had to live with the consequences. One of which was going back like a crazy person to do what had to be done.

So, no choice, really.

He'd give her the ten. Apologize to her.

That sounded so funny. He thought the word slowly, in syllables. Uh-pol-o-gize. . . . But what else could he do?

The plane banked, the engines slowed to a growl, and the steward announced their descent for landing at La-Guardia. Randy Boggs looked down. He believed he saw a beach, but he wasn't sure. He squinted. The moonlight was pale, but it was for certain a beach, though the sand wasn't silver and the waves didn't crash on it in explosions of surf.

*　*　*

Turned out, she didn't need an accomplice after all.

Rune knew there were only two hard parts about breaking into a place: A, if you didn't want anybody to know you were doing it, and B, if you didn't want anybody to know you had done it.

Tonight, the Network's personnel department was empty.

Count one, okay.

And if she found what she thought she was going to, so much was going to hit the fan so fast, that a little thing like a broken lock wasn't even going to be noticed.

This wasn't espionage, it was a frontal assault.

Rune used a letter opener and fire hose nozzle to break the locks out of two file cabinets. Then, she found the bulky file, looked at it briefly, and trotted out with it under her arm.

At an all-night coffee shop in Queens, she ordered take-out: a Greek salad, extra anchovies, and a large apple juice. (Which reminded her of Ophelia and made her feel lonely. She canceled the juice and got coffee; a better idea anyway, she decided.) She walked to Sam's house. It was dark. He was on watch this evening. She sat at the kitchen table. She opened the file and began reading. Her appetite faded by the time she'd finished the watery, salty cubes of feta cheese. But she drank all the coffee. Then she looked up, squinting, walked to the phone and got Lee Maisel's number from Directory Assistance. She punched the numbers in, noticing only then that it was midnight.

Wondering if she was going to wake him up.

She did.

He sounded disoriented, and his voice cracked. He cleared it. "Yes, hello?"

"Lee, it's Rune. I've got to talk to you. It's like an emergency."

"Are you all right?"

"I've got to talk to you."

"You're okay?"

"I'm all right. I found out something about Lance Hopper's killing. It wasn't an accident. Randy and that other man were hired to kill him."

"What are you talking about?" The voice was sharper now; his mind was in gear. A journalist probing for facts.

"It was like a professional hit."

"But who'd want Lance dead? Was it the Mafia or something?"

Now it was Rune's voice that cracked, and the reason it did had nothing to do with being tired. She coughed, then said, "It was Piper."

CHAPTER TWENTY-NINE

He didn't laugh.

Rune heard rustling of cloth, she heard his breath. She pictured Maisel sitting up, putting his feet on the floor, feeling for slippers. Pulling a paisley robe from the foot of the bed.

"What?"

"Piper hired them to kill Lance."

Again, a pause. He was waiting. She heard him clear his throat, then cough. "This isn't funny."

"It's true, Lee."

"Come on, Rune. Why would she want him dead?"

"Somebody took all the Randy Boggs files and tapes out of my desk today."

"They did?"

"Danny Turner, the head electrician, told me it was Piper."

"She did?"

Rune said, "And remember, she didn't want to do the story in the first place, she tried to get me to stop? She was going to send me to London? To get rid of me."

Maisel barked, "What I was asking was why she'd want Lance Hopper dead?"

"Because he was going to fire her. I went through her personnel file—"

"You what? How?"

"I just did. . . . Anyway, I went through it, and you know what she did? He tried to fire her once. She filed two EEOC complaints against him in the year before he died. They were both settled, but there's lots of memos. They carried on this raging war."

"Rune, people don't kill people for jobs."

"Maybe not normal people, but you know Piper. What about her temper? You told me that her job was her whole life. And how much does she make? A million a year? That's enough to kill somebody for."

"How is she going to find killers? This is just too—"

"What were some of her assignments?" Rune let her words rest for a minute. Okay, I'm a little dramatic now, sure. But he's hooked. I can tell. She continued, "In Africa, in Nicaragua."

He considered this. He was less skeptical than before when he said, "She could have met some mercenaries, is that what you're saying?"

Rune felt like a juggler. It was tough to keep all the parts of the story in the air at once. It was too complicated. Her hands were sweating. "When I interviewed Randy, he said that he'd been somewhere in Central America. It was the only time he'd been out of the country. Piper must have met him then. Oh, and then . . ." Her leg vibrated with nervous energy. ". . . and then the new witness died? It wasn't an accident at all. Piper knew his name. She saw it from my story. She sent that fat guy to kill him. And then what happens? All the cassettes disappear. And she knew where I'd put the duplicate cassette of Frost. And she'd know how to get into the computer and steal the master."

There was a faint tapping from the other end of the line. Rune pictured the tip of Maisel's pencil bouncing on the pad he probably kept on his nightside table. She could feel his concentration as he weighed her words, the excitement reporters must feel when they first sniff a lead. When he spoke, it was almost as if to himself. "And she was pretty smooth when she ad-libbed the broad-cast."

Rune said, "Like she'd known all along she was going to do it."

A long pause. "Time out. Time out. This is a nuclear bomb we're playing with. You've got a lot of speculation."

"Look, think about it, Lee. They kill one witness, then they shoot my friend, thinking it's me. If Boggs killed Hopper by himself, why would all these other things be happening? Why would they go to all the trouble to use me to get Randy out of prison? There's something else going on. And I know what it is. It's that Piper Sutton is a murderer."

"Just let me ask you one thing. You're bitter because Piper fired you, and ruined your story. If that hadn't happened. If you were an objective reporter, if you didn't know anyone involved, would you still be coming down the same way?"

She was ready for that. She'd thought about it. And so she could answer without hesitating. "Yep. I'm sure it's the truth."

He said, "Jesus. How are we going to handle it? I'll have to call Dan Semple. . . ." His voice was fading.

Rune asked, "What?"

Maisel whispered, "Semple . . ."

It burst into her thoughts like a firecracker. "I've seen them together. Oh, my God. You think him too?"

"They had an affair, you know. Piper and him. Around the time Hopper was killed."

Rune said, "After Hopper was killed, Semple got his job!"

"Oh, God . . ."

"What are we going to do, Lee?"

Maisel said, "Okay, I'm calling Jim Eustice, getting him over here now. We'll tell the parent, the legal department.

Then, the cops, I guess. We'll have to do the story ourselves and preempt the competition. Otherwise it'll look
like we're trying a cover-up."

He was almost talking to himself, planning, thinking
about who he was going to contact, what he was going to
say, who was going to do the story. . . . She felt hurt, as
if he was snatching her idea away from her. But his next
sentence brought around her attention. "I'll want you to
be lead reporter."

"Wow, Lee, are you like serious? Oh, I'll do a super-
fantastic job. I'll write up my notes. . . ."

"What the hell time is it?" he asked. "Shit. We've got to
get moving. I'll call Eustice and get him and a crew over
here now. Can you be here in an hour? If we really hustle,
we can get it on *Wake Up With the News.*"

His voice faded, and Rune understood that in the excitement of the journalistic bloodlust, he'd forgotten exactly what they were saying. Piper Sutton was somebody
he'd worked with for a long time, somebody that—whatever else you could say about her—he respected. Or had
once respected.

Maisel said, "This's a son of a bitch. . . ." There was a
pause, during which he might have been sighing. And
that was the only emotion he showed. Instantly, he was
Edward R. Murrow again. "You did a good job, Rune. . . .
Okay, let's get moving, I've got some phone calls to make.
Be here as soon as you can." Then she heard his voice,
soft, as if he was speaking through a fog. "Some shit is
about to land."

He hung up.

Randy Boggs stood looking at the burnt hull of the
houseboat. His heart beat furiously, and then his hands
were shaking. God, had Nestor put fire to the place while

Rune and the baby were in there? Tied up, feeling the flames come closer and closer? Lord above . . .

Boggs looked at the black hull, the terrible contrast the yellow police-line tape made in the darkness. Brilliant strips of neon fluttering in the breeze. He smelled a terrible stench. It was wood and rubber, but might also be flesh. There was a wet cardboard sourness about it. He thought he might be sick.

He saw a bar behind him. A gay bar, it looked like. He paused at the door, then walked in. He shook his head when the bartender asked him what he wanted, then asked, "What happened? To the girl who lived there?"

"You know her?"

"Sort of."

The thin young man, wearing a black shirt open to his tight jeans, seemed to be trying to figure out what *sort of* meant to Boggs. He must have concluded that it didn't mean much because he said, "She got shot. Yesterday. I don't know anything about it more'n that. They took her to St. Vincent's."

"And the little girl?"

"I don't know anything about a little girl."

"Where would that be?"

"What's that?"

"The hospital? St.? . . ."

"Vincent's." The bartender gave him directions, the last of which were delivered almost at a shout; Boggs was already walking fast out the door.

"The girl who was shot down by the pier?"

The nurse didn't know who it was. She called to another nurse. "Who's the shooting? The girl?"

Randy Boggs said, "Her name's Rune."

"First or last?"

But the other nurse called out, "She's in eight-oh-five. Her name's Claire Weisman."

The desk nurse said, "What name did you say?"

Boggs answered, "All I ever call her by is her nickname. How is she?"

"You'll have to ask the floor nurse. Are you family?"

"Her brother."

"It's not visiting hours."

"I just flew up."

"You from Texas?"

"Atlanta."

A second nurse said, "Your mother's up there already. We let her stay. I think it'd be okay if you went up."

"My mother," Boggs said. "Thank you, ma'am. Which way'd that be?"

"Take the elevator. Over there."

Upstairs, he found a stocky woman in a dark dress sitting in the room. Boggs stopped, blinked. He checked the room again, then said, "Are you Rune's mother?"

She rose. "Lillian Weisman. Rune's not here. Was her mother coming to visit Claire?"

"I'm not sure, ma'am." Staring at the bed. A lot of bandages. Man, a ton of bandages, and the face half-covered, but, no, damn—this time there was no flood of calm. This time his heart gave a huge gallop. It wasn't Rune.

The woman's face was tracked with exhaustion. "Are you a friend of Claire's?"

He was frowning, looking at the young woman, terribly bandaged. He kept squinting. "I'm a friend of Rune's."

"She was here a little while ago. She had an errand, then she was going back home."

Ophelia woke up. She rubbed her eyes, looked at Boggs, and remembered the playacting from Megler's office. She mumbled "Daddy."

Her grandmother glanced down at the girl and said, "What did you say, honey?"

"Uh," Randy Boggs said.

"Daddy."

The woman leaned forward. "You're hungry, darling?"

"Uh," Randy Boggs said. "Cute little girl." Ophelia pointed at him, but before she could say anything else, Boggs said, "Juice?"

Her face opened in a huge smile. "I want some juice, Grandma."

Boggs said, "I'll send in a nurse." He edged toward the door. "Where did you say Rune was going?"

"That friend of hers."

"Which friend would that be?"

"Sam Healy, I think. In Queens. Here's the address."

He memorized it. "Well, I hope your daughter does okay, ma'am. I hear tell this's supposed to be a good hospital."

As Boggs eased into the corridor, he heard Ophelia say, "Bye, Daddy."

And Claire's mother ask, "What did you say, honey?"

The thought occurred to Rune just after she hung up with Maisel, and she wasn't very happy about it.

What was she going to wear?

You do documentaries, and the only person who sees you is the person you're interviewing. You can wear miniskirts with dinosaurs, or stretch pants and T-shirts or spandex. Nobody ever knows or cares. But you do TV news, and bang you're in front of an Ikegami and a set of lights and ten million people are staring at you.

She didn't even own a trench coat.

And, oh, hell, her hair. The last time she'd used hair spray was when she and a girlfriend got dressed up and went out together, to gorge on ice cream because they hadn't been asked to the junior-high spring dance. Now, she'd have to get her hair all solid and curled under, the way anchorwomen did. She ran into the bathroom. Sam didn't have much hair; why would he have hair spray?

She found some. Rune undid the elastic band that held her ponytail and shook her hair loose, then sprayed on a good dose of Final Net. She tried the sideways sweep that she'd seen in her mother's high school graduation pictures.

It didn't take. Four sticky clumps fell into her face.

More spray.

That pretty much held it in place, but it also changed the color from auburn to more of a burnt sienna, the same as those brown Crayolas that she threw out right away because she hated the shade.

Then tufts on the side were sticking out from above her ears. Yuch. This isn't working. . . .

More spray. She started to cough.

Rune opened the window.

That was why she saw Randy Boggs getting out of a taxicab in front of the house.

The spray fell to the floor. She stepped back and swept the light switch down. The room turned eerie, lit from other parts of the house.

He'd come back to get her. He'd heard that he'd shot the wrong person, and here he was now, come back to get her. Through the open window, she heard his footsteps on the narrow sidewalk leading up to the house. Rune dropped to her knees, then crawled into the living room, she reached up to the wall and shut the light out, thinking just as she finished: No, no, no . . . What a stupid thing to do. Now he knew someone was home.

A knocking. She could see the outline of his face, peering through the small triangular window in the center of the door.

"Rune, hello?"

The phone was across the room, and another one beyond that in the kitchen. To reach one, she'd have to crawl past him. He'd shoot her in the back. Besides, so what if she got through to 911? What good would it do her? This wasn't Manhattan; out here, the cops were probably fifteen, twenty minutes away.

Behind her were the bathroom, with a window too narrow for her to climb out, and the bedroom, which had plenty of windows, but was right next to the front door.

More knocking.

"Rune." The voice still had the pleasant, goddamn lying drawl in it. "I know you're there. Claire's mother—"

The son of a bitch was in her hospital room?

"—told me you were here. I know you're kind of miffed. I want to talk to you."

Bastard. He thinks I'm stupid. He wants me to walk out just like that and he's going to gun me down.

More knocking. Louder. Insistent.

"Come on, Rune. I've got something for you."

I'll huff and I'll puff. . . .

That was when it occurred to her. She crawled backwards into the darkened bedroom.

She heard cracking branches. Boggs had walked away from the doorstep and was circling around the house. He'd be looking for an open door or a window. Rune, on her belly now, crawled toward the bed. Her hair flopped forward and the lash of still-damp spray stung her eyes. She twisted it into a braid and furiously wrapped it with another elastic band.

I'll huff and I'll puff. . . .

A shadow passed the window, then disappeared as Boggs stepped closer to the house. Rune huddled beside the bed. She reached up and opened the bedside table.

Oh, thank you, Lord.

Her hand slipped out of the drawer holding Healy's .38 special Smith & Wesson service revolver. It was in a sweet-smelling leather hip holster. She pulled the gun out, dropping the holster on the carpet. She held it awkwardly, but pistols didn't scare her. The shadow reemerged, and then vanished. Boggs continued his circuit of the house. "Rune, are you there?" she heard him call from the backyard.

She wiped her palm on her skirt and took the gun. She cleared her throat and called, "I'm here." Then: "Randy, come on in. . . ."

Was the back door unlocked? Sam was always forgetting about it. So was she.

It had to be open. Please let it be—

She heard the creak of the door swinging wide, then he was in the kitchen.

"Rune?"

She stood up, surprised at how calm she was. She'd learned enough from Sam to know that this wasn't like Goetz. Anybody breaks into your house, you can pretty much do what you want and the prosecutor isn't going to do diddly to you. Justifiable homicide.

She walked to the darkened doorway and looked across the living room into the hall that led to the kitchen. When Boggs came out, he'd be a perfect silhouette framed by the ugly fluorescent fixture that Sam had been talking about changing.

. . . and I'll blow your house down. . . .

She saw the fuzzy shadows begin to coalesce, as Boggs walked closer to the doorway. Rune lifted the gun. Waiting for her heart to start pounding madly, waiting for a volcanic urge to scream and cry. But no, she felt completely tranquil.

Boggs was walking closer to the door.

She thought of Claire, she thought of Ophelia. . . .

Rune squinted along the black sights of the gun.

Calm.

He stepped into the hallway, looking around him. He couldn't see her.

She thought about the betrayal, about Claire lying wrapped in her ghastly bandages, hovering near death, about how maybe if Ophelia had been with Claire, she'd have been shot too. . . .

She began to squeeze the trigger.

Boggs opened the door to the basement and looked in. "Rune?"

Rune, thinking: I hate you, I hate you, I hate you so much. . . .

She stood that way for a moment. Paralyzed but quivering. Then she lowered the gun and stepped back into the bedroom, leaning up against the wall.

"Rune," the drawling voice called again.

She slipped the gun into the pocket of her miniskirt, backed to the window, and opened it. She scooted up on the sill, then pushed off, and dropped the five feet to the ground, rolling in the soft dirt where she had helped Sam plant bulbs in February.

Then she ran the two blocks to Northern Boulevard, where she found a pay phone. She dialed 911 and told the dispatcher about the break-in.

She'd been wrong about the twenty minute part. Maybe it was because she'd told them it was a cop's house. She didn't know if that gave it special priority or something. But in any event she'd just stepped into the big street to look for a cab, when a blue-and-white went tearing the wrong way up a one-way street, toward Healy's house.

No cabs, but an old bus pulled up just as she reached the bus stop. She climbed on board, sat in the first seat, and began counting out change.

* * *

Lee Maisel said, "You're late."

He closed the door behind her.

"Well, I kind of had this, like, problem," Rune said, then thinking that out of spite, she was going to work a *like* into her broadcast, and hope that Piper Sutton heard it.

"What happened?"

"I almost got killed."

Maisel looked at her with his keen eyes. He was fully dressed now, and completely awake, full of energy. For a big man, a middle-aged man, he had great energy. "What happened?"

Rune saw the bar, and said, "You mind if I have a drink?"

"Go right ahead. Name your poison."

She'd been drinking fuzzy navels a lot recently, a peachy orange thing, but that wasn't what a real reporter ought to be drinking. "What do you have?"

"How about Scotch? I've got MacCallum. Twenty years old."

"Good, that's my usual."

"On the rocks?"

"With Coke."

"Coke?"

"Or Pepsi. Whatever you've got."

"How about just with club soda?"

"Sure. That's good too."

Maisel poured the drink, and handed it to her. She hated Scotch. He poured two other drinks. "Come on, we're meeting in the study." He led the way. She followed.

"Who's here already?"

"You're the second."

Maisel took both glasses in one hand and opened the

door. He put his free hand on Rune's shoulders and escorted her over the threshold.

Jack Nestor, sitting in a red-leather high-back chair, looked at Rune closely and nodded. "There you go, Lee, she looks just like the other one. No wonder I made a mistake."

CHAPTER THIRTY

Like the time she had three frozen margaritas, crazy drunk—her mind giddy and spinning, her body sick.

There was no place to go, if she'd even had the strength to get past Maisel, which she didn't. He closed the door and leaned against it. He sighed. She'd never seen a man's face look this clouded and dark.

Her mind was racing, trying to pin down the speculation. "It was you?" she whispered.

Nestor stood up suddenly, moving fast for a big man, and lifted the glass out of her hand. He smiled in a snotty way, and said to Maisel, "Could be a weapon, you know. I've heard about people doing nasty things with a glass."

"You bastard," Rune hissed at him.

He ignored her and sat down. He wore a short-sleeved striped shirt and gray baggy pants and some kind of rounded, scuffed brown work shoes. He looked her over, then picked up his drink.

"Sorry, Rune, I'm so sorry." Maisel gave her a grim smile, but disappointment and disgust overwhelmed it. He swallowed, then blew air slowly out through his rounded cheeks. Rune could see he was suffering. It pleased her. "You killed Hopper?"

Maisel poured his drink down in one swallow. "I don't know what to say to you. I tried to stop it all without hurting you. I stole the tapes. . . ."

Nestor said, "Yeah, he's right. We tried to ice Boggs in prison. That would've solved—"

"You tried to . . ." Rune looked at Maisel; he wouldn't meet her eyes.

He said, "Why did you keep at it?"

"It wasn't Piper? But she did everything she could to stop the story."

"She's a Network politician. The story would've been bad for her. She didn't want it to run, but she wasn't going to stop it."

"But you encouraged me."

"I had to control you. If I'd told you, no, you would've gone somewhere else. Maybe another station. The story would've run, and they would've found me."

Rune said to Maisel, "Why did you do it?"

"You really curious? You really care?"

She was suddenly abrasive, Piper Sutton tough. "It doesn't matter to me. It might to the police. Remember my boyfriend's a cop. He's waiting downstairs. If you don't let me—"

Nestor was sitting up, frowning.

Maisel shook his head. "She's got a vivid imagination." He walked to the window and looked down. Then he frowned. "Shit, actually I do see somebody."

Nestor said, "Let me go look."

"Uh-uh. I don't want you to be seen here. Better for me to go."

He walked to the door and disappeared.

Nestor kept staring at her.

"Don't touch me," she said. "I'll kill you."

And he just laughed, as if touching her were the last thing in his mind.

"Why?" she asked.

"Why what?"

"Did you kill Hopper?"

He shrugged and frowned. She was asking a stupid question. "That's what I do. I'm a professional soldier. I got hired."

"But why did Lee hire you?"

" 'Causa what happened in Beirut."

"What was that?"

"You know Lee's big scoop a few years back?"

She remembered his Pulitzer.

Nestor looked around toward the closed door. "Mercenaries and journalists hang out a lot together in combat zones. Isn't much difference between them, really, you think about it. Anyway, word was that he was over the edge. A has-been. He'd lost his nerve, and was really into the bottle. All he'd do was sit around and talk about how great he'd been in Nam or Angola or Nicaragua. People were starting to laugh at him. It was only a matter of time until he was fired. But then he gets this big story, about a plot to blow up the American University. It was, what do you guys say, a scoop? Suddenly he's hot again. Nobody else got the story, and he's a hero because the Marines beefed up security, and that scared off the terrorists.

"Then after he gets the award, they brought him back to New York, and eventually he takes over that show of yours. Then I go off to Sri Lanka, and come back to California, where I do some funny stuff that lands me in Obispo for a while, doing easy time. When I get out, Lee calls me and flies me into town to talk to him.

"He's one nervous dude. He's talking to me about hiring somebody. . . . They always do that. It's never 'you' and 'me'; it's always 'somebody.' He asks me about hiring somebody to threaten somebody. Around Robin Hood's barn, you know. And finally I say, 'Lee, you want me to ice somebody, fucking say so. Here's how much it'll cost, here's how I want payment, just like that. He says he was just talking about threatening somebody, and I tell him you can't ever just lean on anybody and expect that to be enough. He shits, and I go to Florida and don't hear from him for a while, then he calls me again and wants to talk some more. Turns out this guy Hopper was looking for ways to cut costs and is looking over everybody's performance the past couple years, and then he comes to Lee, and keeps going over and over the Beirut story."

Nestor took a tiny sip of the whisky. "Which was fake."

"Lee'd made up the story?"

"The whole ball of wax. He paid some local stringer for footage of missiles and grenades and got this asshole looked like the Sheik of Arabic to recite lines that Lee wrote. He was supposedly an informer, but the guy ran a deli in the Christian quarter. Lee paid him a couple hundred for the whole thing." Nestor sat back. "That was it. Nobody ever found out, and he's still got his million-dollar job."

She sat back in the chair, huddling, her shoulders drawn together. "I'll pay you. I have a lot of money."

"Do you now?"

"How much do you—?"

The door opened, and she thought about running for it. But Nestor would only grab her and pull her to the floor. There was a reason she didn't want that to happen; he might frisk her.

Maisel didn't look good. He was pale and sweating. Beneath his salt-and-pepper beard, you could see his lips pressed together. He said, "There's nobody there."

She said, "Look, just let me go. I won't say anything to anybody. I promise. Not even about the fake story, or anything."

Nestor gave a short, embarrassed laugh, and Maisel looked at him. "Been doing some talking, huh?"

"Didn't figure it'd matter much now. . . ."

Rune said, "What about Randy?"

"Boggs?" Nestor snorted. "That loser? We set him up. He didn't know anything about the hit. He couldn't kill anybody if he was about to get whacked himself. He lost his job in Maine and called me looking for work on a fishing boat in Florida. I had him meet me in New York. I made up some shit about a credit card deal. Lee and I were going to make it look like he hit Hopper, then I'd waste him, and leave the gun. A few loose ends, but basically there's a perp and there's a vic, so the DA's happy. But the son of a bitch managed to walk right into a cop car. Well, he doesn't know what we'd planned, so he plays stand-up guy and doesn't turn me in."

Lee said, "We paid him a hundred thousand to take the rap for a few years. He agreed."

Nestor said, "Everything was going along fine, but then I read in the paper about you. So I come to town and talk it over with Lee. We try to make the story go away, and in the meantime I have this asshole buddy of mine happens to be in Attica try to move on Boggs, but that doesn't work. Then you get him out, and things go to hell. He's got his money, and is gone. And now you know exactly what happened."

The wave passed over her like a fever. Thinking she'd almost shot Randy. He'd come back to warn her, or explain what had happened or ask her to forgive him, and she'd almost shot him. God. . . . She swallowed. "Please let me go. I won't say anything. I don't care about Hopper. Just let me go, please? I'll be quiet about it."

Maisel looked at Nestor, who was shaking his head no in a humorous, exasperated way. "Can't, Lee. You can't trust her."

Maisel said, "Rune, Rune . . ."

She stood up. Nestor's hand slipped into his pocket. Her teeth were pressed together, and she felt anger, hot and searing. Oh, what she wanted to say to him. . . . But the words were logjammed in her mind, and even if she found the strength and the calm to sort them out, she knew he wouldn't comprehend them.

Nestor stirred. She understood. This was his show now. He'd seen Lee weakening, and knew it was time for the pro to take over, before more mistakes were made.

Maisel said, "Jack, I don't think—"

Nestor held up his hand, like a patient school teacher. "It's okay, Lee. I'll take care of it."

Rune said, "No, please, I promise I won't say a word." Her eyes were in Maisel's. He opened his mouth to speak, then looked away, and sat down in his chair.

"Lee!"

Nestor opened the door. "Come on. Car's downstairs."

Then they were in the corridor, walking silently. They got to the elevator, and Rune knew, positively, that when it opened there'd be a crowd of people inside, and then she'd start talking with them, and then when they got out, whatever floor it was, she'd get out with them, and keep them around her. This guy was crazy, probably, but he wasn't crazy enough to shoot a whole car full of people.

Yep, the elevator was coming down, and it stopped on the floor just above theirs. She felt Nestor's hand go into the waistband of her miniskirt and hold her, like a dog on a leash. The way she'd held Ophelia. The door opened.

Empty.

They got in.

Okay, that's the way it was going to be.

She was thinking: When they got downstairs into the street, she'd pull out Sam's gun and just start shooting. She'd aim for his legs, pulling the trigger six times, then just run like hell.

"I really do have a lot of money," she said. "You want ten thousand dollars?"

"No."

"I can get it for you right now."

"No."

"Fifteen?"

"How about fifty?" Nestor said.

"I don't have fifty."

"Well," Nestor said, "you give me fifty thousand cash in the next hour, and I'll let you live. I'll let you walk away."

"I don't have fifty, I can get—"

"Then, it's no deal. Fifty or nothing."

She started to cry, "But I don't have it."

"Tough."

And she saw he was playing with her, and whether she had fifty or a hundred, he wasn't going to let her go. This was business, and the bargain he'd made was with Lee Maisel. Nestor's job was to kill her.

Just before they got to the lobby, Nestor said, "What would it be?"

She looked at him.

"Whatya carrying?"

"I don't know—"

"No, don't tell me. I'll guess a Colt Python, small barrel. Three inch."

"I don't know what you mean?" Her heart was slamming, sweat springing onto her palms.

Nestor said calmly, amused, "You wear a skirt like that, with pockets, it's tough to conceal a piece."

Oh, no . . .

"I know what you're thinking. How come I was so calm? Seeing you sitting upstairs with a gun in your pocket. . . . Little lady, you forget this is my business. I knew you were carrying from the minute you walked into the place. I knew exactly what your face would look like before you reached for it, and I knew exactly where I was going to draw a bead on you before you could get your hand into your pocket. You know, if you hadn't come here with a gun, I might have been willing to let you go, sure, if you'd come up with a decent price. But that gun means I can't trust you."

Suddenly, he pinned her to the wall of the elevator and had the gun out of her pocket. He frowned. "A Smittie. Police issue. Lost my bet."

She put both hands against his chest and pushed him as hard as she could. He stepped back a few inches, then laughed, and hit her in the cheek with the back of his hand, hard. It bobbled her head into the elevator wall and for a moment, she was blinded by the pain.

He put his arm around her shoulders, maybe going to pretend she was drunk if anybody was downstairs waiting for the elevator. But it was three A.M., and there was no one in the lobby. And she knew there'd be no one on the street.

Just like there'd be no one wherever he was taking her. No one to see her die.

CHAPTER THIRTY-ONE

Except for a drunk at the corner, his quart can of Fosters dangling from his hand, the street was empty, shimmering with a light rain that wasn't so much falling as hanging in the air.

Nestor said, "This way," and tugged her east toward a dark block. Ahead of them, on Second Avenue, cabs bounded southward. Horns honked, suspensions clattered.

Maybe there she could tear away and run. Just charge right into traffic and hope for the best. Maybe she'd be lucky the same way Randy Boggs was unlucky and a cop car would be cruising past.

But they didn't get that far.

Nestor stopped at a car. He kept his hand firmly on her shoulder as he reached into his pocket to get the keys.

"Hey," the drunk called. He started staggering in their direction. His head drooped in his stupor, his hair fell down into his face. His cheap suit was drenched from rain and he looked like a straggly mutt. "Change? For something to eat." He was still twenty yards away. "You got some change?"

"Shit. Fucking people in this town," Nestor muttered. He opened the car door. He said to Rune, "I can feel you, honey. You're thinking the guy comes up and he's going to distract me, and then you'll run for it. You think I'm stupid?" He shoved her in the car.

The voice called, "Change, please?"

Nestor, his eyes still on Rune, said to him, "Fuck you."

"Fuck you too, Jack," Randy Boggs said and slammed the Foster can into the side of Nestor's head.

"Run!" Boggs shouted as he grabbed Nestor around the waist and tried to pull him to the sidewalk.

Rune scooted out of the car fast. She hesitated, watching them scuffle. It wasn't a fight. More, they were wrestling. Boggs was gripping Nestor's shoulders, pinning his arms so he couldn't grab the gun. Nestor, blood streaming from his temple, tried to knee Boggs in the groin, but couldn't get his leg up without falling over.

"Run, damn it!" Boggs shouted again.

She did. To the nearest corner, to a phone stand. Hitting 911 as she watched the men, on the ground now, in shadows, a dark squirming mass, half in, half out of the street. She told the calm voice about the fight, about the gun, and by the time she'd hung up, she heard sirens. Distant, but moving in close. She thought she should go back, distract Nestor, hit him with something. But she didn't move. She didn't run away, but she didn't walk closer to them.

Then Rune saw one of them, Nestor she thought, break free and scramble away. The other one leapt into the street. Nestor fired two fast shots at him, just as the first blue-and-white squealed around the corner. The officers were out, shouting like madmen for Nestor to stop, to drop the gun. He fired at the car twice, then turned to run, but he skidded and went down on one knee.

"Drop the weapon," a metallic voice came over the loudspeaker.

Nestor lifted the gun again.

The big sparking explosion of a shotgun was like a thunderclap. Nestor tumbled backwards. He said something inaudible. He tried to get up, muttering. He lay back, his body convulsed once, violently. Then he was still.

* * *

Three squad cars, with lights flashing, screamed to a stop in front of Maisel's building. An EMS ambulance pulled up. Lights went on in windows up and down the block. Windows opened. People began materializing on the street.

Rune ran up to where she'd seen Randy trying to get away from Nestor. Two cops were helping him up, leading him to an unmarked car.

She caught up with them. "You all right?"

"I guess, yeah."

"How—?"

"I followed you. I seen you run from that Mr. Healy's house and get on a bus. I got me a cab and followed you here. Didn't know what you were about, so I waited out here. Had me a beer."

Rune looked at him for a moment. She turned to the detective and said, "There's a man in there, Lee Maisel. Fourteenth floor. He and that guy . . ." She nodded toward Nestor. ". . . were going to kill me. Don't let him get away."

The detective said, "Could you maybe give us a few more details, miss?"

Rune didn't answer. She said to the detective, "Can we be alone for a couple minutes. Just him and me? I'll tell you everything." When the detective didn't answer right away, she said, "I'm telling you about Maisel so you can put men on the doors. He's about fifty, balding, beard."

The detective looked at her cold eyes and told two uniforms to cover the building exits. Then he walked over to the EMS attendants, who were putting Nestor on a gurney. They weren't moving quickly.

Rune watched them, then said to Randy Boggs, "Why didn't you tell me?" When she said it, she had her hands on her hips and her head was tilted to the right, like she was sighting down a rifle barrel, and her voice sounded like a gunshot.

"Was a new suit," he said, looking at his torn sleeve. His arm was scratched and blood had mixed with the rainwater. Then he looked up, focused on the flipping lights that were on top of a squad car. "Was the deal I made with him."

"Him?" Rune asked. "That gross guy, the yucky one?"

"Way I was brought up, you don't snitch. Man was my friend."

"He used you!"

"Know that now. Didn't then. Didn't until just a few days ago."

"Didn't you think it was kind of funny that he took you along on this credit card thing? Then somebody gets killed?"

"Guess at the time, I didn't think 'bout it. And he give me all that money. I needed a nest egg. A hundred thousand dollars. Where'd I get money like that otherwise? Nowhere I know of."

Rune felt a painful fullness, as if she'd taken too big a bite—swollen up with anger and emotion. She wanted to slap him, to scream, to grab his thin collar and shake him.

Randy Boggs said, "I'm sorry."

She didn't answer.

"I could've left. I had me a ticket to the Bahamas. I was going there. I was going to open a bar. You know, those kind that sell drinks in glasses that look like pineapples. With umbrellas in them. You like them drinks?"

She didn't answer.

"I was going to give you some money."

Rune said, "You were?"

"I brung ten thousand, and I was going to give it to you. It was on account of me that your house got burned down."

"I don't want your money."

"Maybe your little girl—"

"She's not my little girl," Rune snapped.

Neither spoke for a moment. Boggs said, "I'm just trying to tell you I'm sorry."

Rune said, "I wanted to help you. That was why I did the story in the first place. Everybody told me not to. Everybody told me to forget about you, that you'd killed a man and that you deserved to go to jail."

Boggs was nodding. "I'd appreciate it if you'd consider taking the money."

"Give it to Claire. She needs it more than me."

"I'll give her this ten. But you want another ten, I'll give that to you."

Rune slapped the top of the car. She seemed to be angry for a moment, then she laughed. Boggs was looking around him, smiling too, though he didn't know why. She said, "Shit, Randy, no wonder you never made any money, you give it all away. Damn."

"Haven't held on to it too good. That much is true."

She turned to him, and said, "I need to do my story again. I'll have to interview you. Will you talk to me, tell me the whole story?"

"I do, will you forgive me?"

She said, "I really don't know."

"Could we go drink beer some time?"

"I don't go out with felons."

"I've done some bad things, but I'm not sure I'm a felon, exactly."

A cop took Boggs to the EMS van to bandage his elbow. For a moment, Rune was alone, surrounded by a pool of dull colors, reflections from neon signs in a deli storefront.

The detective leaned against his car, talking on the radio. He looked up and lifted a hand into the air, mouthed

"Give me a minute." For a moment, Rune had been eager to get home, go back to her houseboat and Ophelia. But she remembered that, no, the little girl was with her grandmother. The boat was gone. And Sam would be on watch until six A.M.

So she was in no hurry. She stood and gazed at the scene. It had almost returned to normal. Only a couple cars remained, and the EMS ambulance. There was no crowd anymore—the rain had seen to that—and the few passersby that paused didn't do anything more than glance at the cars, and at her, maybe wondering if she was an undercover cop.

It was totally incredible how fast the incident was over with. Like the explosion of the shotgun and the swirl of violence had been pulled into the huge gears of the city and ground up into nothing. Even the blood—it didn't have to wash away to become invisible; the ragged patch was part of the mosaic of the street, just another stain slowly fading under the motion of every day's events. Rune sat down on a doorstep to wait for the detective.

Wrestle with it, punch it down, fight it.

They stood in front of Claire's hospital bed, Rune in a white sleeveless T-shirt and black miniskirt; Ophelia was no longer post-New-Wave preschool. No more black and Day-Glo and studs. She was in her new Laura Ashley cornflower-blue dress and lopsided hair ribbon (it had taken Rune a while to get the navy-blue satin to impersonate a bow—she'd overheard five music videos come and go on MTV while she struggled).

A sharp, sweet smell was in the air. Rune didn't know whether it was disinfectant or medicine or the smell of illness and death. She didn't like it; she hated hospitals. A hundred feet below was the emergency room, and the boxy ambulances were dropping off patients like taxi passengers at rush hour.

"Where's your mom?" Rune asked.

"At her hotel," Claire said. "She was with me all night. She left at seven this morning. That's something about mothers, huh? Abuse 'em all you want, and they keep coming back for more."

Ophelia clumsily set a paper bag on the bed.

One-handed, Claire shook it open. Out fell a stuffed dinosaur. Claire made it walk across the bed. "Rune helped me buy it," her daughter told her.

"How'd I guess?" Claire examined the plush face with serious scrutiny. "He's like sensitive and ferocious at the same time. You can really pick them."

Rune nodded absently. "I'm sort of a connoisseur."

Fight it. Fight it down. . . .

Claire didn't look real good. She could sit up okay, with some help, but otherwise she was pretty immobile. Her skin was paler than Rune had ever seen it (and Claire was somebody who last Halloween didn't bother with a costume and who everybody thought was a great vampire).

"I won't see in my left eye," she announced matter-of-factly. "Ever again."

Rune looked her straight in the good one, but before she could say anything, offer something sympathetic, Claire was on to another subject. "I got this job. At a department store. It's kinda bullshit. I have a couple bosses, and they're like, 'Well, we'll try you out,' And I'm like, 'What's to try?' It's not like orgasmic, but it's working out okay. Like listen to this—I've got health insurance? I got it just before I left to come down here. Man, they're going to get some friggin' bill. Surprise, surprise."

This room was better than the ICU suite. Claire had a view of rolling Jersey hills and the Hudson, and, closer to home, one of Rune's favorite hangouts: the White Horse Tavern, where she'd spent some afternoons with an old wiry-haired poet who'd claimed he used to listen to Dylan Thomas recite booming poetry there.

Hospitals were pretty icky, but here at least you got a view and sunlight and history.

Claire was talking about her mother's house, and how weird it was that nobody in the neighborhood wore black leather or had shaved heads, and she hadn't met any musicians or short-story writers but the one guy she met who she liked worked for a textbook publisher, as a salesman, and wasn't that like crazy wild? . . .

Rune nodded and tried to listen. The muscles in her abdomen clenched against the crawly feeling, like she was possessed by a space creature that was getting ready to burst out of her.

Then Claire was into a travelog, telling Rune and Ophelia about Boston—Faneuil Hall and Cambridge and Chinatown and the lofts and antique stores around South Street Station. "There's this one really, really neat place. It sells old bathtubs must be three feet deep. Totally humongous."

Rune couldn't work up much enthusiasm for tourist attractions. She nodded politely, and a couple times said, "Wow, that's interesting," in an uninterested way, which Claire seemed to take as encouragement and kept going. Rune found she was holding Ophelia's hand tightly. The little girl squirmed.

Fight it. . . .

Rune didn't say much about Boggs or Maisel or the *Current Events* story. Just the bones. She wanted to keep it to a minimum—Claire must have known Rune was the reason she'd been shot, and Rune wanted to steer clear of that. Not that she was racked with guilt; you could also look at it that another reason Claire got hurt—maybe *the* reason—was that she had abandoned her daughter, which if she hadn't, she never would have gone back to the houseboat when she did. . . . But that got into the way the gods and goddesses and the fates work, and if you start thinking too much about cause and effect, Rune knew, it'll drive you bonkers.

There was silence for a minute. Rune said, "Look, I bought 'Phelia a new dress."

"Look, Mommy."

Claire twisted her body as far as she could so the unbandaged eye got a good look, and the way her damaged face blossomed, it answered the single scorching question had been on Rune's mind for the past couple days.

When she considered it now, she figured there really had been no chance at all, and she was mad at herself for letting her thoughts get out of hand.

Fight it, fight, fight. . . .

She should have known; she'd read *The Snow Princess.* She knew how it ended. This business about fairy stories having happy endings: Well, she'd always known that was bullshit. People melt. People go away. People die. And we're left with the story and the memory, which, if we're lucky, will be good stories and good memories.

Oh, Rune, you keep her with you. Just for a year or so. You two get along so well. . . .

Claire was reaching forward, awkwardly, across the bed with her good arm, saying, "Did you miss me, honey?"

"Uh-huh." Ophelia let go of Rune's hand and tried to climb up on the bed. Rune boosted her up.

In fact, I've thought about this a lot, Rune, and I'd like you to bring her up. Oh, I know it's a lot to ask. But would you mind? You can read her fairy stories every night. I know she'd love that, and if you want, you can even teach her there are dragons and trolls and . . .

Rune said, "You're going back to Boston, huh? The two of you?"

Claire said, "Yeah, like, we'll live at my mom's until I can get some money saved up, but apartments are cheap there. It shouldn't take me much time."

Fight it. . . .

Rune swallowed. "You want, I can keep Ophelia with me until you get settled. There's no hurry. We're pretty good buddies, huh?"

The little girl was playing with the dinosaur, and didn't hear what Rune said. Or didn't want to. In any case, she didn't answer. Claire shook her head. "I kind of want her with me. You know how it is."

"Sure, I know."

"Look, Rune, I never really said it so good, but I like really, really appreciate what you did. It was a groady thing for me to do, just leaving like that. A lot of people wouldn't have done what you did."

"True, they wouldn't," Rune said.

"I owe you."

"Yeah, you do. You owe me."

"The doctor says I can be transferred to Boston in a couple days. And, guess what?"

Rune's face burned. "A couple days?"

"I'm gonna take an ambulance, like, the whole way. Is that crazy audacious, or what? My mom's paying for it."

A couple days?

No good fighting any more; Rune had lost. She took a deep breath and said, "Well, ciao, you guys."

"Aw, come on," Claire said, "stay for a while. Check out the doctors. There's this cute one. Curly hair you won't believe."

Rune shook her head and started for the door.

"Rune," Ophelia said suddenly. "Can we go to the zoo?"

Rune stopped and hugged the girl briefly. She managed, somehow, to keep her voice steady and to hold back the tears for the time it took her to say, "Before you leave, honey, we'll go to the zoo. I promise."

Steady and calm, for those few seconds.

But not an instant longer. And as Rune turned quickly and walked into the corridor, the tears streamed and the quiet sobbing stole her breath, as if she were being swept away, drowning and numb, in a torrent of melting snow.

"A dragon. I always knew it'd be a son-of-a-bitch dragon got me."

Piper Sutton looked at her. "You and your dragons."

They stood on the pier, where the glistening black hull of the houseboat floated, hardly bobbing, in the oily water of the Hudson.

Rune bent down and picked up a soggy dress. She examined the cloth. The collar was a little scorched, but she might be able to cover it up with paint. She thought about the lawyer, Fred Megler, an expert at repairing clothing with pens.

Rune sniffed the dress and shrugged and threw it into the discard pile, which looked like a miniature volcano of trash. Both the fire and the water from the NYFD had taken their toll. On the deck was a pile of books, pots and pans, some half-melted running shoes, drinking glasses. Nothing real valuable had survived, only the Motorola TV, and the wrought-iron frames of the butterfly chairs.

"The fifties were indestructible," Rune said. "Damn, that must've been a hell of a decade."

It was a stunningly gorgeous Sunday. The sky was a cloudless dome of three-dimensional blue, and the sun was as hot as a lightbulb. The air smelled of spring. Piper Sutton sat on a piling she'd covered with a scrap of blue cloth—one of Rune's work shirts—before she'd lowered her black-suede-encased thighs onto the splintery wood.

"You have insurance?"

"Kinda weird, but yeah, I do. It was one of those adult things, you know, the sort that I don't usually get into. But my boyfriend at the time made me get some." She walked to the water and looked down at the charred wood. "The policy's in there someplace. Do I have to have it to collect?"

"I don't think so."

"I'm going to make some serious money there. I lost some really hyper stuff. Day-Glo posters, crystals, my entire Elvis collection . . ."

"Worth a lot, you had a complete Presley."

"That's Costello. . . ." Rune explained. Then considered other losses. "My magic wand. A ton of incense. . . . Oh God, my lava lamp."

"You have a lava lamp?"

"Had," Rune reminded her sadly.

"Where're you staying?"

"With Sam for a while. Then I'll get a new place. Someplace different. I was ready to move anyway. I lived here for over a year. That's too long to be in one place. I think I was putting down roots. Scary."

A tugboat went by. A horn blared. Rune waved. "I know them," she told Sutton, who twisted around to watch the low-riding boat muscle its way through the river.

"You know," Rune said, "I've got to tell you. I kind of thought you were the one behind the killings."

"Me?" Sutton wasn't laughing. "That's the stupidest crap I ever heard."

"I don't think it's so stupid. You tried to talk me out of doing the story, then offered me that job in England—"

"Which was real," Sutton snapped. "And got filled by somebody else."

Rune continued, unfazed, "And the day of the broadcast, when you ad-libbed, all the tapes were missing. Even the backup in my credenza. You were the only one knew they were there."

Sutton impatiently motioned with her hand, as if she were buying candy by the pound and wanted Rune to keep adding to the scale. "Come on, think, think, think. I told you I was on my way to see Lee. He asked me if you'd made a dupe. I told him that you had and you'd put it in your credenza."

"You also went through my desk after Boggs escaped."

"I didn't want any of that material floating around. You were really careless, by the way. You trust too many people." She realized she was lecturing and she reined herself in.

They watched the tugboat for a few minutes until it disappeared. Then Sutton said, "You want the job back, you can have it."

"I don't know," Rune said. "I don't think I'm a company person."

"No, you're not. You'll probably get fired again. But it's a peach job until you do."

"The local or the Network?"

"Current Events, I was thinking."

"Doing what? Like a script girl?"

"Associate producer."

Rune paused, then dropped a pair of scorched jeans into the trash pile. "I'd want to do the story. The whole thing. About the Hopper killing. And I'd want to add the part about Lee."

Sutton turned back, away from the water, and stood up, looking over the huge panorama of the city. "That's a problem."

"What do you mean?"

"*Current Events* won't be running any segments about the Hopper killing. Or about Boggs."

Rune looked at her.

"Network News covered it."

"Briefly," Rune added. "I saw the segment. It was, what, about sixty seconds? They did a longer story on Ivana Trump."

"Well, you know whose fault it is, don't you?"

"Mine, you telling me?"

"The powers-that-be—at the parent—decided the story should go away."

"That's bullshit."

"Can you blame them?"

"Sure I can," Rune said. "It's easy."

In her prototype Piper Sutton voice, Piper Sutton snapped, "It wasn't my decision to make."

"Wasn't it?"

Sutton took a breath to speak, then didn't. She shook her head slowly. She avoided Rune's eyes.

Rune repeated, "Wasn't it?" And surprised herself again by hearing how calm she sounded, how unshaken she now was in the presence of this woman—a woman who wore suede and silk and bright red suits, a woman richer and smarter than she would ever be. A famous commentator, who now seemed abandoned by words. Rune said, "You'd rather that *Prime Time Tonight* or *Pulse of the Town* did the story?"

Sutton stepped up on a creosoted railroad tie bolted into the pier as a car barrier. She looked in the water; her expression said she didn't like what she saw. Rune wondered if it was her reflection.

She said simply, "The story won't run on *Current Events.*"

"What'll happen if it did?"

"If you want to know, I posed that exact question. And the answer was if it does, the parent'll cancel the show. That's why." Then she added, "And I'll be fired. You need a better reason than that?"

"I don't think I want my job back, no," Rune said. She'd found some of her old comic books. They'd miraculously been missed by both the fire and the looters. She looked at the cover of a 1953 classic—Sheena Queen of the Jungle, who swung out of a tree toward a startled lion. The cat stared at her spear and radiant blonde hair and leopard-skin-clad hourglass figure—a physique that existed only in the envious imaginations of illustrators. "That's me," Rune held up the book. "Queen of the Jungle." Sutton blinked at her.

Rune stacked the books in the small "To Be Saved" pile and asked, "Your conscience bothering you yet?"

"I've never had trouble sleeping at night. Not in forty-three years."

"You want my opinion?"

"Not really."

"You're caving, just to keep your paycheck."

Rune expected a tirade, but what she got was a small, hurt voice that said, "I hope you know it's not that."

And after a moment, Rune nodded, understanding that Sutton was right. It wasn't the money at all. Sure, she'd caved, but the reasons were complex. She'd caved partly because she was hooked on the prestige and excitement that went with being a prime-time news anchor. Partly to keep a job that she'd fought for, and fought hard.

And partly because Piper Sutton felt the world of journalism, and her ten million viewers, needed her.

And maybe they did.

"I put it in context." Sutton shrugged. "Boggs was innocent, and you got him out. That's a good deed. But it's still a small story. There's a lot of news out there, a lot bigger news. Nobody says I've got to cover everything."

"I'll produce it independently." Rune sounded more threatening than she meant to.

Sutton laughed. "Bless you, babes, and more power to you. All I'm telling you is the story won't run on the Network. Not on my program."

Rune turned to face Sutton. "And if I do it, I'm going to mention the part about how they wouldn't do the story on *Current Events.*"

Sutton smiled. "Why do you think I told you? I'll send you the backup, the stuff I saved from your desk. That should give you a pretty good head start. Give us your best shot."

Rune went back to her pile of trash. "It'll be a son of a bitch to do by myself."

Sutton said, "Sure will."

Rune continued to stack soggy books. "You know, I could use a business partner. Somebody who was smart. And, like, real abrasive."

"Like abrasive."

"You wouldn't be interested, would you?"

"Quit my job and go to work with you?" Sutton laughed, genuinely amused.

"Sure! We'd be a great team."

Sutton laughed again. "No way in hell."

She walked over to the messy pile and began to help Rune pick through it. She'd hold up an object, and Rune would give her instructions: "Save." "Pitch." "Pitch." "Pitch." "Identity unknown pile." "Save." "Save."

They worked for a half hour, until Sutton stood up straight, looked at her smudged hands with a grimace. "What time you have?"

Rune glanced at her working watch, one of three on her left wrist. "Noon."

Sutton asked, "You interested in having some brunch?"

"Some time, sure. But I can't today. I'm going to the zoo with somebody in an hour."

"A date, huh?"

"Not hardly," Rune said. "Hey, you want to come?"

Sutton was shaking her head, which Rune figured was probably her reflex reaction to invitations of this sort. "I haven't been to the zoo in years."

"It's like riding a bike," Rune said. "It'll come right back to you."

"I don't know. It's not my style."

"Come on."

"Let me think about it." Sutton stopped shaking her head.

"Aw, come on."

"I said I'll think about it," Sutton snapped. "You can't ask for more than that."

"Sure I can," Rune said, and gave her a Cheshire grin, which the anchorwoman elegantly ignored. Together they crouched down in front of the huge pile of mystery artifacts and began picking through it, looking for more of Rune's damaged treasures.